the last place you want to be
is the last place on earth

Bunker, a novel by David Lineberry
Published by Ashen Pawn Publishing, 2013
Baltimore, MD

www.ashenpawn.com
ashenpawn.wordpress.com

To contact the publisher for any reason, including requests for book signings
or special events, write to: ashenpawn@gmail.com

ISBN: 978-0615931494
1st Edition, 2013
REV020614
Also available in eBook formats wherever sold.

Printed by CreateSpace, An Amazon.com Company
Manufactured in the U.S.A.

*This book is dedicated to
my friends and family.*

*Thanks for humoring me
and putting up with my nonsense.*

BUNKER

A NOVEL

DAVID LINEBERRY

ASHEN PAWN PUBLISHING

骗局

Be extremely subtle, even to the point of formlessness.
Be extremely mysterious, even to the point of soundlessness.
Thereby you can be the director of the opponent's fate.

Sun Tzu,
The Art of War

Prologue

Getting away with murder is tricky enough, but trying to slay a giant, especially one as robust as the United States, can be thoroughly problematic. It can't be fought head on as it would take notice and once awake, the giant's strength is too overpowering. The easiest way, perhaps the only way to defeat a titan as powerful as the U.S. is to have it poisoned in secret until its strength is gone; then, it only takes the stealthy severing of a few crucial arteries for it to fall on its own sword. That seemed to be the plan.

Call it divine intervention or dumb luck, but discovering the infiltration was unquestionably improbable. It had gone unnoticed for years until a single Mourning Dove somehow managed to find its way into a secure mountain structure in North Carolina and defecate directly on the air vent of a critical mainframe computer. The usual tech would have left the functioning computer alone as protocol suggests. At most, he may have wiped the violet ooze from the surface, figuring that not enough would have gotten through the filtered vent to cause a malfunction. He probably would have been correct. The usual tech, however, had woken up with a 24-hour sickness and his replacement for that day was much more thorough. The substitute technician's compulsive tendency to clean uncovered the poison that would eventually keep a homeland security agent from sleeping soundly at night some three-hundred miles away in the nation's capital. Foster was the agent assigned to keep that threat from destroying the United States.

There was no urgency in his steps, no sense of foreboding in his voice as he stepped off the elevator and greeted the uniformed guard with a slight nod. The slick soles of his monk-strap shoes slapped the marble tiles as he sashayed around the security desk, just as he had done for years.

"Morning, Krinski," Foster said as he removed his glasses and bent slightly to peer into the retina scanner.

"Mornin', Director. You're early today," Krinski replied. He barely peered away from the rack of security monitors long enough to place his thumb on the print reader, signaling the thick glass door to slide open and allow passage inside. It was a daily ritual that had become comfortably monotonous.

"Well, like they say: be first or be fucked," Foster said.

"Oh, come on. Who says that?" said Krinski.

"Scared sheep escaping lonely farmers, I'd imagine," he said, his feeble attempt at humor garnering him a pity smirk.

Foster's expression was perpetually calm, almost bored. Typical. It would be difficult to perceive that under his arm, wrapped in a cheap, China-made folder, tied shut with a thin string and small metal eyelet was information regarding the next great world war, the potential downfall of America. When every workday consists of the eliminating large-scale threats, part of the mind must become numb; it's vital to the individual's sanity. For Foster, his duties had become almost like swatting flies. Even though he found this particular situation more troubling than most, he refused to let it show to those around him.

His silvery gray suit was neatly pressed, pristine and dull. His balding head brightly reflected the fluorescent light as he made his way beyond the bland hallway of doors to the biggest corner office in the Agency's structure. The confidence he exuded was usually genuine but always visible. That was a calculated strategy. Foster's job often required him to act the part of diplomatic salesman as much as defender of freedom. He had learned early on in his career to play the game, to satisfy those above him on the food chain. It's the only way to truly get anything accomplished in government.

Foster often commented to the few he trusted that working within the confines of the United States Department of Homeland Security seemed a lot like working without confines. An agency of agencies, indeed an ambitious idea, formed from bowels of tragedy and, as Foster often thought, remained tragic thereafter. Rising from the flames of the razed Twin Towers in New York City, those within the tightest circle of government intelligence formed the USDHS.

The USDHS, a maestro conducting a symphony of information in a world of violent dissonance. The agency was intended to become the United State's central hub for coordinating efforts from any and all government departments. It became infamous for taking liberties for and from the citizens it protects, spending the budget it was given, plus whatever else was needed to prevent terrorism from allowing Americans their due wet dreams. Yet even through the many missteps since its inception, even when it stumbled clumsily about like the twenty-foot toddler it was, Foster realized it's necessity. For as many embarrassments as it had to claim publicly, it maintained hundreds of successes in secrecy.

"Jordan," he heard, stopping him short as he raised his fist to give the obligatory knock on the open door. The man behind the desk, Deputy Secretary Woodward, snugly leaned back into his office chair and signaled Foster's entry. He was a stocky man, cleanly shaved and freshly groomed, his short curly hair looking ever impenetrable. He stood to drape his blazer over a wall hook near his Columbia University law degree, pausing to scrape a speck of dirt from the framed glass with his thumbnail.

"How are you?" Foster asked.

Woodward folded up his sleeves unveiling forearms so consumed with layers of thick hair, the Semper Fi tattoo he proudly bore was nearly indecipherable.

"Well, if I'm being candid, my sciatica's been acting up lately, kicking my ass again. Really sucking the sport out of masturbation, you know? And now this shit," Woodward replied. He placed two blue, oblong pain relievers on his tongue and took a swig from a glass of water before he sat back down.

"I know the initial report was scant, but we've since learned the source and named the mark. I brought a follow-up," Foster replied.

"We made him already?" Woodward said.

"NSA initiated, global data taps. His profile is on the bottom," Foster affirmed. He sat across from the deputy secretary and handed Woodward the brown folder, prompting him to skim through.

"Well damn, would you look at this piece of shit," he said, staring at the picture on the profile. "I can assume he hasn't been confronted?"

"Not at all. The immediate threat has been isolated. He's clueless that we even know about it and we can get to him at any given time, but we were unsure how you'd want to go about–"

"Holy shit. Is this right?" Woodward interrupted. He stared intently through his thick-framed reading glasses and held the pages closer to his face as he read. "How much of the threat assessment is conjecture?"

"More than I'd like but not enough to disregard any possibilities. We know what was being corrupted and how, we know that bastard there is in on it and we know he can't be doing it alone. We're still trying to figure out exactly what they intended to do but we're narrowing down probable scenarios. As far as who he's working for or with, we're eliminating suspects and preparing for the worst." Foster paused as he shifted forward in his chair, "This could be a domestic faction, but everything is pointing towards alien."

There was a moment of silence as the two men let the potential hazard of the situation absorb. Foster leaned back into his chair again, awkwardly crossing his legs and folding his arms. As good as he had become hiding his anxiety, traces of unrest still sometimes leaked into a fidgety display of body language.

"Hopefully," he continued, "this is a rogue cell. Isolated."

"Hopefully," Woodward responded, "but if it turns out to be government sanctioned or a widespread faction, well... fuck."

"Fuck is right, sir," Foster said.

"I love this country, Jordan, love it more than I love my own mother and you know I love that woman," Woodward said laying the file down on the desk. "But a bombshell like this could literally start World War III, the whole globe in one big damn death match. Makes my stomach churn to think about it because, frankly, I don't think we'd win this one. Not against an enemy this size." The deputy secretary removed his glasses and massaged the lump of flesh between his eyes. "This could turn out to be the most devastating act of treason in American history and I'm going to treat it as a terrorist attack," he said.

"I couldn't agree more," Foster responded. "This asshole needs to talk."

"So, read me the red letters. What we do know about the bastard?" Woodward said, tapping the file with his index finger.

"We know he's a natural-born U.S. citizen, conceived by illegal immigrants, then homeschooled by a guardian after his parents were deported. All sources suggest he's culturally adaptive, surprisingly well-educated and, of course, militarily trained. We have financial records that indicate his involvement—steep deposits that correlate with intercepted correspondence. Much of it still coded, but we have it. One of the messages we were able to decipher labeled him outright by his original native name, mostly a jumble of vowels. Good luck pronouncing it. As far as the initial psych test, he was likely coached to pass it."

"What do you think, Jordan? You, personally," Woodward said. He leaned back and interlocked his fingers, allowing his hands to rest on his rounded belly.

Foster looked towards the wall and rubbed his chin down to his neck, "The fallout could be devastating. It's one of the scariest things I've ever read and, obviously, the potential repercussions justify extraordinary rendition. We have to find out what he knows, regardless of the means."

"Just skip the foreplay and give me your recommendation," Woodward said.

"That being said, we can't exactly throw this guy down a black hole in Gitmo," Foster said. The detention center at Guantanamo Naval Base in Cuba had come under too much scrutiny to be used effectively but couldn't be shut down without admitting the evils it had housed. So it remained ineptly alive—gimped by public moral pretension, protected by stubborn bureaucratic pride.

"Oh, hell no. I already can't wipe my ass without some liberal tapeworm calling for a congressional enema. So, what do you suggest?" Woodward said.

"The consensus within my group is that we try the Dolus Initiative," Foster said reluctantly.

"Ah shit, Jordan, not the doctor," Woodward said. "He's a smug lunatic."

"I know you don't like his methods, but—"

"Damn right I don't. They're insane," Woodward interjected. "What about using one of the guys we pulled from Bucca? Strazio maybe?"

"Are you looking for an interrogator or an inquisitor? The doctor gets results," Foster continued more aggressively. "You kill away a man's family, destroy his world, take away his hope... you want information extracted, his team is effective. We've held prisoners at Guantanamo for years that still won't talk. He claims his team can get in their head in two weeks."

"Two weeks? This guy won't crack, not for them," Woodward said sharply. "His team is unproven and the stakes are too high to waste time."

"The doctor will personally lead it. If he fails, then we'll still have the other options," Jordan said. "And you'll have a strong case for his permanent dismissal."

Woodward tapped his fingers on his lips as he leaned on his glossy, cherry wood desk. His mind played out his options while his eyes stared at the inspirational art prints that hung on his wall—one of the flag raising at Iwo Jima and another of Trumbull's Declaration of Independence.

Foster adjusted his position on the square, black chair, sitting upright on the edge to accentuate his confident display. The quiet buzz of the fluorescent lights was punctuated by the flatulent sound he made sliding on leather. Its echo reverberated through the office.

"I'm trusting your judgment," Woodward said, his eyes as solemn as his voice. "He has two weeks to work him."

Foster's countenance hinted a slight relief as he began to stand, "I'll initiate it immediately."

"But Jordan, just to make sure we're clear. This suspect is technically an American citizen and, shit, just look at his record," Woodward said glancing down at the open file. "This needs to stay buried. The threat, the operation. Plausible deniability is priority, second only to getting this Judas shitcan to talk. Have your guys fabricate a more public-friendly alternative and email it amongst each other in case we need to leak a time-stamped back story. And if your ass gets exposed, I never heard of this."

Foster gave an affirmative nod and turned to leave, his gradually-softening footsteps sounding off his departure.

01
ASSESSMENT EXCERPT

To Whomever Finds This Letter,
As I write, I retain hope that people will survive and rebuild. I have less hope that I will be found, not soon enough to wait anyway. Depending on when you've come and who you are, I suppose I have a duty to report what happened, but my mind is too weary to chronicle every event since we've been here. I've lost track of the days but it couldn't have been more than a few weeks. Maybe it could. I honestly don't know now.

To my fellow soldiers, I've given up hope for you and I could wait no longer by myself. I'm sorry if you've returned to this mess on your own but I awoke to find I am the only one here now, alive or otherwise. I cannot leave and I'm too afraid to stay. To the army for which we served, all you need to know is that we failed. To my countrymen, the ones that know my mission, I failed, for I can no longer do the task I was assigned. I say all of this to my shame. I can't imagine though that my personal success would have made any difference to the world as it is now. That makes me both relieved and depressed.

It seems ridiculous to address my family now, but in the off-chance that you did survive and somehow get to hear the contents of this letter, I hope you will find some honor in what

I've done. We were never a people to say "I love you" and while I feel foolish for finally writing something that you will never read, I feel I need to do so even if it's only to admit it to myself. There *is* a special place in my heart for you, regardless of the choices you made for me.

My precious Lin, you know how much I love you. This will be just one more note stating so, another letter ironically sealed in a box. I only wish I could see your face again.

To anyone else—to you reading this, whoever you are—congratulations would be in order I suppose. You must have survived.

I want it on the record that the blood you see scattered all over the last room at the far end of the hall, it's not mine. I mean it didn't come from my body, nor did I spill it. I never entered that room. I won't. I didn't know what I was coming into, didn't participate when I got here, and didn't want to stay. Now, I can't leave. There's nowhere to go.

The electronics no longer work. That is to say, they seem to be functional, just not effective. All attempts to use them end in frustration for me. I'm no electronics engineer. If there is still power when you get here, try them if you like. You may have more success contacting someone than I did. Also, the CD player works if you like what's there. I've lost my taste for it.

There is still a little food in the pantry, some cans of beets and beans I think. For now, the plumbing is still producing drinkable water. The alcohol is gone but there's a lot of stale cigarettes in the closet if your interested. I wouldn't recommend it though. That shit will kill you. It amuses me to add that warning now.

There are some clothes and blankets here too. They're dirty but it's better than being cold I suppose. You probably won't need them if you stay inside as the body heat keeps the place warm, but outside it gets consistently chilly. That's what I hear anyway. The temperature doesn't change much down here, being far enough underground that it's insulated from the shifting weather as well as nuclear radiation, if that's a concern.

I've also been very conservative with my ammunition. My M4 rifle, which I left on my bunk beside my belongings, hasn't been fired at all. My M9 will have all the ammunition I was issued, less one bullet.

As for me, since you found me, I suppose you will move my body out of here. I would. I just request that I be buried outside when possible, close to here. I have to admit, while this bunker probably saved my life, I hated this place. It started as a mission station, turned into a shelter, then a prison, and now it will be my tomb. But I confessed my wrongs here, learned a lot about who I am. This is where life brought me so I'd like to stay.

I still have hope of a future for this world even if my own demise is imminent. Should life endure on Earth, sow good seeds with all you meet. Make things better than they were before.

Specialist Kenneth Khu,
"Amish"

Writing that, I flipped the plastic pen in the air, watching it bounce across the floor and hit the far wall. The room was silent, my ears gathering only signs of my own mortality. My lungs sighed deep breaths of warm air. My pounding heart created a rhythm I could feel simultaneously resonating through all my pulse points. I carefully wrapped my dog tags in the letter and placed it neatly on my lap, sealing it with a fold at each end. I then seized the glass bottle of Russian vodka from the floor beside me and swallowed the last warm swig.

The concrete structure felt cold against my legs and back as I sat on the floor, leaning against the wall. From this position, the pistol slid easily from my holster and into my hand. For the first time since I had entered this place, I cocked the handgun, pointing it into the air just as I was trained.

I closed my eyes and emptied my thoughts. Seconds passed into minutes and I remained still. My breath began to become more shallow, my heart rate began to slow. My mind was clear. I then put the cold steel barrel in my mouth and quickly pulled the trigger.

02
Flight, Two Weeks Earlier

I didn't know why I had been called, only that the mission was urgent and my station was classified. I hadn't asked to be transferred and I definitely hadn't achieved anything that seemed worthy of recognition. Regardless, when this special assignment came up, I was recommended. Actually, they told me my name "topped of the list of designated personnel." Same thing, I thought.

Of course, I didn't want to go but in the United States Army, or any branch of the military for that matter, options are run through a filter and at the bottom there's nothing left but orders. Refusal to your superiors really isn't an option even when you're armed with the best excuse and I didn't have one. So, I did as commanded and went to North Dakota. That's where they brought all of us together. Hoo-ahh.

It was unusually warm weather for that time of year but the air was still chilly around twilight. When I arrived on base, stars were clearly visible in the sky as it had just began to shift from black to royal blue. The change in color made it easy to visualize the silhouettes of a several military police against the skyline. Some were patrolling the area on foot; a few others were methodically making laps around the entire base in a Humvee, circling in ways so the headlights could hit the most dimly lit areas.

Off in the distance, beyond the multiple office buildings and rows of barracks, small weather resistant bulbs outlined landing strips and taxiways. An organized pattern of light posts lined the asphalt roadways, creating illuminated cones that sat on the blacktop.

Beyond the boundary of the base, there was nothing even remotely close. No houses, no businesses. Just open land residing in eerie darkness. At that time of morning, everything outside the military borders looked like a void in geographical space.

I was dropped off near an isolated office structure in the northern-most sector of the base, residing nearly a full klick away from the bevy of other buildings. The MP who drove the Humvee told me that in the fifty years of its existence, its use had been increasingly geared towards storage. Newer structures, engineered with updated equipment, made the building nearly obsolete. Its greatest value was its secluded locale, a quality that made it ideal for operations that required cover from anyone that might decide to take notice.

The building was situated next to a small hangar, complete with a runway pointing northwest and a small helipad slickly hidden behind it. As the cool breeze blew through the bolted rooftop, its seams composed a foreboding choir of high pitched whistles. I could have sworn I heard ghostly voices sing "flee away" at one point. That was probably just my instinct. I should have listened.

One other soldier was already there when I pulled up. He remained at ease just outside the large open doorway, sitting on his military-issue duffel bag against the ribbed aluminum wall and peering out across the vacant tarmac apron.

We didn't speak. We hardly acknowledged each other's presence as we waited, giving only the occasional glance. He was a young Caucasian fellow with short red hair, an acne scarred complexion, and a stable relationship with tobacco. The sewn name tag on his army fatigues read *T. Farrell.* He removed a pack of cigarettes and lit up, blowing smoke out into the sky. No more than a few minutes passed before he repeated the procedure.

"They're trying to take that away, you know?" I said, breaking the silence that, until then, seemed mutually agreeable.

He sized me up for a moment, one eye squinting as he read *K. Khu* stitched across the name bar on the right side of my chest. I admit, being examined made me uncomfortable; it does every time. It's not that I'm ashamed of being an Asian male even if most Americans *do* make us the butt of so many racial jokes. Or that I feel self-conscious about the scar that prevents hair from growing completely on my right eyebrow. Or the grouping of moles that litter my cheeks like an invading army aiming to take over my face. It's not even because I'm so svelte—some have said scrawny though I don't agree. I'm not vain about any part of my physical appearance, a mindset that fits well with such flaws. I just don't like attention for obvious reasons. I reside in the background, away from the spotlight. I do it for the good of my country.

"What's that, chief?" Farrell replied, puffing a light gray cloud into the air again.

"Smoking," I said. "They're trying to ban it on bases. You hear about that?"

"Yeah, I heard. Bastards," he said, bending to extinguish the half smoked cigarette to the ground. "Kinda makes you wonder what we're fighting for sometimes."

"What do you mean?" I said.

"We fight for freedom all over the world, right? But I can't smoke a damn cigarette outside? In my own country? That's some bullshit," Farrell said.

The distinct growl of a motor could be heard gradually getting closer. The base was quiet that morning with no aircraft coming or going, making it easy for experienced soldiers like us to identify the approaching vehicle so common to American military bases.

"There's no ban yet. You could have finished it," I said. I nodded toward the partially used cigarette, much of which remained intact.

"Nah," Farrell replied, "this shit will kill you."

A Humvee pulled up carrying two soldiers not counting the military policewoman behind the steering wheel. She gave quick nod and pointed towards Farrell and me as we stood watching them exit the vehicle. The insufficient light gave few details of the men as they walked toward the hangar, each carrying their own personal effects in military green bags. They walked with a swagger, the way young men do when they vie for the position of alpha male in any gathering of strange peers. They had to sense our eyes on them, watching them approach. Each step they took exuded an exaggerated machismo, no doubt an intentional embellishment to make their important roles within the group seem more believable.

Looking out beyond them was an open plain that seemed like it vanished into a dark nothingness, a black backdrop for their grand entrance. Air whipped intermittently across the flat land creating a whistling crescendo at its strongest before subsiding but they walked as if their stride couldn't be swayed. The song of the wind nearly drowned out the engine of the Humvee when it roared around a corner and sped away, back towards the cluster of buildings.

As the men entered the fringe of light underneath the nearby lamp posts, the details of their faces began to be revealed. One of the soldiers, a young black man, walked with his chin slightly elevated and his lips perched. His jaws seemed clenched tighter than what would seem adequate and his eyes blinked with what seemed like an excess in both force and duration. The name on his uniform read *R. Simmons.* He dropped his bag upon reaching us in the illumination of the hangar.

"What's up, fellas?" he said. It was rhetorical I think.

I responded anyway with an unenthusiastic, "Howdy." I'm not sure why I answered with such a hokey word. I felt stupid after it left my mouth and I wished I had responded like Farrell who gave a short nod but said nothing.

They were so restrained then, so passive. I thought conversation would be hard to come by with these men but it was too early judge them accurately. I couldn't evaluate their personalities. I would never have predicted their genuine motives.

The other soldier, a Latino man with a thin mustache and chubby cheeks, dropped his bags and checked out each one of us as if sizing us up. He was a brawny guy, thick but not obese. The width of his neck and head seemed equal and his extremities didn't seem to taper at their ends; rather, it seemed as though tree branches sprouted hands and feet. He appeared way too cheerful to be there that early, looking at those of us around him with what seemed to be a constant smirk.

"Ah, good day to be alive! What do you say, brothers?" he said. "I'm Rico." His name tag read *I. Delgado* and *Delgado* is what we called him despite his preference—maybe even because of his preference.

Before any response could be blurted out, a door slammed from the nearby office building. A tall, muscular Caucasian man rigidly advanced toward us. His walk seemed to have an urgency to it, but I think it was more of a reverence for his time on duty. I respected that. His arms rocked back and forth with each step as if he were marching to battle. His countenance, at least the little that could be seen of his face underneath the shadowy brim of his army cap held a fierce grimace. It seemed to stay that way all the time.

"Well, well, well," the approaching officer said sprightly. "Just look at the cultural kaleidoscope we have here. Feels like I'm walking into a damn U.N. Meeting."

We four stood promptly and kept our heads forward. My gaze still bounced around at the others after the varying ethnicities between us was called to attention, not that I hadn't already noticed.

The officer walked toward the center of the semicircle we had formed as a group underneath the hangar doorway. "At ease," he said.

We relaxed our tensed, upright postures but no one moved out of position, not a one.

"I am Lieutenant Colonel Charles Granger," he continued as he walked around between us, looking each uniformed soldier in the eyes. "Welcome to Minot Air Force Base. I know that this call to action was done without notice and I know that you have not been briefed. As you may have deduced, there is a special circumstance that has been brought to the attention of the United States government and each of you has been selected to help address the issue based on what I'm told are excellent psychological profiles and superb service records. All you need to know for now is that this is a detainee escort and watchdog mission. I will be leading this excursion."

Granger spoke with authority and his presence commanded respect. We all remained silent, our ears intent on hearing his words, hoping some light would be shed on the reason for our presence. We watched him from our periphery as if a direct stare would garner hostile attention and indeed, it may have.

He continued, "Now, normally if I were to see a picture this pretty, I'd bet balls to Bangkok that some capitol hill ballot chaser was on standby, ready to give us a group hug and ask us to wag our dicks for the camera. However, I can guarantee you that our mission will get as little attention as can be prevented and no politician would be caught sipping misties around our private soirée. So, I have to believe that this wonderful little snapshot of American diversity is either a random anomaly or, more likely, is an attempt to make sure that racial scrutiny be waved away quickly should our outing be brought to the attention of the American people. We can't let that happen."

He spoke as a stereotype. Thick layers of recycled witticisms were piled atop a mix of genuine patriotic concern and government angst. Granger wanted to portray the role of brave American military leadership. He tried to become something he's not and the closest he could achieve was a cliché. I should have seen through his character's flimsy facade even then. I wished I'd foreseen the whole thing was an act.

As we stood there, the faint but clearly recognizable beating rhythm of whirling helicopter blades could be heard approaching. From somewhere amidst the base, a few engines roared as they were ignited. The sky's deep blue was being overtaken from the horizon by orange and yellow hues and the stars above had all but faded into their daily obscurity.

Another large Humvee pulled up behind the commanding officer, the driver killing its engine. A military policeman stepped out from behind the wheel and opened the vehicle's rear compartment door revealing an array of weaponry and gear.

"Now, with that being said, I need you all to bunk your personal effects in the lockers behind you. All cameras, cell phones, media players—any device capable of recording and transmitting images, video or sound needs to be left behind. Empty your pockets, leave your billfolds. You won't need 'em. You will take only the gear you're issued and the key to your locker, not a damn sight more," Granger concluded. "Hoo-ahh?"

"Hoo-ahh!" we yelled. Every branch of the military has their own slightly-varied unifying affirmation, the verbal equivalent of a group chest bump. It's our war cry, our allegiance, our way of saying "go team" or "hell, yeah" or "yes, sir" to anyone else in a matching uniform. Hoo-ahh.

We quickly picked up our bags and moved toward the back of the hangar where rows of large green lockers were bolted against the wall. Every one of us unclasped the door to an empty compartment and removed a small key, the ends covered in a buoyant plastic and numbered correspondingly. The abrupt clash of the metal doors echoed shut, one after another, as each man locked away almost everything that tangibly connected him to his individuality. We were no longer truly free as we were bound by service. Much like the metal embossed tags around our necks, we were uniquely named, but now belonged to the U.S. Military. Hoo-ahh.

The other soldiers and I swiftly walked outside towards Lt. Col. Granger who now stood at the rear of the Humvee. As we approached in turn, he handed us each an M4 carbine assault rifle, a holstered M9 pistol and a personalized army green duffel bag containing two sets of uniforms, a survival kit and personal hygiene supplies.

The helicopter had come closer, landing only a few hundred feet away on the helipad. It was an UH-60, commonly known as a Black Hawk. Its reverberating sound waves made it difficult to hear the orders he barked or the silver sedan that approached from behind us.

"You will not fire these weapons unless I say so," he commanded. "Safeties remain on."

As our training mandates, we popped the clips out of our weapons and looked briefly at the loaded ammunition before slipping them back in. The sky was still so dark though and we weren't standing under light; it was hard to see anything, much less thoroughly inspect our gear. To be honest, I can't remember if I even genuinely tried to give it a good examination or if I was just going through the motions. Everything was happening so quickly, I took the situation for granted and questioned nothing. I obeyed all my orders. I followed every instruction.

Each uniformed man secured the handgun holster around his thigh. I did the same. The supply pack went over the shoulder while the strap of the assault rifle instinctively wrapped over my head and into my dominant arm.

Granger waited and watched as two men in suits left the silver sedan and entered the Black Hawk carrying a few pieces of baggage. We stood behind him vigilant, gazing on as the car pulled away. The radio attached to the commanding officer's hip produced a loud beep and some static along with a faint voice, "10-8, 1 minute out." He lacked any response as if there were no message.

"Sir," Delgado said to his back, loud enough to be heard, "what are we waiting for, Sir?"

"The belle of the ball," Granger said. Without pause, his eyes never left the corner of the building that hid the turning roadway. A large military police transport rounded the corner slowly, stopping as it approached the group of soldiers. Two military police exited the cab of truck and approached the large doors in the back. One of them counted down from three with his fingers in the air, then turned a rotating latch that released two steel bars securing the entrance. The other squarely held a riot shotgun towards the doors as they opened.

"Simmons, Khu, you're lead," Granger instructed, "Farrell, Delgado, you're rearguard. Move out."

The M.P.'s stepped back and nodded at us, signaling their relinquishment of authority. Simmons and I immediately approached the transport and peered inside at the lone man sitting on the steel bench, his hands bound together in his lap and secured to his ankles. His swarthy skin contrasted against his plain white t-shirt; a belt was noticeably absent from his light khaki pants as were the laces from his shoes. A black fabric hood concealed his head and bundled up around the base of his neck.

"Get up! On your feet!" Simmons yelled as he crossed the threshold just enough to grab the man's arm and guide him down the shallow steps. The prisoner stumbled as he was blindly led, his ankles restrained from moving more than a few inches apart.

Granger walked with intensity towards the helicopter while we followed. The four of us surrounded the olive-skinned man, two men beside him gripping his bare elbows, two men behind him watching his movement. The wind rushing from the propeller blades pushed the hood tightly against the prisoner's face, forcing him to turn his head to breath. To us, though, he gave no resistance.

The two men from the silver sedan occupied the flight cabin behind the pilot, separate from the main passenger bay that comprised most of the aircraft. Simmons hopped inside and hauled the prisoner up, roaring at him to comply; I helped guide the man's legs from outside. He was then seated towards the rear. Simmons fastened the straps around his wrists and ankles tightly to the floor, while the other soldiers boarded.

We hurriedly secured our duffel bags to an overhead bin and buckled ourselves to the seats lining the walls of the fuselage. As we began ascent, we could hear the faint sound of 'Reveille' playing over speakers scattered throughout the base. The lively trumpet tones quickly diminished with the growing distance. The sun was starting to peak over the horizon and gleam through the windows. The day was just beginning. It looked to be beautiful.

03
Arrival

That Black Hawk soared above lush hills and valleys and what appeared to be an endless array of trees and farmland. Occasionally, the landscape was broken up by small communities and clusters of buildings, but the flight seemed to travel along a course that avoided any densely populated areas.

Normally, I love to fly. Every time I'm able to do it, hovering off the Earth even if only by a few hundred feet, I find it so liberating that my stress subsides and I begin to truly feel free. Having a detainee, however, took away that feeling. It's ironic, I think, that my feeling of freedom was bound by his lack of it.

None of us spoke. We couldn't. It was a given that all those aboard were trained to keenly observe our surroundings. Just like me, every one of us had undoubtedly noticed the sun shining in through the starboard windows since our departure. Only Simmons, however, broadcast his curiosity to the group. "North?" he questioned. It seemed like thoughtless verbal ejaculation at the time. Maybe it was intentional. Regardless, that single word, spoken in the earshot of an otherwise blind captive, earned him a vicious scowl from our commander.

Simmons' eyes shut tightly in rapid succession. His jaws clenched and released repeatedly. The silent reprimand incited his nervous childhood tic into a mini facial seizure and was enough of a warning that not another word was spoken by any of the soldiers during the remainder of the flight.

He was right though: North of North Dakota. Flying somewhere over Canada meant we weren't going to an American base. Extraordinary rendition they call it. That's the glossy term the government hogs came up with to describe taking someone out of the country to interrogate and often torture them. Hogs is a term many of the uniformed servicemen use when referring to politicians. I think our jargon is more accurate. Hoo-ahh.

The men sitting with the pilot exchanged words periodically, none of it audible through the thick steel wall and glass window separating them from the us. The barrier was a physical manifestation of their superiority, their elite status in the bureaucratic hierarchy. Only their heads were visible, turning occasionally when they spoke, not looking at each other or at any of us behind them.

The two men, both Caucasian, seemed to be acquaintances at most. Seeing only the sides of their faces as they would turn toward each other, the expressions they exchanged appeared civil but not friendly. Communication was forced in short statements and even shorter replies. Maybe they just didn't like each other but my hunch is they knew each other no better than they knew us.

With little warning and without a clear destination in sight, the helicopter began its descent. It touched ground in the middle of a large grassy field, surrounded by trees in a mile-wide circumference. It was flatland as far as could be seen in all but one direction. No structures or power lines or any other signs of human development were anywhere close.

A monstrous green truck came rolling towards us, leaving a trail of impressions in the grass with its deeply treaded tires. It had a cloth covered truck bed, ribbed from the high supporting frame, with an open back above the tailgate. Its engine growled within the thick steel chassis, shaking the whole frame as it moved. The front of the hulking vehicle, with its squarely shaped hood and sharp linear grill design appeared intimidating if not menacing as it parked a short pace away. Its headlights looked like staring eyes, its exhaust pipes like horns. On the front quarter panel, appeared the words, "CFB Moose Jaw."

We exited the helicopter, Granger leading, the prisoner in tow. The air was crisp and clean, the sun shining brightly. A fellow American soldier, the driver and only passenger of the beastly military transport, exited and swiftly met us in the middle carrying a clipboard and the keys. Granger ordered us to continue on as the two strange men from the helicopter passed by and entered the cab of the truck. As we walked away, I heard the driver speaking of rations and preparations, loud enough to compete with the aircraft's rotating blades.

The prisoner walked without struggle, obeying every command, entering the bed of the truck and sitting beside large transport boxes as he was guided.

Granger advanced to the open back of the vehicle and observed how we had situated ourselves, surrounding the prisoner on all sides. "Watch him. Keep him controlled," he ordered. "Use force if needed—just keep him alive." A few moments later, he fired up the truck's mighty engine and began to drive us away. As we departed, we could see the driver of the truck board our helicopter and rise up beyond our range of vision.

An hour or so drifted by, traveling off-road almost exclusively. The terrain remained as lush but the flat landscape had given way to a sea of rolling hills. The single farm they passed, enclosed by a neglected post and wire fence, gave signs that it had been abandoned for years with wildflowers and weeds growing throughout. While we had seen no humans, wildlife was abundant. Foxes and rabbits darted away, birds flew overhead, and even a few grazing moose could be seen as the truck plowed its own rogue path across the green environment. The motion of the vehicle continued to quickly rise and fall with the ground's curvature; then it slowed and circled the same small area several times before coming to halt like a dog positioning itself on a rug.

I poked my head out from the back and saw nothing. No base, no building, no structure... only hills. My expression must have shown my befuddlement as Granger walked behind and gave two forceful knocks on the tailgate, signaling us to follow. We all jumped down from the vehicle with the same look of confusion, Simmons and I guiding the prisoner by the arm, Farrell and Delgado walking two steps behind.

Granger walked around to the side of one of the steeper hills and knelt down beside a large metal door, slanted to the same angle as the ground and painted with camouflage that convincingly blended it to the surrounding grass from a distance. One of the men in suits handed him an oddly shaped key that allowed the long lever to turn, releasing the latch. As he opened it, everyone peered through for a moment. The darkness inside was exposed enough to see immediate access to a set of spiral steps leading down into the Earth.

He began to descend the concrete stairs, illuminating the cold gray walls with a flashlight. We followed, inhaling the musty air from within. The passage felt much more constricted than it first appeared from the outside; the low ceiling, being only a hand width above some of our heads, gave the illusion that it narrowed even further as it spiraled down. Every step was outlined with a strip that glowed a dim green in the dark, the only guide we had to keep us from tumbling down.

One of the men in suits behind us had a flashlight as well, but the two flashlights were hardly sufficient in a tight spiral for seven men forced to walk in single file. And the prisoner, that poor bastard still had the hood on. He had no chance of seeing.

He stepped down slowly and carefully, guided by my words. I admit I took pity on him. That's easy to do before you know a man's sins or the depth of his capability for evil. Knowing what I know now, I should have pushed the lying bastard down the steps and let him break his own neck.

Granger flicked a switch at the bottom of the stairway, illuminating our station: a concrete underground bunker. The central corridor comprised the bulk of the place, all rooms leading off from it. Every open eye briefly scoped out the areas as we were led past. There were two small sleeping quarters, two twin bunk beds squeezed in each, a large storage area with a wooden table set, and a bathroom with a toilet and stand up shower, all furnished decades ago with scarce a change since.

The end of the hallway opened up into a relatively wider area, a modest assembly room of sorts. Despite it being the most open space available down there, I still felt like the confining gray walls were squeezing us together. One corner of the room was occupied with a slim desk, on top of which rested some vintage electronics and a fairly modern laptop computer. The opposing corner was sectioned off with newly constructed walls, complete with a door that locked from the outside. I knew before he even said so, that was where we were going.

"Secure him in here," Granger said.

We followed, pulling the prisoner by his arms. Simmons and Farrell walked him inside and sat him down on a wooden chair that had a large hole cut in the seat. The chair was bolted to the floor underneath some overhead cabinets, its legs already connected to shackles with chain. The space inside was tight, too confined for me to go in with them, not that I felt it necessary or desirable to do so anyway. So, I stopped at the threshold to watch. I watched them bind his ankles to the legs of the chair, watched them bind his wrists to the handles. He appeared so helpless, so completely at our mercy.

I hadn't given much thought to the non-uniformed strangers at that point. The two were government men, obviously, but until we arrived I didn't know their supposed function. Maybe I should have guessed it from the start, but I had never been on this type of detail before. During the conflicts in the big sandboxes, both Afghanistan and Iraq, I was in the states on guard duty. I never interrogated anyone, never watched while someone else did. I was naive.

Their appearance gave no clues either. The bald man wore thick black frame glasses that accentuated his deep eyes. The thick lenses probably made them appear more sunken than they actually were but I hadn't seen him take his glasses off. That was the most disturbing thing about him though. He was fairly stocky and his belly was somewhat round and protruding; it made him look harmless, docile even. He just appeared to be an average American, someone's husband, someone's dad. He probably was.

The other one looked like a young businessman dressed to impress his corporate boss. He had a jet black head of hair that would probably crunch when pressed. It was slicked straight back, shiny like freshly polished boots. The dimples on his cheeks looked big enough to hide a thumb and his cleft chin was so sharply cut, it looked like his bottom lip was growing an ass. The two of them could just as well been seen having lunch together, discussing stock reports or going door to door trying to convince people to let them demonstrate the latest technology in vacuums.

I didn't like those guys from the beginning. I know I'm biased. I'm from a different sect with a different mindset and I don't like American bureaucracy anyway, but even beyond that, I didn't trust those two.

As soon as I saw the stocky man walk into the interrogation room alone, shutting the door behind him, the roles they were to play struck my brain as an epiphany. It was then that I realized what should have been obvious, maybe blindingly so, to anyone down there about these two government men. This was their party, and their requited invitation fulfilled specific functions necessary to achieve the mission's goals. One was a pit bull, the other was his leash.

Granger gathered the four of us to give us our orders. Just as he had stated before, our mission was simply to escort and guard. We were all trying to gather our bearings; none of us seemed completely at ease, none of us seemed to give full attention. We listened, looked at each other and took in what we could. As far as I was concerned, we were eight strangers trying to get to the end of 14 days as quickly as possible. That's what they had told me. This mission had a maximum time line of 14 days.

04
The Bunker

The way the schedule worked out, the five of us had guard duty 8 hours on, 12 hours off to cover two posts around the clock. Post A was 4 hours just outside the prisoner's door; post B was 4 hours at the top of the spiral staircase. Granger had sequenced our shifts according to rank which meant I was up first, followed by Simmons, Farrell, Delgado and even himself, then starting the whole cycle over. I sat down on the wooden chair beside the prisoner's door, beginning my first stint almost as soon as he was securely locked inside.

Our commander told us, ordered really, that we were not expected nor allowed to interact with the prisoner and that our part was strictly a supporting role for Dr. Hanna and Agent Ekwall. We were only reinforcements making sure interruptions never entered and the prisoner never escaped. That's all.

I had only been on duty for five minutes when the prisoner's door swung ajar and Hanna walked out, his pudgy fingers gripping the handle making it look like a golden egg wrapped in sausages. For a brief moment, I could see the prisoner through the open doorway. He remained just as he was seated before, still shackled, still blindfolded.

Hanna sat down at a table across the room and crossed his legs in way that struck me as rather effeminate for such a husky man. He opened the canvas bag he carried with him, pulled out a copy of *Madame Bovary* and began to read.

"So, what now, *Doc?*" Ekwall said.

"Now, we wait," Hanna replied.

"What for?" Ekwall said.

"For enough time to pass," Hanna said.

"And how will we know when that is?"

Hanna looked up from his book, obviously becoming annoyed by the inquiries.

"I'll let you know," he said.

"I didn't come all this way to sit here and watch you read," Ekwall said, his impatience becoming readily apparent. "There has to be something you can do besides sit on your ass."

Hanna tilted his glasses and squinted his eyes with a glower. "Time weakens men. We wait for him to get sleepy, hungry, thirsty. We wait for his legs and wrists and bladder to become sore, for his mind and will to become weak. Every man cracks in time; then, I will break him. Not before," Hanna said calmly. "Not before." Then he returned his attention to the book.

Ekwall shook his head and retreated to his briefcase, looking through a stack of papers in a folder. I wanted to have a look through that folder and dig in his briefcase. Therein assuredly hid the information about why we were here, the sins that caused this man's detainment. There's a universal allure to forbidden fruit, and knowledge is no different, possibly even the most desirable fruit of all. Gathering classified information, however, takes patience and every little comment exchanged, every odd glance or awkward action a clue. It takes time and time I had aplenty, sitting in a wooden chair, watching a locked door for hours on end.

To be honest, I initially didn't mind the first post at all; it wasn't much different from being off duty. The door to the interrogation room, the cell as it started to be known, was right off the assembly room, primarily where everyone congregated anyway. The 12 hours we weren't guarding either the cell door or the gate—that's what we nicknamed the entrance to our dungeon—we could sleep or play cards or use the Internet or do whatever we wanted to keep our minds occupied until our next shift. Hanna even said that the prisoner couldn't hear us in there so, unless he gave a warning otherwise, we were free to talk. Frankly, post A was a nice excuse to just sit there and listen to the conversations without having to contribute. I enjoyed the banter, no doubt, but really I was more interested in why we were down there to begin with.

There were restrictions to our free time, of course, which they gave at first opportunity. By they, I mean Granger, the soldiers' ranking authority, Ekwall, the mission's apparent resident overseer, and Hanna, the prisoner's supposed solitary liaison.

First, they reiterated, there was to be no unauthorized interaction with the prisoner. This was crucial to the success of the mission. Only Dr. Hanna was to speak to him. They drove this point into the ground with unrelenting redundancy. Then they said it again.

Next, use of the Internet was extremely limited. There was to be no personally specific outgoing information. This meant no email, web text messaging, instant messaging or any other social network communication; we couldn't even use a site that required a user name to be entered as that could be exploited to reveal our location. They stressed there was to be absolutely no pictures but since we weren't allowed to bring any of our own devices and the mini web camera built into the laptop had been removed, forcefully it appeared, I'm not sure how we could have anyway.

Lastly, we had to stay within the confines of the bunker. We couldn't walk outside or rest in the sun or even open the door.

Farrell and Delgado had the task of unloading our rations when we arrived. When finished, they moved the truck a few hundred feet away and covered it with a camouflage tarp so it would be impossible to spot on satellite photos. After they came back in, the door was shut and locked. It wasn't supposed to be opened until the end of the mission, 14 days later.

Under these restrictions, there weren't a lot of options for restless minds. At all times, there was supposed to be two soldiers on guard duty, which meant there would be three soldiers free to roam the bunker. From my chair, I could see Farrell and Delgado nosing around, exploring the small confines. They would walk down the hall, poke around in the rooms and soon after end up back in the assembly room. That first day, off-duty exploration of our new surroundings stemmed from natural curiosity and boredom. Things were very quiet, very calm.

Delgado was the first to notice a pair of handles hanging by rope in the far corner. Oddly, they were coming out of holes in the ceiling next to a large vent. I thought they were for exercise when I first saw them, like gymnastic rings maybe, something that could be used to do pull ups or inverted sit ups. Delgado probably did too when he first approached them. It seemed like every time I looked up, he was doing crunches or push ups or squats, anything to maintain his thick build.

He pulled the handles simultaneously and they didn't move. Then he tried pulling on only one which made the other rise to the ceiling. Moving one, then the other, then again and again with greater force, he initiated a large waft of air coming down through the vent.

"That's a Kearny Air Pump," Granger said.

"A what?" Delgado asked.

"Kearny Air Pump. Brings in fresh air from the surface, evens out the temperature. This many bodies down here, we would bake in here without using it sometimes," Granger said.

"What the hell is this place?" Delgado said.

Granger looked to the Agent sitting next to him as if yielding to his authority or at least his clearance level. Ekwall seemed reluctant to divulge more information than we absolutely needed to know, not just this time but all the time. He would always pause before speaking as if he was carefully reviewing what he might say and editing it down to a satisfactory bare minimum.

"It's a fallout shelter," Ekwall said.

"No shit? An American bomb shelter on the Canuck turf. Everything looks so old. It is, right? Has to be twenty years old, at least." Delgado said.

"It's a remnant from the cold war," Ekwall said.

"It's a pothole, man. It can't be the only one, it's too damn small. This was made under Reagan?" Delgado said.

"What the hell. You writing a book, slim?" Ekwall said.

I could see it in his eyes, the way his jaws clenched, Delgado wasn't happy about the nip. He reminded me of a hulking banger I once saw in a documentary about street gangs in Los Angeles. I half expected a glimpse of a steroid induced rage, maybe even him ripping his shirt open to reveal Latin King gang tats.

"Easy, Suit. I'm just passing the time," was all he said. Then he walked away. I was surprised by his restraint, impressed, really.

Ekwall didn't respond but the tension that he created lingered, keeping the chatter down.

Delgado made some good points though, logical even. That one small bunker could house ten people, maybe a dozen in a disaster. It would seem rational that, since the government hogs decided to build shelters, they would have built enough to house the president, probably the whole first family, select members of Congress, and key scientists or scholars. This one was right in between the east and west coast, far enough away from likely targets to be out of danger but they could have built them anywhere. The States, Mexico, Cuba make sense. This is all my speculation, of course. Ekwall wasn't talking. Nobody was.

It was a welcomed relief when Farrell walked in and lightened the mood.

"Poon porn?" he said. "Who the hell stocked the library down here?"

He tossed a few romance novels on the wooden table beside Hanna, who paid little attention. I couldn't see them very well from where I sat, but they all looked basically the same. A well built man holding a woman, both of them with long hair flowing in the wind, their clothes held on their bodies by threads and faith.

"Seriously, who reads this garbage?" Farrell said. "I thought they planted these down here for you, Delgado, but they're not in Spanish."

Delgado smirked, "I'm glad your here, Ginger. I'd hate to go two weeks without the smell of vagina."

That's what started their war of friendly fire. At least, that's the first I saw of it. They constantly tossed insulting little digs back and forth, all spoken in jest and taken as such. Granger never seemed amused but didn't hinder it either. I was happy about that too. As juvenile as it was, I often found it entertaining. It broke the quiet stiffness and passed the time, got everyone to open up. It kept me out of the line of fire too, at first anyway.

"What's your story?" Farrell asked as he turned to me.

"That seems pretty open ended," I said. It probably came off as sarcastic, but I didn't mean it that way. I always try to keep things friendly, at least that's my intention. I guess I can be a little socially awkward.

"I mean, where are you from, chief?" he asked.

"Lancaster," I said. "Originally from Lancaster, Pennsylvania." I'm not sure why I said that. It wasn't true, of course, but it was too late after it left my mouth to retract it.

"Yeah, that's what I thought. I had you pegged for an Amish," he said, cracking a grin at his own remark. Delgado smiled too.

And that's all it took to make the name stick. They found it an amusing handle for a soldier with an obvious Asian ethnicity and I guess I can see the humor in it. Even so, I'm proud of my ancestry and my country; I didn't want to be associated with a strange people. My gut reaction was to get upset but I didn't let that show. That might only make it worse. Some people, especially men amongst a group of men, like to pull emotional reactions out of their peers to separate the weak from the strong. I thought by not reacting negatively, the nickname would go away quickly. I thought the joke would die once it became stale, but I was wrong. From then on, as if it were my purposefully given name, the other soldiers called me *Amish*.

The first 4 hours, the easy time on post A, seemed to fly by that first day, but it had to come to an end. "Shi-ift," Granger roared, loud enough to be heard throughout the whole bunker as it reverberated off the concrete walls. Simmons, regaining a clear mind after an abrupt end to a short nap, sauntered out from one of the bedrooms to relieve me of my uncomfortable wooden chair. His eyes were at half mast and his body movement seemed to drag through time. Certain parts of his brain still hadn't awoken. I suppose it was irrelevant. He was still alert enough to guard a man bound and gagged behind a locked door at the back of secured bunker in the middle of nowhere. At any rate, he was calm and relaxed enough that his nervous tic wasn't detectable and that was fine by me. It was painfully hard to watch sometimes.

I got up and strolled toward the entrance, toting my rifle on my shoulder, getting a second glance at the rooms as I passed, getting only a teased hint of what I'd expect to find when I was allowed to explore at the end of my second shift. Everything seemed so confined. The cramped walls seemed suffocating as I walked up the spirals stairs. The stale air didn't help.

As I reached that top step, I sat on the cold concrete and stared into the darkness. The tiny luminescent strips glowed with enough light to see the contour of the walls but nothing more. It didn't really matter though. That narrow stairway had nothing interesting to see but the bare gray concrete. I could almost feel my pupils dilate as my eyes adjusted to the dark, stretching open to gather as much light as they could.

I leaned against the door, knowing that just on the other side still remained the last third of a pleasant day. Warm sun, fresh air, and green grass all mere inches away, kept from me by a few layers of steel and the official mission parameters.

That shift, post B, was the hard shift. Time limped by. A few minutes in that dark, quiet space felt like a whole shift among the other soldiers. I tried to find a way to sleep but my efforts were thwarted by the rock-hard steps against my back that prevented any comfortable position. I remembered reading about solitary confinement, how it was used in prisons to discipline unruly behavior. I now understand how it works, how someone kept in a condition like that could have his spirit broken, if not his sanity. My mind would drift off into memories and dreams and fantasies and my eyes would start to form shapes in the dark void. Day one, and I was already growing weary of that duty.

05
Free to Roam

"Shi-ift," Granger yelled again. His forceful roar was surprisingly difficult to hear at the top of the stairs, and sincerely, I was listening in near silence for that sweet call of relief. The spiral walkway seemed to be a decent sound insulator and kept noise from traveling up so easily. It didn't occur to me until later that sound probably had just as much resistance traveling down.

This change in posts was how I kept track of the days without nagging my superiors for the current time. I tried anyway, at least near the beginning. It sounds like it should be easy enough, strictly alternating 8 hours of duty with 12 hours of rest, but we were essentially living 20-hour days. Two 4-hour shifts down plus a few full hours of transport, the time must have been around 2000 that first day when I was finally relieved of my detail and I was starving.

I crept down to the bottom of the steps, greeting Simmons and his prodigal facial tic as they passed. My growling stomach afforded me no patience for genial chatter, not that it would be welcomed otherwise. I'm no racist, but I've never been able to really connect with a black man, or any black people for that matter. And I wasn't about to try again just then. After 4 hours in darkness, even the light made my hunger-induced headache pulsate with the rhythm of my heartbeat. I had to eat.

I walked into the meager storage room/mess hall combo, eyeing up food crates, ready to tear into anything remotely edible. There were cartons of field rations, separated and labeled by name for each of us; each box contained 42 meal kits, enough food for 14 days. These meals were built with uncompromising military guidelines for basic sustenance, not pleasure, and it was evident. Don't misunderstand what I mean: someone purposefully designed food just palatable enough to satiate hunger and nourish soldiers without making it so tasty that anyone would want more. A small pouch of dry chicken or tuna or pork, a few crackers reminiscent of solidified sawdust, a packet filled with a spreadable topping like unsweetened peanut butter or jam, and a piece of hard candy for dessert—all designed for the military with a minimum shelf life of a year at room temperature. It made me wonder, how many soldiers, fighting in wars for their country's freedoms and beliefs, have violently died after eating something like this for a last meal? Serial murderers sentenced to death eat better before they get peacefully injected. Hoo-ahh. I ate every crumb.

Evidence of an aging origin was rampant throughout the bunker, nowhere more than that room. The chairs and table, a complete wooden dinette set circa 1980, provided little comfort as I ingested the last morsel and took in my surroundings. The refrigerator was an awful shade of olive green and exuded an unidentifiable musk whenever opened. The microwave, the most up to date appliance in that room, was still older than me.

The small open pantry housed stacks of canned goods, supplementals they were called, that we could use at our discretion to enhance our dining experience in the off chance that some dry crackers and a few bites of meat didn't quite hit the mark. At a quick glance, it seemed to be mostly vegetables, a disproportionate amount of them being beets. I hate beets.

The inquisitive impulse for exploration I had postponed started to get the best of me. I walked into each bedroom, feeling the flimsy mattresses sitting atop a springy steel latticework. I explored the drab latrine, amazed that such weak water pressure could possibly carry away solid waste. I crossed my fingers that none of the other soldiers were prone to large movements and had a greater appreciation for the small meals given us. I ended up, as I often did, in the large assembly room, sitting with the other soldiers. It didn't take long to realize they liked to talk. As it so happens, I liked to listen.

"Do you shake it or flick it?" Farrell said.

"What are you talking about?" Delgado said, reluctantly diverting his attention away from an Internet news site.

Farrell, on duty by the cell, often initiated juvenile debates with Delgado. When you wipe your ass, do you crinkle or fold the toilet paper? What's the most important part of a sandwich, the meat or the bread? Often sexual, sometimes disgusting, they usually evolved into another battle of insults. I'd often wonder if they only took breaks to come up with new material, passing the time trying to create a dig the other couldn't top.

"Your dick," Farrell said. "When you get done pissing, do you give little Pedro a slap or choke his neck dry? Me personally, I just bang it against the side of the toilet, but I figure you probably don't pass up an opportunity to touch yourself."

Comments often contained thinly veiled ethnic slurs, the Latino versus the Irish. This always led to a return fire that continued on way too long. I was a little envious. I'm not a worthy opponent to either of them though; I don't think with a humorous mentality. I understand it. I enjoy it. I just can't duplicate it, not on my own. They were doing more than just talking smack though. They were building a perceivable camaraderie, earning respect for each other with every creative verbal jab.

"Usually, I just leave it wet because your mom likes the taste," Delgado said as he stood and headed toward the latrine. "Speaking of which..."

"My mom is a 350 pound, one-legged diabetic in a wheelchair. If that's your thing, have at it, you sick fuck," Farrell said.

As entertaining as it was, I tried to tune it out for the more subtle conversation between the two government men. Hanna had started visiting the captive in the cell every few minutes and I heard him say something about "Stockholm Syndrome" to Ekwall who continually shot sour glances at Hanna as though the sight of him induced bouts of spontaneous constipation.

I ended up researching it when I was able to get online. Stockholm Syndrome: a psychological condition where victims feel trust, even compassion for their captors. I had no idea what was going on behind that door. I didn't think any of us did. I was gullible.

Granger seemed like he couldn't care less about what was happening to that man. He would patrol the hallway every few minutes and speak minimally. As long as we were stationed during our shift, he gave no instruction, information or rebuke. The other men seemed indifferent about him as well, at first anyway.

"Oh, hell yeah," Delgado said as he returned, holding two large bottles of vodka. "Look what I found in the storage locker."

"Shit," Farrell said. "How the hell'd I miss that?"

"I know, a hearty Irish breakfast like this? I thought you people could sniff this stuff out. What do you say, Colonel?"

Granger took a bottle and read the label, nodding his head approvingly as he handed it back.

"Put them in the freezer. No more than two shots after every second shift," Granger said, "If I see anyone intoxicated, I flush the rest. Hoo-ahh?"

"Hoo-ahh," they returned.

"No. That is *not* a good idea," Ekwall interjected abruptly. "It's not appropriate, Colonel. We have a mission and I can't allow any conduct that could be detrimental to the success of this mission."

"You and I have different missions, Agent Ekwall. Everyone you see around you wearing camouflage is only here to make sure *that* asshole doesn't escape or kill you. I see no harm with a couple drinks for my guys when they're resting," Granger said.

"Bullshit! I don't want them drinking."

"Lucky for them, they're under my command."

"You want to piss a line in the sand, I'll make a few calls and have those stripes ripped off your shoulder. You'll be dragging your balls across the boot camp gravel, teaching recruits how to fuck up a military career. Don't challenge my authority here, Colonel."

"Your authority only extends to your mission directive, not my men. That was made very clear to me and it should have been explained equally as well to you. Just let me know what you need done and it will get done but you will not tell me how to do it."

Granger turned sharply and headed towards one of the bedrooms as Ekwall glared on fumingly. Delgado nodded towards the bottle in his hand as he walked towards the kitchen as if to offer me first crack at the unopened supply. I smiled lightly as I declined. I've never been much of a drinker. I prefer to keep my wits about me.

06
The Interrogation Begins

The screams woke me. That was the first time I'd heard them. They were intense but muffled and brief. Still, they woke me. I had wanted to sleep before my next shift and I did for a time, but was startled awake and sat upright instinctively. I remember I had been dreaming just before, although I don't remember the dream, and when I awoke I wasn't sure if the screaming was real or not. Then I heard it again.

I entered the assembly room to see all eyes pointing towards the cell. They were as surprised as me I thought; at least, surprised enough that they didn't acknowledge me when I entered the room. I looked around briefly, then joined their visual focus towards the cell door, as if awaiting an explanation. The screaming had ceased.

Slowly the door opened and out came Dr. Hanna, meeting each glare with his own. His shirt was unbuttoned, his sleeves rolled up. He had a bit of sweat shining from the top of his bald head and rolling down his brow.

"Don't look so surprised," he said. "You're not children. You know why you're here." Then he sat down and began to read his book once again.

Maybe he was right. We had all known about the detention centers and we'd all heard the rumors and rumblings of black sites and torture but I, at least, had never seen it. Not first hand. Not irrefutably so close.

One by one, every man went back to his own corner, back to minding his own business, maintaining his own sanity. Farrell was at the computer looking online, Agent Ekwall buried his face in a report, and Granger sat uncomfortably upright as he guarded the cell door. My shift was approaching.

I followed Simmons into the kitchen, entering just as he was pulling the top off one of the sealed punishments they deemed food. His facial tic was in a full tizzy as if his forehead was having an orgasm. I have to admit, part of me was becoming fond of the facial tic. His blatant weakness, so predominately displayed, somehow made me feel less vulnerable. He gave a slight glance over his shoulder, opting to disregard me.

"What do you make of that?" I asked.

"I don't know, man. I ain't tried it yet. It look like shit though," he said.

"I mean the prisoner. What do you think is going on in there?"

"I don't know nothing about that neither. Man must have done something and now he paying the price, right?" he said.

"Yeah, I guess," I said. But I didn't guess. Diplomacy be damned, I already disagreed with whatever was happening to him. Regardless of what he may have done, I had no desire to be part of some black-op witch hunt. "Do you think this is right though? What if he's getting tortured? Maybe even to death?"

"You ask me," he said, "you do wrong, you get wrong back. That's just the way shit works. And as far as I go, I keep sparks out of my eyes by not blowing the fire, you feel? That's also how shit works."

"So, just follow orders and keep your head down, that it?" I said.

"Damn straight," he said. "I'll let the men in the suits and stars process the shit no one else want to deal with. They can pull the trigger, they can taste the blowback. I advise everyone of you do the same. We don't get paid enough to lose sleep over what's right."

I sat there for a few minutes as he ate the last of his sad meal. I didn't want to argue with him. I'm always the one making every effort to stay unnoticed so I shouldn't expect anyone else to behave differently. Especially down there, in a place so isolated, I didn't want to cause a commotion or make enemies. Who am I to question their authority or tactics? Take up a cause based on assumption? I truly didn't have all of the facts. My disagreement was with what I imagined was going on behind that closed door. But, I started to reason that was probably just empathy putting myself in his place, a traitor accused and no matter how guilty, I'd want someone to end my suffering.

"Where are you from?" I asked, perhaps getting some sociable inspiration from Farrell's banter and confidence from Simmons' facial spasms.

"Baltimore, man," he said. "It's my home. I miss it."

"How long have you been away?" I asked.

"I ain't been back since I enlisted," he said. "Not sure when I'll get to go back neither."

"Yeah, why is that?" I asked.

"It's a long story," he said.

"We have time to kill," I said.

"It's personal then," he said. "I just don't want to talk about it."

"Fair enough. We all have our skeletons," I said.

"You ain't lying, Amish," he said, "you ain't lying."

Farrell walked into the room, slowing down as he heard our chatter turn to silence. He looked at us like we were startled deer and headed towards the refrigerator.

"Relax, ladies. I didn't come to bust up the sewing circle," he said, displaying a cocky smirk at his own remark. "Although, I could go for a few hands of hold 'em. Either of you play?"

We both shook our heads.

"You gals fancy yourself more of Bridge crowd, huh?" he said. "Perfect. I'll teach you."

I must admit, I enjoyed the game of Poker much more than I thought I would. It contains so many compelling aspects: the statistical strategy of trying to create a winning hand with whatever your given, the psychological challenge of trying to read others' faces for signs of deception while withholding your own, the thrill of outwitting opponents by betting for escalating risks which, for us, ranged from candy and money to rations and eventually, shifts. Most of all, to my own surprise, I truly enjoyed just sitting around with a group of my peers and bonding freely, being socially accepted even. It was the first time I had held that feeling, I think, ever. Yes, actually. Looking back on my life, I'm sure of it.

We played quite often at first. The players would change with the shifts, and on occasion, even our superior, Granger, would sit and play a few hands with us.

They said I was a natural at it too, that I had no *tell*. I was too embarrassed to admit I didn't know exactly what that meant so I didn't ask, but I quickly reasoned they could not easily detect any physical cues when I bluffed which makes perfect sense and I consider that testament to my training. I didn't win every time, of course, the most extreme of my mistakes following a lengthy winning streak and resulting in having to take one of Farrell's dreadful shifts at the gate.

"Damn you, Amish!" they would say when I laid down my winning cards. "Damn you, Khu!" I would think to myself when I'd lost. No matter the outcome, I was damned just for playing their game, even if it took some time to realize how true that was.

Shift change had come, initiated by Granger's growling yell down the cement corridor. My commander passed me as I took over his duty at the cell. I found it unusually respectful, very admirable even, for him to share in the responsibilities, alleviating some of the tedium from the four of us. It garnered him a lot of respect; indeed, my fellow soldiers made several comments about his character. In retrospect, I know it wasn't so selfless.

I placed myself in the hard wooden chair beside the entrance to the cell, toting my rifle at my hip, only feet away from the door. I peered through, trying to get a glimpse as Hanna entered inside. I could see him, the prisoner still shackled at the ankles, sitting where he was placed, his wrists still bound to the arms of the chair. The white shirt he wore was soaked with what I assumed was sweat. His hood was removed now, but I couldn't see how he appeared as his head rested downward; his thick hair, wavy and black, created a veil that covered his face completely. Large headphones were strapped to his head and I could hear the faint sound of heavy metal music rhythmically pumping from inside.

I saw some tools hanging from the wall and scattered about, but I was so focused on the hostage, I couldn't make myself look directly at them to see what they were. The door closed too quickly behind Hanna, sending out a big waft of hot air towards me. I could smell burnt hair.

"Oh shit," Delgado said. He sat at the computer desk, hunched over the small laptop screen looking at a news site. His thick, meaty hands smothered the mouse as he maneuvered.

"What's wrong, Esse? Find some dirty pictures of your mom online again?" Farrell said, shuffling the deck of cards against his thigh. I think he was beginning to consider himself somewhat of a card sharp. His insults were becoming tiresome.

"The news, man. I don't know why I read the damn news. It's depressing as hell," Delgado said.

"How can you be depressed serving two weeks in this little chunk of heaven? I'd call it a wash at least," Farrell said. That bit of sarcasm even made Simmons crack a smile, his facial tic receding to a nice calm as he rested in a dark corner.

Agent Ekwall didn't flinch though. He hardly acknowledged any of us, as if to dismiss us all for wasting his time. I could feel animosity emanating from him, especially, although not exclusively, towards me. I attributed that to being a Specialist, the lowest ranking grunt here; I could see no other reason for him to single me out. His body language—clenched jaw, sighing breaths, piercing glances—all displayed his contempt for us, maybe this whole process. He kept to himself, sitting alone at the table, alternating between reading reports and doing brain teasers from a puzzle book he kept in his briefcase.

Damn, that briefcase. How I wanted to explore its contents but there just was no opportunity. When he left the room to go to the latrine, the briefcase went with him. When he went to sleep, it was locked and on the other side of his mattress. It never left his sight. None of the other soldiers ever expressed interest in what it contained. I was though. Very much, I was.

"The stock market just got ass-pumped again and that Jersey bitch, the one who killed her own kids, she walked free on a technicality," Delgado said. He emphasized the most troubling current events as he scanned down the headlines, "Murders, rapes, space rocks, hijackings–"

"Space rocks?" Simmons said.

"Yeah, a meteor shower it says. May cause major satellite disruption on the other side of the globe," Delgado said. "And the worst part is, access to porn is blocked on this damn thing, so there's not much else to look at."

"Anything about Baltimore in there?" Simmons asked.

"As a matter of fact, I just read Baltimore no longer leads the country in STD's," Delgado said. "I'm not even shitting you, it's right here. So, congratulations on that, Simmons."

"It says that?" Farrell laughed. "Well, that's just because Simmons left. In other news, Moose Jaw, Canada just saw a surge of crotch crickets."

"Did anyone notice if we have toilet seat covers here?" Delgado said.

Simmons couldn't help but smile at their jabs. "Fuck you both," he said. What he meant, I think, was "good one."

Without warning, the screaming started again, followed by a momentary flicker of the lights. We all hushed; our smiling faces turned grim. Even Ekwall looked up from his crossword toward the door. We could hear the faint sound of Hanna talking and occasionally muffled yelling. Even as the closest to the door, I couldn't make out what he was saying or asking or, most likely, demanding.

The prisoner's screams of agony resumed. As they continued, intermittent with moments of serenity and chatter, we all remained silent. It takes a cold heart, perhaps even a sadistic soul, to continue lighthearted banter in the presence of great suffering, even that of your enemies. It was difficult to stomach, despite being unseen. There was a disturbing growl in the prisoner's voice, guttural wailing of pain and fear and torment.

Delgado was the first to walk away, to retreat to another area of the compound. Farrell and Simmons shortly followed his lead, one after the other. I don't blame them for leaving. Had I not been captive to my station, I would have gone as well, possibly even first. Only Ekwall remained, he and his disdainful glances. It made me long for the silent solitude of my shift at the gate.

I don't know how long it lasted. There was no indicator of time around me, natural or otherwise. I felt like it went on for too long though, as if time slowed to keep the end of my shift from reaching me. I walked a few feet toward the computer, just for a moment, to look at the digital clock in the corner of the screen; it read 12:13 am. Ekwall kept his eye on me as I returned to my chair. Then the room fell silent.

Dr. Hanna emerged and with him, another waft of hot air. A thin cloud of smoke seeped around the door carrying the stench of burnt flesh. A small spray of blood swept from one side of his belly to the other. I'm sure it wasn't his own. Inside, I could see the prisoner in the same position as before. His shirt, too, was decorated in splotches of red stain. A rag, saturated with blood, wrapped around his left hand, which still remained bound to the arm of the chair. Hanna closed the door behind him and wiped the dripping sweat from his head with a clean handkerchief.

"Well, what did he say?" Ekwall whispered, seemingly to preclude me from hearing.

"We will break him," Hanna replied just as softly. "Don't worry. In, time he will break."

I watched Hanna guzzle down a bottle of ice water and wipe the condensation across his forehead. A monster, I thought. A demon masquerading as a hero, authorized to unleash his evil.

It brought to mind stories of the famous Romanian, Vlad the Impaler. The man dubbed Vlad Dracul, the dragon, he of such infamy that legends of his cruelty evolved into myths that spread across the world. It's common knowledge that the myth eventually created the vampire, a vile monster with an unequally wicked mind. And yet, in Romania, a statue stands honoring Vlad, the soldier and king that saved his people. The god and the devil, two sides of the same coin. It's only perspective that determines which one you choose to see.

So preoccupied with my surroundings, I hardly noticed Granger standing before me.

"Shift, soldier," my superior said. His tone was unusually calm. Perhaps, I thought, none of us were hardened enough to remain unaffected. I stood, rifle in hand, and headed toward my second shift.

The atmosphere was heavily somber. I saw despair in the eyes of my peers as I passed them, gathered around the kitchen table in silence, pouring shots of ice-cold vodka. Maybe their emotional state was just a hallucination; perhaps the feelings I sensed were simply a projection of my own. At the time it seemed logical though. It's disheartening to see the underbelly of your own country's military tactics and bureaucratic policies, to know what they condemn as criminal from foreign governments is being conducted under a supposed flag of justice. It's a demoralizing betrayal, one which breeds contempt among citizens, one they feel impotent to overcome. I know this well. Hoo-ahh.

I walked up into the spiral darkness, feeling comfort in the solitary that I once dreaded. I reasoned a day and a half had passed and I just had to remain calm and endure this station. In time, everything would be fine.

07
For Mental Health

The quiet darkness was supposed to give me peace. That's what I believed anyway. But as I sat there, waiting for the end of my shift, they continued, those terrible screams of agony continued. Whether they were actually happening or not was hard to tell. The memory of them was enough, embedded in my brain and holding my mind hostage. Not just the sounds themselves, of course, but the thought of whatever actions led to them.

My imagination was all I had to rely on, using the brief visuals ingrained in my mind, guessing what was being done behind that door. Pulling of fingernails or teeth, tearing and burning of skin or eyes or genitals. I had no idea what horrible acts were being perpetrated against that helpless man. And there I was, sharing the same roof, selfishly becoming angry and frustrated that I couldn't get comfortable.

I leaned against the wall, adjusting myself on the angled step. The pistol at my side dug into my thigh and the cold concrete made numb every part of me that touched it for too long. I held firmly onto my rifle, hugging it like a devoted companion, determined not to send it tumbling down the spiral staircase. In the still of deafening silence, surrounded by darkness and rock, I longed for passage of time, to go back to my regular duties guarding government equipment on the East Coast. Back there, every day ended with my lungs breathing fresh air. Back there, I saw no blood shed or suffering dealt.

Then I heard rhythmic beating and melodic tones. It was faint, so difficult to hear but definitely there. I wondered what was outside the thick metal door against my back, the door that led to green grass and blue skies and at that moment, I thought, music. I tried to make out what it was, but I couldn't. I put my ear against the steel hinges, hoping to get more of it, to get something to replace the screams that haunted my thoughts, but it was no louder. Even still, it continued.

When Colonel Granger finally called for a change in post, I couldn't wait to tell the others what I'd heard. I had already planned out how I'd exaggerate the volume of the sounds, perhaps even say I thought I heard gunfire. I'd volunteer to investigate, maybe go so far as suggest a third shift to patrol outside, anything to get a break from within those prison walls. In my imagination, Granger would agree and commend me on my keen sense of perception; the others would thank me for a chance to breathe fresh air and feel sunshine on their face.

But as I began to descend, it became apparent that would not be the case. The music became more audible with every step downward and once I reached the main hallway, it was clear and recognizable.

Oddly enough, it wasn't Simmons but Granger who passed me to cover the position at the gate. He said not a word as he shook his head and maintained the stern, determined expression from which he rarely deviated. I peered in one of the bedrooms as I passed; Ekwall was sleeping, a pillow over his head and the briefcase under his arm.

"...Wanna take my time, change your mind...," the song played on. I had heard it before but I didn't know its title or even the artist singing. I'm no aficionado of music, especially vintage American pop music, so if I've heard it, I can conclude it *must* have been popular, at least at one time.

As I walked in the main assembly room, music filled the whole space. Farrell was dancing foolishly back and forth, clapping his hands above his head, trying to make the others laugh. He looked at me when I entered and pointed fingers at me with both hands. "Check it out, Amish! It's the Party Boss, baby," he said exuberantly.

It was Bryce Fallsteen, I would come to know, singing a song called *Dancing in the Night*. Delgado acted like he didn't enjoy the foolishness but his partially concealed smile revealed otherwise.

"You believe this shit?" Simmons said, serving his post beside the door to the cell. "I ain't sure who they trying to torture down here. I'm about ready to trade places with that tied-up mother-fucker in there."

"Oh, come on," Farrell said. "I could only find two CD's: this and Dick Fastley. All the other cases were empty."

"Granger OK'd this?" I asked.

"OK'd? He told me to play something," Farrell said, "and get this... Hanna told *him* to have us play something. I thought Ekwall was going to shit an angry midget over it. Then he moved our shifts around, which I'm thinking is to give Simmons some more exposure to actual music."

Even then, it seemed peculiar to me that Granger would change his orders and opt to take another shift early. Random changes like that only made it harder to keep track of time, but I didn't want to question his authority. I was in no position to do so. I simply accepted it like I did everything else.

As for the the music, it wasn't my taste and I didn't exactly understand why we had to play anything. I reasoned the possibility that the upbeat tunes were intended to counteract the obvious damage on morale done by hearing what we had. My guess though was that Hanna intended it to cover the ongoing sounds of interrogation as they intensified. Now I'm not sure what sounds they were trying to conceal.

At any rate, it seemed to have worked well enough on everyone else, even Simmons with his obligatory complaints about the genre. Farrell was dancing around like a king's jester on one end of the room while Delgado alternated between doing push ups and jumping jacks in synchronized tempo on the other side. They all appeared to quickly grow callous to the situation while it sat heavily at the forefront of my mind, distracting my focus. I was envious of their apathy and quietly held hope the songs would work on me too.

Music is a simple salve—really, very simple measured against its great effectiveness. Through melody and harmony, rhythm and tones that can be felt as much as heard, emotional wounds can be soothed through terrible situations. Salves, though, are only effective if the wound stays closed. And once the screaming became loud enough to accompany the music or Dr. Hanna would emerge with red stains spattered on his hands, shirt or face, we were quickly reminded that just in the next room, a more serious situation was unfolding. And before too long, out he came.

Dr. Hanna looked around the room as if taking inventory of our reaction to him. Sometimes he'd take a break and read or snack or nap. Every once in a while, he'd rinse off in the tiny shower to the side of the latrine. This time though, he retrieved his leather bag and went directly back in. Moments later, the screaming resumed.

Farrell subtly pulled Delgado and me into the kitchen, leaving Simmons to wallow in the atmosphere Hanna created while the CD player dished out ironically appropriate tunes like *Born in America* and *I've Been Burned.*

We didn't talk about the prisoner. We didn't share exchanges about what we thought was happening in there or how it made us feel to be privy to the whole scenario. It was still out of sight; even if just barely, it was still enough for personal deniability.

Instead, we quietly played cards, hand after hand. Quietly, that is, until Farrell pulled the vodka from the freezer, pouring a substantial amount in three plastic cups without so much as asking us. He was up next for duty and still he drank, ignoring the commander's orders. Maybe Farrell was *trying* to get booted out of here; maybe, I thought, he was just trying to cope.

I've never been a drinker as I've followed the orders that were handed down to me, to abstain in order to survive. I've kept my mind clear and my wits sharp; after all, I know my priorities. But these men, united with me through this service, pushed it in front of me and held their cups high. It was as much an offer to bond with them as it was to soak my sorrows. I partook for both reasons. The acrid liquid was ice on my tongue and fire on my throat. It was fantastic.

I remember at least two refills at that time and it wasn't long before I started to feel the effects. The burdens of my surroundings, the obligations and duties placed on me by my superiors, all of it became easier to bear as I gently slipped into a sweet numbness. It became obvious they felt it too when their lips began to loosen. As conversation rapidly increased, the tone evolved from dismal to untroubled.

Farrell started to reminisce about his childhood growing up near Salt Lake City. He spoke fondly about his sister and him running around the neighborhood at Halloween dressed as a cupcake and a ninja turtle, collecting candy from anyone who'd answer their door and egging the houses of those who didn't. He recalled childhood memories of family road trips, fighting with that same sister in the backseat, exchanging small sharp pinches they called "snake bites" and twisting "Indian burns" in each others' forearms.

Once, he said, his best friend had gotten some bottle rockets from a family trip to Wyoming and the boys decided to set them off together. They walked to the middle of a large, empty field by their home when they came across a heavy lead pipe the length of his arm. It seemed perfect in the mind of thirteen year old boys to combine the lead pipe with the fireworks to create a makeshift rocket launcher. One boy would rest the pipe on his shoulder for aim while the other stuffed a lit rocket in the back. It worked just as they expected, he recalled, until they decided to tie three of the small projectiles together to create a more massive explosion.

As one may expect from the work of such youth, their knot held tightly enough to keep the rockets connected, but not tightly enough to maintain their directional alignment. The three rockets left the end of the pipe igniting at slightly different times and jumped around chaotically until the thin string binding them together burned away. Then, they shot away from each other in different directions, one heading right for the two boys. As they narrowly evaded that single explosive, they looked up to realize the others had landed in two separate areas of dry brush, instantly setting them ablaze. It caused the most expansive brush fire the city had seen in twenty-eight years.

"It was, to describe it in one word... fucking awesome," Farrell said. Having the same passion for fireworks, it was hard not to agree and, smiling widely, I told him so.

I enjoyed the stories quite a lot and especially liked hearing him relive the memories of his sister. Having no siblings to speak of, I don't truly know what it's like to have family I could always return to, kin to share memories with and depend on during times of trouble. I only understood the responsibility that goes along with the blood-ties and the sacrifice that it demands.

When he would speak of her, I pictured myself in his place, and I truly felt jealous.

They asked directly if I had any siblings and I said I didn't. I lied, of course, but it was easier to deny their existence than to explain how little I knew about them. Any details I could have given would have to be fabricated and I've learned that keeping track of complicated falsehoods just becomes too difficult over time. So I shared minimally, as always, and quickly returned a question to get them speaking about themselves again. That disciplined practice not only helped me avoid having to divulge personal information, but hearing them talk about their past was genuinely endearing, even if eventually detrimental.

I became so engrossed in their stories, so pleased with the fantasy of making their memory my own, I lost focus on the game we were playing. Before even paying the debt I already owed, three kings betrayed me and I had to take another of Farrell's shifts. This time though, he made clear I'd earned a shift by the cell. Aside from being the prisoner strapped to the chair, guarding the cell door had quickly become the least desirable position down there.

That hand ended the otherwise enjoyable game on a sour note for me. They showed little sympathy though, Delgado even snickering as he left the room.

"I should have run like a hunted deer when they contacted me about this mission," I said, my lame attempt at contemptuous wit, admittedly more accurate than funny.

Farrell shuffled the cards and asked me if I liked magic tricks.

"As much as anyone, I suppose," I said, "but I don't know any."

He separated out two small stacks of cards and scribbled a small note directly on the table, covering it with his hand.

"Pick one of the stacks," he said. "I already know which one you'll pick."

So I did.

"Go ahead and count them," he said.

I tallied out five cards, a royal flush he had formed. He then lifted his hand to reveal the note he left on the table which read, "you picked the stack of 5." He fanned out the other stack face down and sure enough, it only had four cards.

"How'd you know?" I asked.

"It didn't matter which one you picked," he said. "Had you picked this one, I would have just told you to look at these."

He turned them over revealing the stack with four cards being the 5's of every suit.

"See... no matter what, you were always going to pick the 5 stack. The real trick is making you think you had a choice to begin with."

I understood his point about the military though it was no revelation to me: options are run through a filter and at the bottom there's nothing left but orders. This mission was no different. Hoo-ahh.

"Now if you'll excuse me," he said, "I have some Russian liquor to sleep off and I think you have some shifts to cover."

I stumbled towards the hard wooden chair by the prisoner's door, tired and drunk. I hadn't slept well since I'd been there and it was catching up to me. It was going to be a long shift.

08
Keeping it Clean

I was wobbling. Sitting there with that uncomfortable wooden chair pushing against my back, I'd catch myself starting to fall asleep. Frankly, it was less a gentle beckoning of slumber as a relentless thrust into oblivion. I can only imagine how I looked from an outside perspective, bobbing back and forth, closing my eyes and jumping when I'd feel gravity overpowering my pose. Desperately holding onto thoughts that wanted to drift away into nothingness, I'd shift my attention from one object to another, feeling the delay between fixation and perception. The laptop at the desk, the puzzle book on the table, the air pump handles dangling from the ceiling. To look at them, to really focus on them, took all the effort my drunk brain could muster. I just needed to wait for it to wear off, to collect myself and fight through the intoxication, force my mind to overcome the chemical trying to disarm my consciousness. I closed my eyes at one point and felt the room begin to spin so I bent over and put my head between my knees to stabilize. That only made it worse.

It's amazing how thought processes differ in that state of mind. Things that seem so important in sobriety carry much less weight under the influence. Attempting to remain upright, elbows planted on my knees, staring at my crotch with my rifle propped up between the floor and my shoulder, I should have been concerned about the prisoner, pondering every aspect of my station. The most dangerous man on Earth could very well have been the man sitting in the next room, most likely scheming for freedom that I was charged to prevent. Had he managed to unleash himself from his shackles, he'd have found me completely vulnerable and impotent.

I couldn't know how truly susceptible I was to his attack. I didn't know he was the engineer of my world's destruction, the one to eventually doom us. I should have been focused on my mission, keeping my training in mind so I could continue my work for you.

Instead, resting there with my head between my thighs allowing the alcohol to comfort my anxious mind, all I could think about was the sweaty stench emanating from my nether region. I hadn't bathed since I'd arrived and while I wasn't as physically active as some of the others, hygienic maintenance was long overdue. With so many adult men confined to such a space, the whole bunker had slowly begun to reek of body odors. Every time I'd descend down the spiral staircase from the gate, I'd be smacked in the face with the natural stench dominating the air and clinging to the walls. It was a product we all manufactured. I was becoming afraid though, that I may have contributed more than my due share.

The shower was a cramped but openly visible stall sitting just inside the small latrine beside the toilet. Aside from the steel gate at the entrance and the one separating me from the prisoner—both oddly lockable from either side—there were no doors in the whole bunker, including the entrance to that small washroom. The other men seemed fine walking through the doorway and using the shower while someone else sat on the toilet, inches away with nothing separating them. To do so in those close quarters meant stripping down and stepping over their legs, providing an unwelcome and candid view of our humanity. Most were courteous about it, respecting the awkwardness of the personal invasion of space though no one else seemed as bothered as me. Farrell even made light of it, saying things like, "now you get to see what a man-sized dick looks like," or, "don't worry, having my balls in your face runs in your family."

There was only a small hedge of a wall intended to be a splash guard at the ankles, keeping water from spilling too far from the drain in the floor. The shower head itself was nothing more than a threaded pipe protruding from the wall, spilling out a thick, sad stream of cold water, reminiscent of a garden hose releasing at half pressure.

My tendency to maintain my privacy, combined with my thin physical frame, made it difficult to overcome the embarrassment of exposing myself in full and washing off in plain view. So, until that point, I hadn't. But then, sitting in my own filth and breathing in fumes that would make me nauseated had I known they originated from another, I began to correlate the strength of stench with an increase in people using the air pump to bring down fresh air, surely for olfactory relief as much as environmental comfort. I wanted to wash off, badly. The alcohol had lowered my inhibitions enough that I wouldn't have cared who saw me naked, but at that point I was stuck in a sedentary position, fighting to stay awake.

The music had stopped, probably automatically, but nobody rushed to restart it. There's only so many times a person can hear the same album over and over before it becomes tedious and irritating, even if it's something they like and I was about done with it before it even started. The audible stillness joined forces with the warm temperature to oppose me. I succumbed and drifted in and out a few times.

In my haze, I remember hearing an argument coming from a room over. I could have sworn it was Granger and Ekwall discussing the prisoner.

"It's going nowhere. We need to know what he knows!" Ekwall said. "Hanna needs to push it further, faster."

Granger growled back but his voice, naturally in a lower register, was harder to hear. And before long, Delgado started using the air pump again, wafting a big gust of welcome air across my face but making it impossible to discern any more of the argument.

Further, I thought. Faster. His words stuck in my brain like a nail. I'm not sure what he expected or wanted to happen to that man, how much more ruthless he'd prefer his beast to act. I saw fresh bloodstains appear every time Hanna exited the cell door. I heard screams at regular intervals. What was his limit for abuse? How harsh would it have to get before it was too far? Then I wondered if Ekwall would be able do it himself. Could he get the blood on his own hands or was his cruelty merely in giving orders? I no longer saw him as the leash on a pit bull but a vicious master pressing his dog to bite harder.

I don't know how long I was out, but when I awoke to the commotion, I was balanced upright with my face pressed against my rifle, the steel barrel pushing up my eyebrow. At once, my eyes popped open as I could feel my body fall forward. I immediately began to panic that I'd been seen asleep and fierce reprimands were sure to follow. Hanna aside, everyone was gathered before me, staring at the screen of the computer. I rubbed my eyes and watched them for a moment, expecting them to say something to me, anything. No one did. I walked over to murmurs of shock and disbelief.

I sucked my tongue momentarily, attempting to moisten the dry surface, readying to speak. Before I could open my mouth, I caught glimpse of the headline on the screen:

Meteorites Devastate China, Japan, India with More Possible.
Words escaped me.

"You believe this? It's Armageddon over there. Old Testament wrath kind of shit," Delgado said, then making a sign of the cross on his chest.

I skimmed down the page of written text, next to pictures of desolation and ruin. Buildings razed to piles of burnt rubble, trees stripped bare and pushed to the ground as if stepped on by God's massive sandal.

"What happened?" I asked.

"Those damn space rocks. They hit, man. Hit hard," Delgado said. He continued speaking but I couldn't process the words. My mind was too occupied as my eyes scanned down the page over his shoulder, trying to make sense of the event.

According to the article, NEOs—near earth objects they called them—usually burn up coming in our atmosphere but these didn't. Dozens of large meteors traveling over 100,000 kilometers per hour, many bigger than a house, made it through our atmosphere in tact. Some rained down on the shoreline and the land hitting with forces measured in hundreds of megatons. The deadliest ones exploded in the air just above the Earth, wiping out everything for thousands of kilometers. The pictures were captioned as areas near the fringe of the events where searches for survivors continued. The article said analysts believed survival any closer to ground zero was near impossible; I had no reason to believe otherwise. Hiroshima seemed relatively lucky.

A related article stated that NASA's giant infrared telescope was designed to survey the sky and find galactic rubble before contact, but mysteriously it missed most of these. The bigger ones didn't even make a blip on the radar. The few NEOs that were detected had a vastly larger impact than predicted and the brightest minds in science hadn't even a theory why. That kind of admission seeds concern for what else isn't known.

"Are there any more articles?" I asked. "Did it say what parts were destroyed?"

"Worried about the cousins, Amish?" Farrell teased.

"Oh, I get it, because I'm Asian. Therefore I must be related to everyone in China," I said sarcastically. "Ha ha, dick." I made light of it, but inside, my stomach sank with worry about my family, my blood family that *was* in China. The same family that depended on me for financial support, to provide for brothers and sisters I hadn't even met. The same family that could very well have been reduced to ash without warning. I couldn't tell them that though, to admit my Chinese background. I had sworn my whole life that my family was from South Korea and I couldn't say otherwise now.

I've learned most Americans have trouble discerning races based simply from facial characteristics. Sure, they know black and white or Asian and Latino. But Chinese versus Korean or Arab versus Jewish or even German versus Polish, average Americans are inept. The ones that do have an aptitude won't dispute whatever heritage you claim; they simply shrug it off as anomaly.

"Enough edutainment for today," Granger said. "Back to your positions."

Screams from the cell restarted as I ascended the stairs.

My mind was sobering up. I learned Adrenaline does that. Adrenaline and fear. My head was already pounding from the alcohol and the news only made it worse. I wanted to use the laptop, scour the Internet for more information. I needed to see the damage, find a map of what areas were hit. It would at least put my mind at ease if I knew it was away from Fuxin, where my family lived.

I can only imagine what the victims may have experienced based on what I read. Explosions in the sky larger than the biggest man-made atomic bombs. Tidal waves as tall as skyscrapers speeding out from the oceans and demolishing anything in their path. A flash of light and an intense quake followed by heat so intense, everything close was instantly vaporized or petrified. People just living their lives and suddenly, they no longer exist.

The dismal concrete steps welcomed me. Somehow, I managed to lay back and eventually drift asleep.

I had a dream the day I read that initial report. I was running through a thick forest in the dark of night when I fell into a deep pit, teeming with thin, thorny vines that dug into my flesh. I tried to climb out but wolves surrounded the perimeter and viciously bit my fingers as I clawed at the dirt. It suddenly started to storm and rainwater pooled up at my feet, then my ankles, my knees, my waist. It rose so quickly, I began to panic as I realized death was inevitable. By the time it reached my chest, I remember thinking I had only to choose: be torn apart by the wolves or simply let the water overtake my face and fill my lungs. I woke up, gripped by fear and dripping with sweat.

"Amish, what the hell? You still alive or what?" I heard through the darkness. "Your shift is over, man."

Delgado's voice echoed off the cement. I woke up feeling dazed and disoriented. The lack of quality sleep, somber atmosphere, distressing news and general isolation from the world had affected me much more than I would have expected. I could only guess how long I'd been there when I awoke. The days bled together. I stunk. I was drained. Thirsty.

It was hard to imagine things could get much worse. I slowly dragged myself to the latrine to piss and wash up, unbuttoning my uniform as I walked down the hallway. I should have been paying attention and heard the water, but I wasn't and I didn't. He was already in the shower stall, water pouring on his bald head and down his naked body. It turned into a thin pink mixture, tainted as it washed away the prisoner's blood.

The whole encounter couldn't have lasted longer than a few seconds but it still disturbs me deeply to remember it. My eyes locked onto Hanna's as he stood under the running water, motionless except for the one arm he was using to furiously masturbate. I was so shocked it took a moment for my brain to tell my body to exit. As for Hanna, he didn't pause as he watched me leave. The bastard didn't even slow down.

I needed a shower more than ever.

09
Love One Another

I've never experienced a real fist fight. It's easy enough to avoid confrontation when you grow up without the freedom to socialize with unfamiliar kids. That's not to say I've never been hit. As a child, I'd felt many a knocks at the hand of my Uncle Lee, always in the name of discipline. That's not the same as a fight though. There was no attempt to block or evade; there's no search for an opportunity to strike back. There's only losing struggles to withhold tears, waiting for bruises to heal and learning to avoid making the same mistakes that aroused his anger to begin with.

Once as a child no older than nine years old, I sat looking out my bedroom window when I saw a crowd gathered in the schoolyard down the street. It intrigued me to see how other children lived, piqued my curiosity too much to refrain. So as my Uncle Lee slept, I crept through my window and climbed down the fire escape, four stories to the ground. I remember feeling my heart race and my breath become short as I ran along the asphalt, excited partially to see why the crowd was formed and partially just to be out of my bedroom and feeling a forbidden freedom. My little feet couldn't carry me there fast enough.

Dozens of children, all older than I, formed a self-induced circle around two others. The mob chanted and yelled as the two kids danced around, weaving back and forth in the most intimidating stances they could perform with their gangly frames. In my naivety, I thought it was a game of some sort and I was eager to watch them compete. It only took one of them to throw a punch for it to escalate into a full-on brawl. They grappled and, before long, fell to the ground in an aggressive embrace, hitting each other with closed fists whenever they found opportunity.

As I crouched there, watching between the legs of the other children, I felt two thick fingers grab my ear and pull, so hard I thought it'd be ripped it off. Above me stood my Uncle Lee who dragged me all the way back home and up the steps where he proceeded to angrily beat me.

I remember the laughter of the other children as I was hauled away, some of them mocking me, others enjoying the brutal spectacle they came to see. At least they didn't get to witness my humiliation as I curled up against the door of the apartment and begged him to stop hitting me. My eyes swelled shut with bruises and tears; blood streamed down my face from a gash in my right eyebrow. I hated him; at the same time, I was dependent on him and felt compassion. I understood Stockholm Syndrome much better than fist fights, perhaps because I hadn't seen one since that day. It surprised me all the more then to wake up to one.

"Calm your ass down, now, soldier!" Granger ordered.

In all honestly, I didn't see any of the punches being thrown, only the aftermath. That was probably intentional. The yelling woke me up and I jumped out of bed to find everyone in the assembly room just outside the cell. Granger stood in Simmons' face, their noses close enough to feel each others' breath. Farrell stood at the opposite side of the room, blood running from his nose down his chin.

"Seriously, Simmons, you need to chill the fuck out," Farrell said.

"Fuck you and your racist ass," Simmons said.

"Shut up, both of you!" Granger yelled.

Everyone hushed and looked at our commander. Ekwall remained an object in the background, sitting quietly and watching the show with a subdued grin on his face. It was the first time I'd seen him amused.

"Farrell," Granger asked, "what the hell happened?"

Farrell said, "We were talking about sports. Simmons started to menstruate when I made a comment about how black people are typically better athletes—"

Simmons interrupted, "No. What you said was, 'If coaches want stronger athletes, they should stop half-assing it and train full breed monkeys to throw a ball.'"

"I said 'purebred silverbacks'—'monkeys' doesn't even make sense, dumb-ass," Farrell said. "Take a fucking joke."

"Oh, I'm dumb too now, peckerwood?" Simmons said.

"You were dumb way before now."

"Redneck asshole!"

"Shut up! This ends now," Granger demanded. "Get your collective shit together and go back to your stations or I'll ram my boot up both your asses. Act like soldiers." Then he stared them down until they broke eye contact.

Simmons glared at Farrell as he brushed off his shoulders and returned to his chair by the cell. Farrell looked at the blood on his hand that he had wiped from his face and headed toward the kitchen. It had ended, for the time being at least, as quickly as it started. And just as ordered, they were acting like soldiers once again.

As horrible as it may sound, I wished I could have witnessed it. Don't misunderstand, having seen it wouldn't have satiated some deep rooted lust for violence. Far from it, I don't like blood and lean heavily towards pacifism. It's just that their fight brought back flashbacks as a child, excitedly watching those kids tussle and trade blows back and forth and I can only imagine grown men being much more vivacious. Seeing people drop their guards and doing something based off emotion and desire, breaking away from the constraints of responsibility and diligence and expectations, it was, vicariously of course, very freeing. Almost inspirational.

Louder than ever, I could hear the sounds of Bryce Fallsteen restart behind me as I walked down the hall. It made me speed my pace to get away. Any placatory purpose it served was completely negated by its constant, irritating repetition.

When I entered the kitchen, Farrell blew his nose in his palm and placed the blood-soaked hand under the faucet. Small lines of red beaded down his chest and stained his army green t-shirt a dingy brown.

"How's it look, Amish?" he said, elevating his face so I could see up his nose.

"Not broken," I said. "You missed some blood on your cheek. Aside from that, you don't even look like you got hit."

"Yeah, asshole got in a lucky shot. Barely clipped me," he said.

Delgado walked in and smiled wildly.

"Way to go, ginger," he said. "I mean it—really excellent people skills. Maybe next you should try some gay jokes in your routine."

"Whatever. He can kiss my ass," Farrell said.

A lingering moment passed before the words had been processed. I wouldn't have even noticed what he said, but Farrell didn't let the comment slide by. He stopped washing and tilted his head curiously.

"Wait. What do you mean?" Farrell said. "Who'd be offended by gay jokes?"

"Oh, come on now, don't tell me you don't know. You're always up in everyone's shit—you had to have heard," Delgado said.

"Who? Hanna? I'm not worried about offending that tool," Farrell said.

"No," Delgado said. "I mean, sure, he's probably a packer too, but that's not who I'm talking about."

Farrell got a puzzled look on his face and looked at me. I shrugged my shoulders, signaling ignorance to his unasked question. For a moment, I thought they suspected me. Maybe my quiet mannerisms or meek personality led them to believe something that's never been true. I was waiting for a joke, a thinly disguised probe for information to fly in my direction but it didn't. I redirected my attention back to Delgado, influencing Farrell to follow.

"I'm talking about Granger, dude," Delgado said. "He's a pole-climber."

"Get the fuck out of here," Farrell said. "You're just messing with me."

"I shit you not, man. The guy enjoys dick," Delgado said.

"Yeah, OK. You experience this first hand?" Farrell said, laughing and elbowing me to join him. I'm sure my face still showed traces of shock and skepticism. That's definitely how I felt.

"No, asshole. One of my cousins was stationed over in California, at Fort Irwin, and it was big news on the base when Granger was outed. Got caught getting sucked off by some recruit," Delgado said.

"Let me guess," Farrell said smiling, "Granger was looking forward to a discharge?"

"I'm not joking, man. This happened," Delgado said.

"Then why didn't he get kicked out?" Farrell said.

"This was back when the military was getting blasted for persecuting homos so they couldn't discharge him. Instead, he was transferred to other bases across the country but come on, a move like that don't die," Delgado said.

"Got that right. Shit flies faster than radio," Farrell said.

"The rumors kept following him, causing all kinds of trouble, so they started assigning him shit details to make him bow out. I heard about it from where I was stationed, even though nobody knew his name. But since my cuz was on base at the time, he knew. And I remember when he told me about it, he kept using his name, 'Granger, Granger, Granger.' It stuck with me, man," Delgado said.

"That doesn't mean it's the same guy. I'm sure he's not the only 'Granger' in service," Farrell said. "And this one's such a hard-ass. Can you imagine him biting the pillow?"

"Yeah, I thought that too. But I overheard him telling Ekwall he was from California, then he named all the other places he's been stationed. List longer than my forearm. And look around... details don't get more shit than this," Delgado said.

"Can't argue with that but damn, I don't even want to believe it. That cocksucker saw me in the shower. Probably got him all horny and shit," Farrell said. Then he smiled smugly.

I didn't want to believe it either. Granger was a rough man, very frigid and rugged and masculine. He acted like a walking drill sergeant cliché, an army caricature given life. Delgado said Granger had been raised in a military family and expected to serve the United States Armed Forces from birth, probably fighting those secret urges his whole life. He could never openly be what he was, instead having to mask his genuine nature. Maybe he hoped he could fulfill the adopted persona, acting in prescribed ways until his true identity was too smothered to exist, even to himself. It's no wonder when an opportunity arose, he tore off the chains and let his authentic instincts run free.

Don't misinterpret my sympathy. I find homosexuality repugnant. Yet as I cringe at the idea of two men engaging in a sexual act, it was hard to hear his story and not empathize with a man being shoehorned into an unwanted lifestyle. I'd identify with anyone forced to hide their true desires, to live a counterfeit existence for someone else's happiness. Granger was a fabrication. It was all a big game of make-believe, but to that aspect I could relate. I didn't want to accept it, but somehow they had convinced me. They said he spent his life in service to his country. And what did he get in exchange? The worst details the Army had to offer in a ploy to make him go away. Hoo-ahh.

"I hear you," Delgado said. "In a way though, I feel kinda sorry for him."

"You know who I feel sorry for?" Farrell said. "His boyfriend. Granger's dick probably shoots nine-millimeter hollow-points."

I didn't laugh as loudly as they did, but it was hard not to find the humor in his remark. As weird as it may be, believing our commanding officer was homosexual added an extra layer of awkwardness. It's difficult to explain exactly why. Spiritual roots deeper than conscious thought sent up uncontrollable feelings of disappointment and disrespect and discomfort. If someone were to proclaim their love of beets, I would respectfully disagree, but I wouldn't think less of them. I wouldn't even think less of a woman if she found other women sexually appealing because that attraction I can at least understand. If a man, however, admits he has a sexual appetite for men, it's disturbing to me. It's like someone vomiting up evolutionary instinct.

Together, we three walked back into the assembly room, empty except for Simmons who was still guarding the cell. It was Granger's shift at the gate and Ekwall was hidden away in one of the bedrooms we passed, scribbling down notes in one of the files he kept burying his nose in. Casually but purposefully, I went just ahead of the other two soldiers. My unconcerned facade had lasted long enough; I was eager to see an updated report on the disaster, hoping for better news than what we'd already heard.

Farrell and Simmons avoided eye contact as we entered. I could feel the tension but I couldn't tell if they had calmed down enough to make peace or if they were just lone innocuous chemicals destined to combine into a volatile explosion. Neither seemed eager to initiate interaction regardless.

"Stay the fuck away from me or you gonna eat your teeth," Simmons said softly, barely audible above the music. His twitch had ramped up worse than I had ever seen it before.

"Yeah? Think twice before you swing, bro," Farrell replied. "You have no posse down here and you only get one sucker punch."

Any doubt I had about their feelings was quashed. I kept my eyes focused on the screen though, quickly navigating the browser. So many sites I preferred were blocked by government filters, even seemingly harmless news pages. Every search would grind at a pace just a bit faster than a standstill, bringing up filtered results that gave no information pertaining to what I wanted to know. My anxiety was eroding away all the patience I had.

"Screw it, I can't take this shit anymore," Delgado said. He reached to the stereo and harshly jammed down on the stop button. With the loud sounds of Fallsteen aborted, the stillness of the room made it easy to hear a previously indiscernible banging on the wall coming from the cell. It didn't sound like a torturous beating this time, but more of a steady thumping. It would periodically ascend and descend in volume and tempo, but it was definitely rhythmic. Notably, there were no screams. We could hear a voice though, faintly but distinctly emitting a muffled groan coinciding with the beat. It was hard to ignore.

"Alright, what the hell is going on in there?" Delgado said.

Everyone paused for a moment to listen.

"That," Farrell said, "sounds like sex."

I gave up searching my preferred sites and clicked on the federally-approved military news link bookmarked in the title bar. Information slowly crawled on-screen in small blips.

"Damn it, that's disgusting," Delgado said. "I mean what the hell? You think Hanna's really in there going balls deep in hostage ass?"

"Would that really surprise you? Something's not right with that guy," Farrell said as he started to smile lightly. "Who knows? Maybe it's consensual."

"You think Ekwall knows about this?" Delgado said.

"Yeah, he knows," Simmons said. "Why you think he left the room?"

As the information appeared in front of me on screen, a chill shot up my body making the hair on my extremities stand straight up. I saw the pictures of devastation before I even read the headline. I muttered something to get their attention. I don't remember what it was, maybe a vulgar sentiment, maybe gibberish. Whatever I said, it went unheard.

"What about Granger? You think he knows?" Delgado said.

"Oh, hell yeah, he definitely knows," Simmons said.

"Why do you say that?" Delgado said.

Simmons didn't respond.

"Guys, you have to see this," I said. I know it was loud enough but they still ignored me.

"Hey, I'm talking to you. What do you mean?" Delgado said to Simmons.

He sat back in the wooden chair and looked at Delgado, reluctant to speak. "He knows what's going on," Simmons said, "because he's in there too."

Everyone went silent with that information. Everyone but me. At that moment, I didn't care as much as about what was going in that room as I did about what was happening across the world.

"Is anyone listening to me? You have to see this shit!" I said.

One by one, they all came over and read the report, each one letting out an understated verbal declaration of shock. We didn't know what to think. There was nothing to say. It was too big to comprehend as real, but looking at the pictures, it was impossible to dispute.

Europe Hit in Second Wave of Space Debris, Millions Feared Dead

England, Belgium, and the Netherlands were hit the hardest, it read, but not one country in Europe went unscathed. Germany, France, Italy, Spain. Dozens of images taken from various countries showed the worst damage but the photos all showed the same things. Piles of ash and rubble and burnt bodies. Famous landmarks, icons of humanity, were no longer distinguishable, demolished amid the charred debris. I wouldn't have been able to guess even one location had the photos' tagline not given them away.

Emergency plans were being initiated where government could still operate but the damage was too widespread and relief was stretched far too thin. Riots broke out within hours inciting a hostile martial law. Scared people turned savage while seeking loved ones and food and medical supplies. Others became savage out of greed. Thousands of religious zealots evolved into militant conquistadors vowing to vanquish whatever sin had provoked God's wrath; organized gangs started to command control of areas where devastation had severed access from authorities.

Reports were even worse in China and India where the previous bombardment had wreaked havoc on what was left of society. People slaughtering the weak to conserve supplies of food and water, using stolen children as slave currency, and eating the dead among them. Governments had lost control of the population and there were rumors of some Middle Eastern regimes having their own military forces approach the foreign borders, not to assist, but to seize land. This was happening everywhere the rocks had hit. It was like reading a bad nightmare.

Scientists were still baffled by the exaggerated force and inexplicable stealth of the meteorites with no definite way to predict another incident. As the report read, the hypotheses that were proposed couldn't be tested without it happening again. With the last two incidents mere days apart, forewarning to the general public may not be released anyway. A major city takes at least a week to evacuate; impending doom would only create panic and chaos. For the first time in recorded history, it seemed all of humanity was gripped in a collective fear.

It was surreal. The article painted a picture of civilization eroding away on half the Earth. I couldn't wrap my mind around it. At the end of the text, there was an elementary damage map of all the countries, including China. My family's home town, Fuxin, was one of the places marked as being directly hit. I wouldn't allow myself to shed tears over distant ties becoming permanently severed. I showed no sorrow. I said no prayers. I grieved for my family silently, too numb to be properly bothered by the background sounds of the detainee under our care being anally raped.

Delgado pressed play on the CD player to mask the sound and walked away. They all did. I have to admit, considering the alternative, it was good to hear Bryce again.

10
Cut Off

I was raised to eat for sustenance and nothing more. Throughout my childhood, I was fed small portions of traditional Chinese dishes, most of them containing a combination of rice or noodles and vegetables with various spices. Occasionally, they'd be topped with a meat if my Uncle Lee happened to catch an animal around the neighborhood.

Though we were being raised in the United States, we were sheltered from its ways as much as possible. My Uncle wanted to make sure that the old world values he held onto so dearly were first properly ingrained in our minds. Then, as I had almost reached my teenage years, I began to receive a minimal exposure to American staples like fast food. For future survival and acceptance, to get "a proper and relevant job", my Uncle Lee saw gaining knowledge of the culture as a necessary evil; he was cautious, however, that I not become Americanized in philosophy, influenced to take on a greedy, consumerist mentality.

I remember the first time he brought me a McDonald's cheeseburger and french fries. I was twelve then, the oldest of the boys that lived with us. They seemed so envious watching me eat and pestering me to describe every taste. I had no comparison for them and I wasn't allowed to share, not that I particularly wanted to do so. I found it uniquely delicious; my Uncle Lee said it was pig shit. Even still, he'd get a meal for me every few months and I looked forward to it every time.

My stomach would feel so full and heavy after eating it that lethargy would set in but I was never allowed to be slothful. I was always doing bookwork or chores, tending the communal garden or even taking care of the other boys. After that one meal I'd be more than satisfied for the rest of the day to the point of feeling bloated and uncomfortable. It wasn't until years later that I learned the meal I had been eating was meant for a child half my age.

It came with a cheap toy I'm told, but I never received one. Uncle Lee must have thrown it away before he came home. Ironic he wouldn't allow me the one part of the meal made in his home country. Poorly made Chinese exports made him angry, reminding him how American business "gorged itself with the blood and sweat our people." I was grateful to even get the sandwich though, as physically bad as it made me feel.

Ever since those days, the concept of American comfort food has remained foreign to me. Consuming those items that are typically granted that title always made me feel anything but comfortable. I suppose some people do get an emotional high from eating and for others it's very relaxing. Delgado seemed to be one those people.

After the latest news, I saw a sharp increase in the time he spent walking around with an open can of something in his hand. Potatoes, green beans, beets or small meat sticks. He would slide his thick, beefy hands inside the cold can water and devour whatever dripping food he could pull from it. It wasn't a rare thing to see him put the can to his mouth and drink creamed corn like a beverage.

As minimalistic as our rations were, it's reasonable that a man of his girth just needed more energy to maintain his brawny physique. He would exercise for hours in the corner and bang on his chest between sets, grunting and looking around at the rest of us like he was ready to eat someone's hand for protein. Even still, he admitted to having a weight problem in his youth and watching him scoop potted meat with his bare fingers, it seemed logical to suspect comfort food as probable culprit.

Everyone had their own way of dealing with the mental stress that seemed to be building as time went on down there. Delgado ate. Farrell joked relentlessly. Simmons picked fights with everyone. And Granger, our leader and role model, he made regular visits to the hostage with Hanna. Ekwall's attitude toward the disasters was, in a sense, the most disturbing; he didn't seem to care at all.

Sometimes he would argue with Granger, most times with Hanna. The subject was always the same though: extracting information from the hostage. It was all done in relative discreetness, spoken in a side room whisper, as if we'd been given no clue that some kind of horror was playing out behind that cell door. Ekwall refused to call him a 'hostage' or 'prisoner' or even 'detainee' when he spoke in that quiet candor though; he always said 'the mark'. I didn't understand why at the time but, then again, I didn't really give it much thought. I was obtuse. I was distracted.

That first time Granger came out of the cell, Hanna followed behind him, both tracking bloody footprints from the soles of their shoes. The other three soldiers and I were without words. It was one thing for the monster and his pet to commit heinous acts, but none of us soldiers were supposed to be in there. An invisible line had been crossed and the sense of betrayal was inevitable. Though troubled as we all seemed to be with Granger suspiciously appearing to take a more direct role in the hostile interrogation, nobody wanted to be insubordinate.

In a rare and candid moment, we were together, every one of us in the assembly hall. We all held witness. Agent Ekwall came out of the bedroom, looking around at the group before pointing his finger at Hanna.

"We need to speak," he said, "in private."

"Do we?" Hanna said as he steadily continued toward the table and chairs. "I'm tired. So if you're going to say the same things over again, save your breath and I'll just keep ignoring what you said last time."

"We need to have words. Now, *Doctor*," Ekwall said.

Hanna sighed and reluctantly walked into the far bedroom with Ekwall and Granger tagging behind. They tried their best to talk quietly but in the cold stillness, their words were hard to miss.

"What else do want us to take away? He's unmarried, has no kids. All of the family we know about is halfway around the globe," Hanna said. "We need to stay the course. Trust me, he'll crack."

Their tempers would flare up and increase the volume of their voices before they'd catch themselves and reduce to speaking as harshly as a whisper would allow. I inched my way closer, trying to eavesdrop without making it obvious, before finally sitting at the computer. It was as close as I could get to them without walking down the hall.

"I see no evidence you're having any success at all. Push it further," Ekwall said, "or maybe we should pull the plug and try another direction instead of wasting time."

"Time is exactly what it takes," Hanna said. "Time is a key..."

Delgado started pulling the ropes to the damn air pump, masking the conversation with gusts of fresh air. "I'm sick of hearing it. The less I know about that shit, the better," he said.

"I hear you. I've already seen too much I can't erase off my brain," Farrell said. He then restarted another round of

Bryce. Damn Bryce! Every sound of every song had become too familiar and the constant repetition was beginning to drive me crazy.

I can only guess what was said after that because I heard no more. But, I'd gathered enough to know that Ekwall was determined to see his mission through. His drive to get the information they wanted was adamant and in some ways, more genuine than anyone else's character down there.

I have to imagine that Ekwall pushed Hanna to the point of frustration. That was one of his most keen natural abilities. He'd make snide comments and backhanded suggestions in a condescending tone letting everyone around him know that nothing we did was worthy of his respect. Whatever he said to Hanna was effective. It seemed he had provoked the beast. The beast responded.

Hanna stormed out of the bedroom, down the hall and into the cell, slamming the door behind him. The screams started again, sounding more shrill than they ever had before, cascading up and down in intensity. It went on for probably less than a minute but with sounds of suffering that intense, it was difficult to stomach.

Moments later, the door swung open and Hanna looked around the room until he laid his scowling eyes on Ekwall. The sounds of the wailing prisoner echoed through the open door though we couldn't see inside. Hanna flung his arm, hitting Ekwall from across the room with a bloody mess of a projectile that bounced off his chest and plopped onto the cold, cement floor. Ekwall stepped back, surprised like the rest of us. It took me a moment to recognize that the gooey globs of flesh that waded in the crimson puddle were two whole, dismembered fingers, lopped off beyond the second knuckle.

"The fuck?!" Ekwall yelled, looking down at the red impact marked that stained his otherwise clean, white dress shirt.

Hanna belted out a demented, maniacal laugh that echoed throughout the still structure and down my spine, shooting chills out across my body. "That good enough for now or you want a chunk from his insides, you piece of shit?" he said.

Ekwall lunged at him, knocking him back against the wall and hitting the glasses from his nose. Granger and Delgado stepped in front of Ekwall, Farrell and Simmons in front of Hanna. I jumped in the very center of the commotion, feeling obligated to join but aiming for what I reasoned to be the safest place. I still took an anonymous stray elbow to the back of the head.

In his rage, Ekwall pushed the group together, trying but failing to connect another swing. It surprised me how much brute strength was concealed behind his shiny hair and necktie. I hoped in a panic that I wouldn't be the last obstacle for a man who could push his way through Delgado and Granger. Luckily, they did not fail. He yelled a string of profanities and threats, verbally doing what he physically could not.

Hanna calmly wiped the blood from his lip and picked his glasses up from the floor. He then began to laugh again in a much more subdued way.

"You'll get what you want. Just back off and give me the space to do what I know how to do," he said. "I didn't want you here but since you came to observe, do only that. You get in the way of letting me do my job and the failure will be on your head, not mine."

The tension was getting out of hand. I was hoping Ekwall would dismiss Hanna on the spot, maybe even shut down the entire investigation for now. I was wishing he'd pull a cell phone or radio from his briefcase and signal a chopper for an immediate evacuation. There was even a short-lived fantasy that maybe some other group of men would be brought in to replace us and I could leave that place forever. None of that happened. That arranged nightmare was mine to endure.

Ekwall took a deep breath as he began to unbutton his bloody shirt. "You better know what you're doing. I'm talking to you, *Doctor*, so I hope you're listening. Your time is running out," Ekwall said.

Time. It had gotten so difficult to keep track of, I had nearly given up trying to do so. Down there, surrounded by thick walls and buried under several meters of Earth, there was no day or night, dusk or dawn. People ate and slept when they were actually hungry or tired, not when three ticking hands told them to feel that way.

Granger was the only soldier with a watch and he let the rigid shifts decay into loose approximations. Since the post order had been switched so many times, he appeared to have lost track of the organization and picked people at random, placing them arbitrarily at one location or the other. As if we were second guessing him, he'd get irritated when we'd ask what time or even what day it was, so we rarely did. Ekwall and Hanna seemed bothered by us regardless, so we never pestered them.

I thought I'd use the computer to maintain my mental grip on the passing time, but even that turned out to be impossible once I realized it would often reset itself at irregular intervals, restarting at noon. Farrell said computers have a built-in battery that powers the internal clock. When those batteries die, computers can lose track of the time and date, especially when powered with an unreliable source. Vintage outlets located in a 1980s fallout shelter would qualify I suppose.

As Ekwall retreated in a bedroom to clean off and Hanna in the cell, no doubt to keep the prisoner from bleeding out, I sat down at the computer for what would be the last time. Out of habit, I glanced down at the on-screen clock knowing that I could randomly guess and have just as good of chance at being accurate. A triangular yellow icon surrounding an exclamation point popped up beside the incorrect time, but I was too interested in world affairs to give it my attention.

I felt shaken from the scuffle and dazed from the whack to the back of my head. Even still, I held just as much anxiety about what may be happening across the globe.

I was hoping to read something positive, maybe good news on how there were more survivors than expected or how people had banded together to help one another in crisis. As I opened the browser, though, I discovered something that felt instantly worse than the previous reports. I had no network connectivity at all. Like a stranded imbecile kicking the door of his broken car on the side of the road, I hit the refresh button repeatedly and with greater force as if it merely needed to be awakened.

But it was gone. My one window to the outside world was gone. I'd never felt so isolated.

11
Master Plan

None of us had seen the open sky in days. Cabin fever had set in and become more of a plague, killing us with dormancy. I found myself becoming fidgety and easily agitated, and I was more even-tempered than most. My mind started to scheme like a prisoner with nothing but desire for freedom and plenty of time to think of ways to get it.

I'd imagine excuses to leave, to feel the sun on my face and breath air that hadn't first traveled through a metal shaft burrowed through ten meters of dirt. No matter how plausible I thought my excuses were, I never actually tried to use any of them. I suppose it was my upbringing, years of indentured servitude that taught me freedom wasn't something I was entitled to or should even strive to obtain.

I could tell I had lost weight, even after only that short amount of time. Between the stress of my surroundings and the lack of desirable food, my appetite had diminished out of existence. As a further deterrent, I found alcohol much more effective on an empty stomach and I increasingly began to welcome the intoxicating numbness with open arms.

Hanna's outburst initiated a voluntary but universal spell of silence as we four soldiers sat together as peers, sipping cups of vodka like a group in mourning. That one disturbing act of rage created an uneasy tension that made going back to lighthearted conversation seem impossible. My thoughts were becoming undone before I could even complete them, turning my tongue into a useless appendage. Luckily, some of the others were more capable than I.

"I've been thinking about all that shit going down," Delgado said. "All those people, dead."

"God seems pretty pissed about something, huh?" Farrell said.

"Exactly," Delgado said. "What if God did it on purpose?"

"What? That's some bullshit," Simmons said.

"I mean what if God's cleansing the Earth. He did it before, right? The flood and the dude with the boat?" Delgado said.

"Oh, come on man. I was just kidding. Don't make me have to agree with that asshole," Farrell said looking at Simmons who responded by putting up both middle fingers.

"Seriously, think about it for a minute," Delgado said. "The Earth's surface is mostly water, right? Seventy percent or something. Rocks start showering down from the sky and not only hit land, but nail countries with high populations, the highest in the world? Think that's coincidence?"

"No. It's bad fucking luck," Simmons said, "but it ain't God. You can't pin that shit on Him."

"You attorney of the divine, now?" Farrell said.

"First off, fuck you. I still ain't talking to your cracker ass," Simmons said before turning to Delgado, "but I ain't seen God do nothing and I know plenty of chumps pray 'til their knees turn raw, calling to God and He ain't never pick up. Jesus, Muhammad, statues of fat little bald bastards and elephants and shit. Doesn't matter who you think He is, because He ain't here. We're a failed experiment, man. I think He just cut His losses and ran. I don't know where He went to, but way I see it, He gets no credit, He gets no blame."

"So, you think God created everything and then left us to fend for ourselves?" Delgado said.

"Maybe. I wouldn't blame Him if He did. World's a fucked up place," Simmons said.

"So we're an ant farm sitting on Jesus Christ's nightstand? I don't buy that either. I know a ton of stories about God intervening for people in trouble," Farrell said.

"Is that right?" Simmons said. "You in any of 'em? Or you just got some bullshit about a cousin of a brother of a friend? Stories like that something everybody heard, but you meet someone that got a story of their own, seem like they also have their hand out for something."

"I like it better when you're not talking to me," Farrell said. "Really, how can you think that God's not looking out for us to some extent? I mean, why keep us around if we're so awful? Yeah, so bad shit happens. It's always happened and always will. Any time there's an earthquake or volcano or Mother Nature queefs a giant tornado from her flora-laden vaj, you have every religious nutcase either cursing God or repenting because the world's about to end. But you know what? We're still here. Sure, a lot of people are dead and that sucks for them but I'm going with statistics and betting most of them were probably assholes anyway. Besides, how many times have we been told the Earth is getting overpopulated. I say it's all just nature thinning the herd. Go Darwin."

"Damn, you're a dick," Delgado said. "Am I the only one who thinks this stuff might just be some kind of divine retribution? What about you, Amish?"

They looked at me, waiting for me to step in and pick a side. I didn't really want to participate. I just wanted to drink my booze until everything went black. But they stared. Stared and waited.

"I don't believe in God," I said.

"Well, ain't that just great?" Delgado said. He took the last swig from his cup and looked around at each of us. "I was raised Catholic but I was never really strict with it. And I've done a lot of things I regret, things I'm afraid I might have to answer for. Millions of people thought they'd wake up and go about their day, eat breakfast, hug their kids and go to work. They had all the time in the world. Then, no warning, they're just gone and here I am, knowing one day I'm going to die too and I don't know when my end is coming anymore than they did. All this dirty shit in my past, I never confessed. Everyone needs to confess before they go, man. I ain't ready to be judged."

"Holy shit, will you take it easy? We're all fine," Farrell said. "Another week, we'll all be back to our own normal, slightly less miserable lives and never have to see this place again. Just relax, you'll see."

I needed to be comforted and I took Farrell's simple re-assurance to heart. The rest of those men, they didn't know how I was feeling and I couldn't tell them. They hadn't read about the probable loss of their blood families in a news report and they didn't know I had either. I wouldn't admit my true heritage, not out of shame, mind you, but out of fear. I was afraid of the questions that would follow, questions that I'd feel impelled to make up lies to answer. It just wasn't worth the risk. So I comforted myself about my family, swallowing liquid that was starting to remind me of rubbing alcohol.

Granger approached us from the hallway, emerging from the spiral staircase that led to the gate. I always expected him to get angry about the slow increase in our drink consumption but he never did. I wondered if maybe he felt guilt from doing whatever he had done in the cell; maybe drinking just seemed trivial after everything else that had happened. He turned a blind eye to it, to us really, not saying a word as he walked by and tried the computer once again.

"Ekwall," he yelled out. "Ekwall, you up?"

Agent Ekwall walked out from one of the bedrooms, undressed down to his boxers and undershirt. His hair looked unusually disheveled, sticking straight up in places normally held down with excessive amounts of product. His vocal response wasn't as much a word as a grunt.

"Our connection is still down," Granger said.

Ekwall rubbed his eyes and stubbly chin as he repeated Granger's failed attempts to connect to anything across the Internet. He then clicked the mouse repeatedly on the refresh button with no better results.

"Yep, sure is," he said. Then they stared at each other in a moment of awkward silence.

"Well, can you get it fixed? It's been down for several hours now. It's obviously not coming back up. Do we even have another lifeline in case of emergency?" Granger said.

"OK, right," Ekwall said. "Uh, all of our communications run as a courtesy through a hub at the nearest Canadian base, CFB Moose Jaw. We can contact someone there." The agent's delivery had the stale enthusiasm of an actor who couldn't remember his lines. His brain was still half asleep and the portion that awoke seemed annoyed to do so.

"Fine. Can you call now?" Granger said.

"My phone isn't working down here but we were provided some emergency radios in the truck. They're supposed to connect directly with an operator at Moose Jaw. That should be enough of a lifeline, but if you think we need online access that badly, I'll call," Ekwall said.

"I do," Granger said.

We listened attentively, we all heard what he said and I think we all had an idea of what that meant. At least one of us was going on a short field trip outside.

"Khu," Granger said.

"Sir?!" I said excitedly, smiling like a man reading a winning lottery ticket. I could almost taste the fresh air, feel the breeze on my face, and see the sunshine or starry sky, whichever was out at the moment. I didn't care. Time had escaped me but it didn't matter what it was like outside as long as I could be out there with it.

"You're on post at the cell," he said. "Delgado, I need you to get some equipment from the truck. Farrell, guard the gate while it's open and help him if he needs it. Hoo-ahh?"

The excited smile I had remained. It just transferred to different faces.

"Hoo-ahh!" they said, both hopping up and readying for departure. I watched them tighten their boots and grab their guns, almost giggling like kids as they walked out. I was completely envious of their task; Simmons seemed apathetic about it. He was just happy to be away from Farrell and, hell, it could be worse for him. At least he wasn't stuck guarding the hostage and was free to walk up with them and see the outdoors if he wanted. I know I would have.

Instead, without that option, I moped to the familiar wooden chair, rifle in hand, and waited for the prisoner's inevitable wailing to begin once again. Hoo-ahh.

12
Reason to Smile

The tedium of sitting alone in a dark room and watching a closed-door is more mentally taxing than you'd probably imagine. The popular analogies of watching ice melt or grass grow might seem comparable scenarios at first glance, but those things actually change given enough time. This door remained closed and relentlessly boring in the best of times and opened to reveal a showcase of horror in the worst of them. As I stared at that thick slab of wood, watching it remain the same for hours on end, I tried to escape my surroundings by clinging to the happiest memories I could muster, just shutting my eyes and reliving them.

That always brought me back to Lin, the closest I ever had to a girlfriend. I'm told love is fleeting during youth and most would probably doubt the depth and sincerity of my feelings. I was only thirteen and she was a year younger than I, but naive as I may have been, it was the most passionate love I've ever felt.

The first day I saw her, she was working in Turner's Field, a large courtyard enclosed in between the two apartment buildings we lived in, she in one, I in the other. Though close to central Philadelphia and set amidst a diverse, low-income community, both buildings housed primarily Chinese residents that used the semi-enclosed field as a communal garden to grow their own vegetables. Everyone that worked to maintain it could eat from it and Uncle Lee had the rest of the boys and me labor regularly to help supplement the needs of all those hungry mouths.

As far as chores go, cultivating the garden, arduous as it could be, was one of the most desirable tasks and the one I always picked whenever I had the choice. Working outdoors and sneaking a few bites of a fresh tomato or a sweet apple was incentive enough, but once I had laid eyes on her, all of the other reasons seemed secondary.

Lin had the sweetest round eyes partially veiled behind a tuft of hair that always hung down over her face. Her restrained smile conveyed an innocence that made me feel so drawn to her. Over the years, I've studied the English language intently, but I'm at a loss of words to describe just how beautiful she was to me. The best compliment I can say is that looking at her, just seeing her face made me happy. Even now as I write, I can't help but smile when I picture Lin in my mind's eye.

She caught me staring at her more than once. I'd turn away and she'd grin at my shyness and that only encouraged me to look for opportunities to get closer to her. It wasn't long before I found one.

That wonderful day, I remember her walking through the garden, carrying a large metal bucket full of produce. As she traveled from plant to plant looking for what she needed, Lin would blow air upward through her lips to move the hair away from her eyes. It was as dark brown as you can get without being black and she always wore it in a ponytail, tied with a bright red ribbon that flowed down her back. The one gathering of hair not fastened though, would fall back down on her face and every few minutes, she would repeat the procedure of blowing it away. It made me smile to watch her do this. It made her smile to see me notice.

The wind rapidly became strong enough to cloak the sun behind dark gray clouds and bring gusts that carried the ribbon right off her head. I watched it float through the air twenty or thirty meters, finally landing on a nearby pepper plant an arm's length away from me. As droplets of rain began to fall, I rushed to get the ribbon and moved quickly to return it to her. We exchanged a greeting followed by a few kind words before the incoming storm forced our conversation to an abrupt end. Then she kissed me on the cheek. That was the moment I fell in love, but that was a long time ago.

I find it sad that as I stared at that door, the happiest memory I had to keep me company occurred half my life before. I relived it in my mind often to keep the memory alive, to keep her with me, to make me happy. Down there in that underground bunker though, happiness was short lived.

My fantasy quickly faded away when I heard a woman's scream.

"Move it!" Delgado said. It was distant, but I could feel the harshness in his voice as they walked down the hallway.

"Hey, take it easy, man! She's not a fucking hostile," Farrell said.

There was a cry and whimper and then I saw her face, a beautiful Caucasian brunette, tears streaming down her cheeks. Delgado held tightly onto her upper arm, tossing it lightly toward the wall once they were completely in the assembly room. Farrell followed behind them, his scornful glare making it apparent he was displeased with Delgado's undue aggression.

Granger and Ekwall came rushing out of the kitchen, Simmons out of the bedroom. I remained seated in my wooden chair, confused but excited to see the new face. What a beautiful face.

"What the hell is this?!" Granger said.

"We caught her stealing from the truck," Delgado said.

"She was only sleeping in the truck," Farrell said.

"She was trespassing," Delgado said. "She broke one common law, we have to assume she'd break the other."

"Enough!" Granger said as he turned toward her.

She sat against the cement wall in an upright fetal position, looking around at the military men who dragged her into what had to look like a dungeon to a civilian. After all, it looked like a dungeon to me. Granger squatted down to her level and smiled as much as his battle-hardened face would allow. He wasn't used to doing it and we weren't used to seeing it. Being out of practice then, I guess it's hard to place blame that his smile appeared more creepy than friendly.

"Ma'am," he said. "My name is Lt. Colonel Charles Granger of the the United States Army. What's your name?"

She sat there and stared at him, shaking like a scared puppy.

"Bitch wouldn't talk to us either," Delgado said.

"Damn it, Paco. What the hell's your problem? Why don't you just waterboard her for fuck's sake?" Farrell said.

Granger looked up at them, shutting their mouths with just a glance before turning back to her.

"Ma'am," he said. "What were you doing in our truck?"

She still didn't say a word.

Just then, Hanna exited the cell, his clothes spattered with blood and his face dripping with sweat. It was a horrible sight for us to see. I could only imagine what went through her mind as she looked at that butcher and screamed, sliding back away to the furthest corner.

"Who the hell is this?" he asked.

"We're working on that," Granger said.

"You need me to ask her?" Hanna said, sporting a sinister grin.

"Stay the hell away from her you sick bastard," Farrell said.

Hanna looked at him as if ready to attack. Farrell looked more than ready to retaliate.

"Alright, that's enough!" Granger said. "Keep her in the mess hall until we make sure there's nothing missing or damaged in the truck. Then we'll cut her loose."

"Bullshit!" Ekwall said. "Your boys brought her down here and now she's seen things she shouldn't have seen. You want to just let her walk?"

"What has she seen, Agent Ekwall?" Granger said. "A few men in uniform and the underground bunker they're stationed in?"

Granger's eyes followed Ekwall's as they looked over toward Hanna, wiping blood on his shirt from the sides of his fingers. Our commander paused for a contemplative moment and peered around the room at the high emotions most of the men had. Then he looked at me.

"Khu, take this girl to the mess hall while we figure this out," Granger said.

I didn't hesitate but in actuality, I may have been just as afraid to be around her as she was around us. I laid my rifle on the floor and walked over to the girl who sat with her arms wrapped around her knees. She didn't look afraid as I approached, but rather relieved. I guess my non-threatening appearance, the same that had been a continual detriment to gaining respect amongst group of male peers, made that woman feel more at ease. Even still, when I bent over and reached out my hand, she wouldn't take it.

"Are you thirsty? We have water," I said. "Food too."

She stood up, keeping one eye on the group of men around me, particularly Hanna. She couldn't have been more than twenty-five years old with her lovely face and clear, smooth skin. The girl showed signs of being well-groomed until only very recently, but she *was* dirty. Her clothes were stained with brown splotches and her bare feet were covered with grass stains. I imagine even vagabonds still look decent the first few days after they become homeless.

She followed me into the kitchen and sat down facing me, responding to my courteous gesture toward the table. I poured her some water but she wouldn't drink it until I'd poured some from her cup into mine and I drank some first. Her reluctance was understandable.

"Are you hungry," I said. "Food?"

"Food," she said, nodding her head softly.

I opened one of my own rations and gave it to her, signaling for her to open the individual packets herself. She ate slowly at first, but quickly finished the rest once she had a taste. As I watched her eat, I looked at her eyes and Lin came back to mind. I missed her.

"I'm sorry, I know it's not very good. You should have come by yesterday. It was lobster night," I said. I thought it was funny.

She didn't even crack a smile.

"Merci," she said.

"French? You speak French? Uh... Francais?" I said. I knew only a few words so while it was a great thing to discover, it was going to be a short conversation.

"Oui," she said, "I know small English too but not so well."

Over her shoulder, I could see Granger listening from the doorway, motioning a circular pattern with his fingers for me to continue with her.

"My name is Kenneth," I said. "What's your name?"

"I am Eva," she said.

"Eva? Are you hurt anywhere, Eva?" I said.

"Je vais bien," she said, shaking her head a moment later, "I am fine but I am afraid."

"We're not going to hurt you. We do need to know why you were in our truck though," I said.

She got a puzzled look on her face even after I repeated myself. I may have been talking too fast, I guess. I do that when I get nervous.

"What happened, Eva? Why are you here?" I said.

"I saw things. There were death and fires and people... train de devenir fou," she said taking a moment to think. "They started being crazy."

"Where were you?" I said.

"I lived in Quebec and I tried to leave in an airplane. I tried to run from the crazy people but people on the airplane started to be crazy too. It fell and I run from the people. They tried to hurt me so I run," she said.

"You were in a plane crash? When?" I said.

"One day earlier," she said. "I did run for one day. Then I found your truck. I needed to sleep so I hide to sleep."

"You can sleep here. You're safe here," I said.

She took a deep breath and looked into my eyes. It felt really nice, like she was genuinely looking at me as an individual, beyond the allegiance I displayed on my fatigues. My whole life, I've felt like I wasn't my own person, rather a utensil to be used for someone else's purpose. But that stare that she gave made me feel like she was reading me, wanting to know what I was about. I didn't want her to look away and break that connection.

"You damn Americans invade my country now too?" she said.

"No. America's not invading Canada," I said. The thought of it made me grin even though she didn't look like she was kidding.

"Why then are you here? Do you too run from the crazy people?" she asked.

Granger shook his head affirmatively behind her. That was a command.

"Yeah," I said, "we're running from the crazy people too."

I lied. I didn't want to but I had to lie to her. Granger gave me a silent order and I had to follow it. All of the soldiers, myself included, had lost respect for our commander, but there's a hierarchy and it has to be followed. Without hierarchy there's no order; with no order there's only chaos. That's the last thing we'd want. We wouldn't be able to function in chaos.

13
Keeping Order

As I watched Farrell assemble the radio equipment that he and Delgado hauled down from the truck, I was impressed by the aptitude he had for connecting machines that he had never used before. He put three large electronic boxes on the desk and roughly tossed the computer aside as it had largely become a paperweight since the Internet had gone missing. He stripped cables with his utility knife as if it were second nature and manipulated the wires like a surgeon trying to get a signal that would reconnect us with the outside world. Having found it earlier and realizing its purpose, Farrell stretched a thin antenna wire that protruded from the wall under the desk and hooked it onto the back of the radio system.

I watched them work and felt a little guilty for not helping but I know next to nothing about radio technologies and I admitted as much when they asked. Farrell was the sole communications technician and with Delgado already looking over his shoulder, he didn't need two of us slowing his progress. Besides, I had been granted duties elsewhere in which I had found a solace I hadn't expected.

I had given water to Eva and fed her from my own supply. I'd pulled a blanket from the bed and offered a quiet place to lay her head. I had even stood guard in the doorway of the bathroom while she urinated and showered, my back turned to her, of course. Fighting instinctual desires, I didn't try to peak at her nakedness, not even a glance. I'm sure my honor in that regard didn't go unnoticed. In any event, I'd unofficially become both her warden and guardian.

She asked me to stay with her while she went to sleep and I did. I sat there in that small bedroom, watching her drift off and dream. Once I could see her eyes move rapidly beneath her eyelids, I felt as if I were invading a private moment and I left her to slumber. A short while later, she peaked out of the bedroom and saw me in the large assembly room, sitting on the floor against the cold concrete wall. Still wrapped in the rough flannel blanket, she quickly came out and sat beside me.

"Why did you leave me?" she said quietly.

I couldn't really explain my answer. I suppose I just wasn't used to somebody wanting me around, rather, wanting to be around me no matter where I was. I hadn't realized that in the little time that I'd helped her, I created a bond that made her want to cling to me. Maybe part of me wanted to gently distance myself just to see if she'd return. To my delight, she did. And she sat so close, cocooned tightly in her blanket, leaning on me and resting her head on my shoulder. She used the same soap we all used, but it smelled so much better emanating from her. I began to feel an infatuation, one I hadn't known since Lin was taken from me.

"What's with all this?" Granger asked.

"Well, we have two separate systems here," Farrell said. "We have a two way system with four handsets. They connect with each other and, supposedly, with a console located at CFB Moose Jaw."

One of the handsets sounded off a beep followed by some brief static, then Ekwall's voice.

"Testing, testing, 1-2-3," he said. "Testing, 1-2-3."

"They seem to work fine. Ekwall's outside on a field test now," Farrell said to Granger.

He then picked up the radio handset and pressed the talk control with his thumb.

"We hear you. Did you get ahold of Moose Jaw?" Farrell said to Ekwall.

"No. I tried every channel, all the modes. You sure these damn things work?" Ekwall's voice said.

"Can you hear me?" Farrell said.

"Yeah," Ekwall said.

"Then they work," Farrell said before releasing the button. "Douche bag."

"Maybe we're just out of range," Granger said.

"Doubtful, sir. These things use digital and analog satellite in addition to traditional long range, ultra high frequency transmission. They're military grade and encrypted. There's no reason the signal shouldn't be making it there and there's no interference that I can tell. Even if a few of the satellites got knocked out from the meteor shower, they're supposed to have a 100 mile range without them," Farrell said.

"So why else would we not get anyone?" Granger said.

"If I had to guess, I'd say someone at Moose Jaw is sleeping on the shitter," Farrell said.

Ekwall walked in from the outside and tossed the handset on the desk with an agitated look on his face.

"Piece of garbage," he said. "My mobile doesn't work either."

"Not surprising unless you built a cell tower while you were out there," Farrell said.

"What's the other system you found? You mentioned we have two," Granger said.

"Yeah. I also found some old ham radio equipment in the supply closet. We have two receivers and a transmitter... I'm working on hooking them together but they're old, like Korean War old. They may take a some jiggy-rigging," Farrell said. "They're also not encrypted, so we have to be careful what we transmit on them."

"What's ham radio?" Delgado said.

"Amateur radio, and I mean pretty much anyone can get one. People can get a license for recreational use even before they're old enough to grow pubes," Farrell said, "so even Simmons' girlfriend could use it."

"Kiss my ass," Simmons responded.

"No!" Ekwall interrupted. "You can't use that thing if you can't encrypt it. It blankets a signal everywhere around us, right? Like throwing out a fishing net out and seeing what bites?"

"Fish don't bite nets. Otherwise, yeah, that's generally how radio works," Farrell said.

"If you haven't noticed, this isn't a goodwill tour so broadcasting a signal from a classified location for no particular reason probably isn't in the best interest of the American government," Ekwall said.

"We can't stay isolated," Granger said. "We either broadcast or you have to go to Moose Jaw. You're the only one with contact authorization."

Ekwall stared at him wearing contempt on his face.

Granger continued, "If you don't, I'll pull the plug myself. Seems to me that you may have purposefully cut us off from our superiors so you can gear the mission towards a personal agenda."

"What personal agenda?" Ekwall said.

"I don't know. To satisfy an appetite for suffering. Maybe that guy slept with your wife and you're getting revenge," Granger said.

"That's bullshit and you know it," Ekwall said.

"Probably. But that suspicion puts me well within my power to end this now. Hell, I may even get commended for my keen sense of situational awareness. Think your guys at the DHS will give you the same accolades if the mission ends now?" Granger said.

"You bastard," Ekwall said.

"I have my moments," Granger said.

Ekwall turned his back and muttered what sounded like some profanities under his breath as he momentarily thought.

"Just sit tight and don't do anything stupid," Ekwall said facing Granger once again. "I'm taking the doctor with me to deliver his report firsthand. The truck is military use only so I need an escort to drive it. That's protocol."

"I'm sure I'll find a volunteer," Granger said as Ekwall walked into the cell, shutting the door behind him. Then he turned around and looked at each of us.

"A road trip watching that jerk-off compare pecker sizes with Dr. Frankenstein? I'd rather drive that truck up my own ass," Farrell said.

"That sounds to me like volunteering," Granger said.

"Bullshit, sir. No disrespect, but Delgado and I just spent the last hour humping equipment down the tiniest spiral staircase ever created. I still have work I need to do just to get it to function," Farrell said.

"Well I had my black ass stuck in this chair damn near two shifts," Simmons said.

As Granger looked at me, Eva took her arm out of the blanket and held onto my mine. Before her, I would have gladly gone with them just to be outside and see the daylight, but I found something that felt even better and I didn't want to leave her behind. Maybe I was a little worried about her, even jealous. I was the only one who'd connected with Eva and I guess I preferred it that way. I'd seen the way some of the others looked at her. Delgado with animosity, Simmons with lust.

Granger then did the oddest thing I've ever seen a ranking officer do. Looking back, it was almost unbelievable. He pulled a pen from his pocket and wrote down numbers on a five strips of paper and folded them up tightly, putting them in his hand. Then he walked around to each of us and we chose.

"Russian roulette isn't a spectator sport so I'm even putting myself in the mix. Whoever gets number *1* goes now, number *2* gets the next unwanted task and so on. It's fair as fair can be so give your all to Uncle Sam and leave your complaints with Jesus. Hoo-ahh?" Granger said.

"Hoo-ahh," Farrell said smiling. "I got *4*,"

"*3* for me," Delgado said.

I quickly unrolled my slit of paper, unleashing a sigh of relief as I looked at the favored digit and held it in the air so all could see. "*5!*" I said.

"Damn it," Simmons said, rolling up his paper into a wad and tossing it across the room. His facial tic began to flare in agitation.

"I guess that leaves me with *2*," Granger said, dropping his still folded paper on the floor and kicking it to the side. "Get your gear together and take a couple rations for each of you, just in case."

As a military man, I found the whole process bizarre. I'd never seen a commander do something like that, never putting himself as an equal with the men he was charged to lead. In my career, orders are given and orders are followed—nothing is left for the fates to decide. But, he ordered us to choose numbers, so that is what we did. I tried to fathom why he would opt to act so unorthodox, but at the time, the last thing I wanted to do was question a deck that was stacked in my favor. I thought maybe he was trying to compensate for abusing the detainee, to make up for the respect he'd lost among us. Cracks in his machismo and hard-line attitude had already exposed him as a sham. The pretense behind the charade never crossed my mind though. It's a brilliant strategy I suppose, to reveal one flaw so it deflects attention from a more important one. I thought I had won that game. I just didn't understand the game we were playing.

"Now I gotta drive a damn truck. I don't know how to get to no Moose Jaw," Simmons muttered lowly to no one in particular.

"It's easy. Just head north once you find a moose knuckle," Farrell said. Delgado and I snickered, partly from Farrell's vulgar joke, mostly from relief that Simmons' misfortune wasn't our own.

Eva snuggled against my arm, holding it tightly. I was getting lost in her touch and feeling more comforted by it than the vodka ever could. We watched the three men preparing to leave, carrying with them only what they thought they might need. Simmons took his issued gear and Hanna a blood-stained notebook, no doubt chronicling whatever information he'd been able to obtain. Ekwall grabbed a radio handset, a few rations and his jacket, but that was all. I should have noticed it then, should have looked for it even, but I was too distracted by that beautiful woman to care that he didn't take his briefcase.

Besides, between the disasters and my situation, I had more pressing things on my mind.

14
Reaching Out

The three men couldn't have been gone for more than thirty minutes before Granger slipped his way into the cell. It made me wonder who was really acting toward their own agenda. Delgado, Farrell and I looked at each other, waiting for someone to be the first to react or, at the very least, comment. No one did.

I was dreading the moment when the noise of sodomy would begin. I imagined the look of horror Eva would have once she realized what was behind that door and why we were really there. I worried she may even question my character by association. While she would sometimes surprise me with the handle she had on American English, there was still a language barrier that prevented full comprehension. How could I explain my impotence in the matter due to chain of command or justify my own inaction against such blatant abuse? Many would-be judges might condemn me, but nobody could understand without being in that position firsthand.

To my surprise, though, the noise never began. No rhythmic thumps on the walls or screams of agony. Only silence. My dread was replaced by relief, tainted with a morbid curiosity. I don't think I was the only one, even though most comments sidestepped the subject.

"You know," Delgado said, "for a minute there, I thought we were gonna have to bring Bryce back."

"I can't do it. I hear Bryce one more time, I think I'll shoot out my own eardrums," Farrell said. He stood up, wiped the sweat from his forehead and momentarily admired his work before bending back down to plug in the radio system.

"Besides, I got something much better for us to listen to," he added.

"Whoa, hold up. You're not going to use that, are you?" Delgado said.

"Sure, why not?" Farrell said.

"Ekwall may be a dick, but in this case, he's not wrong. There's too much risk to broadcast from down here," Delgado said.

"I think his assessment of the risk factor is ridiculous. You know how hard it is to source trace a broadcast signal? And who's even looking? Besides, we don't have to broadcast ourselves to listen to other broadcasts. Listening is impossible to detect," Farrell said.

He pushed down on a silver toggle switch and the front panels illuminated with a soft yellow glow. Crackling static, intermixed with squealing twangs, flowed from the speakers that rested atop the three transmitter boxes. Farrell sat down in front of the system, pressing different buttons and working with the large knobs trying to tune into a solid signal. It wasn't long before he found one.

The female voice that came from the speakers was panicked and fighting through terror to deliver her message. The emotional distress that her voice carried made it seem as though her words would cease as soon as the imminent crying would overpower her ability to speak. It was also in German so we didn't understand a word of it. Farrell tried again passing through several signals of intermittent static.

The next signal played, "...and we can use whatever help you can give. Again, we're in the old shack at the end of Marsha's

Till. Please bring food or water or whatever you have. We have shelter for now, we'll share...," then it too disappeared into static.

Farrell worked with it, tuning in signals as best he could, then changing them if they were in a language foreign to all of us. One of them was in Chinese. He paused on it long enough to say, "Hey, I think they're speaking Amish." Then he repeated "ching-chang-chong" until even he didn't find it amusing anymore.

I wanted to tell them I understood what was being said, but I couldn't. I could hear only a little over Farrell's mockery but what I heard disturbed me deeply. The voice said things like, "Please someone help! They've eaten my children," and "the clouds are killing us." I wanted to hear the rest but even at that point, I thought it better to continue my ethnic facade.

Another signal soon tuned in, this one being a looping recorded message amidst more static. I don't remember the whole thing but a male voice with a long, southern United States drawl talked about being part of a "reformation of the Union before the inevitable rising of the beast." There was a bunch of references to biblical prophecy that made it sound like the rant of a madman. I couldn't take it too seriously at face value but the inference was still troubling. Farrell changed the signal as it began to repeat.

Eva started to cry as we watched them work, tears running down her cheek and onto my sleeve. I supposed the stress of the whole situation was weighing heavily on her and I was empathetic. Granger dismissed her story as a lie or even lunacy, but her fear seemed genuine to me. As I looked over at her face, completely beautiful even with her eyes welling with tears, I realized that she wasn't trying to escape and never asked to leave. We wanted to keep her there under our surveillance but, aside from Delgado's initial hostile detainment, we hadn't threatened her or made her feel like a prisoner. She seemed content to remain with us. I was confident that she was hiding. All I knew for sure

was that sitting down in that concrete prison, cut off from a
world to which I no longer had a connection, I felt so much
better having her beside me. And together, we watched as the
world around us appeared to collapse.

The longer Farrell continued to fumble with the machine,
the more his frustration seemed to build. He bypassed another
static-laden signal only to find another, finally sitting back and
looking at the meters on the front panel of the receiver boxes.

"This doesn't make any damn sense. I've never seen static
so strong, almost like someone is trying to amplify it
intentionally," Farrell said. "I've used it during hurricanes and
never had this much…"

"Shh, listen," Delgado said. "There's a pattern to it."

We all remained still and listened to the noise fade in and
out with varying intensities. I didn't hear what he was remarking
about at first but as difficult as it was to notice, it was equally as
difficult to ignore once it was pointed out. At my previous
station, in all those months of guard duty in North Carolina, I
never needed to use Morse code and, to my discredit, I had not
kept it fresh in my mind. It was definitely in the pattern of static,
though. Although too rusty to decipher the code, I could
recognize its presence.

Farrell grabbed a pen and began to transcribe the letters as
they were transmitted, listening until the pattern repeated. He
then turned his attention towards the knobs, changing them as
he spoke, "It's a number, written out in word form: 2-5-2-
PERIOD-8-0-MHZ."

"It's a frequency," Delgado said.

Farrell rechecked every setting while we listened to the
sounds of the quiet speaker hum. "It's a frequency filled with
dead air. This is it," Farrell said, "and nothing is being broadcast
on it."

"You sure you're working that damn thing right?" Delgado said.

"Back off, chico, I know radios like your people know lawnmowers. I'm doing it right," Farrell said. "I just don't think this is an invitation to listen. I think it's a call to speak."

"Now you want to broadcast?" Delgado said. "You don't even know who you're broadcasting to."

"It's military, English speaking military, probably U.S." Farrell said, "and they only want other military personnel to contact to them."

"How they hell can you tell that?" Delgado said.

Farrell explained, "They're sending controlled interference in a Morse code pattern. Only people trained in Morse code would be able to recognize it and these days, who else knows it besides military and radio operators? The message itself is just a frequency reserved for military aviators. They also used the word 'period.' That's English. Other countries would have said 'comma.'"

"But why pattern interference? Why not broadcast as clicks or beeps?" Delgado said.

"It may have been to make it less obvious to anyone who doesn't use Morse Code regularly. Hell, I use it and I missed it at first. More importantly though, it's difficult to broadcast on every frequency simultaneously because you'd have to send out a specific signal to every frequency. But interference, you can interfere with every frequency at once pretty easily, even the ones that already have a broadcast on them. You control that interference in a Morse code pattern and you have a yourself a wide reaching message that's veiled just enough to keep most civilians from jamming up the one frequency you want to keep clean."

"We should get Granger, man. I'm telling you, cover your ass," Delgado said.

"You really want to walk in on him doing whatever the hell he's doing in there? Fuck him," Farrell said. He flipped the switch and watched the meters and gauges on the front panel of another box illuminate. Then he reluctantly put his mouth to the large bulbous microphone, pressed the call button and said, "Outpost for actual. Come in."

We waited a moment in anticipation, but heard nothing.

He repeated, "Outpost for actual. Come in."

A short static burst came through the speakers, followed by a man's voice, tinny and shallow but clear, "Outpost, this is R.O. Actual unavailable, state your file and position."

"I knew it was military," Farrell said pressing the button again. "This is Sergeant Tommy Farrell. Position classified."

The radio operator paused for a few moments then spoke adamantly, "R.O. For actual. State your position. That's a direct order from President Dixon."

Farrell looked puzzled. We all did. At that point, I held out hope that the signal may have been a gag. Farrell acted like he did too as he held a slight smirk on his face. Perhaps, I thought, it wasn't best that he was the one using the microphone. "Pardon me for speaking plainly, but who the fuck is President Dixon?" he said.

"Sergeant, are you the highest ranking officer at your position? That question comes directly from the United States commander-in-chief," the radio operator said.

Farrell's smirk abandoned him as he looked around to us.

"OK," he said to Delgado, "I guess we could get Granger."

15
Bad to Worse

I find it fascinating how children are molded into who they become by those that surround them. Nobody chooses where they enter this world or the situations that they're thrust into when they get here. We all learn from our experiences and most of us, as children at least, believe the situations that we go through are normal, as if there is such a thing. Those lessons that we learn, both typical and unique, carry us through life and influence every decision we'll ever make.

For example, I had learned early in life to not defy my authorities. The summer that Lin first kissed me, the summer I fell in love, was possibly the greatest time of my life. Her peck on the cheek turned into another and another and soon moved to my lips. From our window four stories up, Uncle Lee would oversee all of the boys while we did our chores and it didn't slip by him that I'd found a friend, a female companion. I remember one time in particular, she had kissed me and I looked up as if I could feel his burning gaze; sure enough, there he stood on the other side of the glass, looking down on me, on us, with stern disapproval.

"Stay away from girls," he said to me when I returned. "They can only distract you from your responsibilities."

I couldn't though. I told Lin what my Uncle had said, but she didn't want me to leave her alone and honestly, I didn't want to anyway. She convinced me to sneak away with her for minutes at a time, hiding together in a secluded alcove behind the stairwell in my building. We talked and laughed and, of course, kissed like the innocents we were.

As we grew to know one another, our physical affections escalated and our kissing became passionate. This caused the quality of my chores to suffer even though they took noticeably longer to get done. With growing frequency, I'd lose track of time during our continued rendezvous and be forced to make up excuses for my delay. I doubt he ever really believed me.

The last time I kissed her, she pushed her body against mine. We had already been kissing for several minutes and male physiology being what it is, my nearly prepubescent erection poked right into her hip. She may not have even known what it was at the time. She never got a chance to ask. I gasped and felt instant panic as I opened my eyes to see my Uncle Lee standing right above us. The bastard slapped her across the face with the back of his hand, knocking her to the floor. At first, I was so in shock, I did nothing. She broke out in tears and ran away to the sound of him yelling "whore dog" at her back.

Enraged by his assault, I tried to tackle him but he was too big. I punched his meaty stomach but my young arms could do no real damage. He was just too strong. His punches, however, were much more effective on me. The last thing I remember as I sat there on the ground, staring at trails of my own blood and tears and snot on the cracked vinyl floor, was him pulling my ear to speak into it. He told me that if he caught me with her again, he would forcefully take her innocence himself and he would do it in front of me. He said he'd make me watch.

I didn't think it was fair and I didn't think anyone should act so evil, but this was my childhood. To me, this was normal.

Maybe he was bluffing, but I don't think so. He never bluffed. At any rate, she still tried to talk to me a few days after that but I loved her enough to tell her I wanted her to leave me alone. I lied to her to keep her away from danger. I hated him for it, but I learned not to defy him.

To this day, the act of defying authority makes me feel as queasy as that young boy laying on the hallway floor. I was already worried about my family and my country, but watching Farrell and Delgado bicker about who was going to get our commander's attention, or whether or not we even should, made my stomach knot up even tighter. Granger had lost much of the respect of his men and with it, some of the willingness to acknowledge his authority. Nobody really wanted to listen to him, but nobody wanted to tell him that we collectively and deliberately disobeyed an order either. I sensed an inevitable power struggle drawing near.

Delgado finally threw his arms up in frustration and walked toward the cell. He stood there for a moment listening, then loudly beat on the door three times with the bottom of his fist before stepping back towards the desk again. Granger didn't respond immediately. In my mind, he was cleaning up or getting dressed or covering his tracks. That thought made me feel a little sicker.

He finally opened the door after a minute of quiet and stepped out, looking around the room to all of us for a response. Eva squeezed my arm, hiding her face partially behind my shoulder as he gazed in our direction. It was an awkward moment of silence, as if he was anticipating some kind of intervention, maybe even mutiny. Farrell opened his mouth to explain the developments in his own terms, but he didn't get a word out.

"Sergeant Farrell, this is R.O. for actual. Come in," the radio operator said through the speaker.

We all exhibited surprise on our face as we looked over at the radio, Granger most of all.

"What the hell did you do?" Granger said, brushing Farrell aside in agitation. He walked toward the desk and sat down as if to take the reins, scowling as he looked at the multitude of knobs and switches and gauges. He seemed reluctant to admit his ignorance, especially to the person who had just angered him, but he had little choice. "How does this damn thing work?"

Farrell pointed out the send button and pushed the microphone toward Granger's face. Granger aggressively grabbed it from Farrell's hand and turned his back toward him.

"This is actual commanding officer, Lieutenant Colonel Charles Granger. To whom am I speaking?" he said.

"State your position," the radio operator said.

"To whom am I speaking?" Granger repeated forcefully.

"Sergeant Riley, U.S. Air Force. State your position, Colonel," the radio operator said.

"Negative. Our station is classified. State your purpose for contact," Granger said.

"Colonel, we need your position. This is an order from President Curtis Dixon, United States commander-in-chief."

"Curtis Dixon? The Secretary of Education?" Granger said. "Is this some kind of joke to you, son?"

The speakers went quiet as we sat there for a full minute, waiting for information, trying to grasp what was happening.

"Sergeant Riley, do you read me?" Granger said.

Then the radio operator responded, "Lieutenant Colonel Charles Granger, 45 years old, born May 15, in Norfolk, Virginia to father Harold Oswald Granger and mother Beatrice Rae James. Never married, no kids. Religious affiliation: none, party affiliation: Republican. I'm reading this out of the Department of Defense's classified personnel database, Colonel. I can go on if you'd like. Rest assured, this is no joke. I'm asking on behalf of our newly appointed commander-in-chief."

Granger sat down in the chair, as worried as I'd ever seen him.

"You were sent from Minot to Canada. Is this correct?" Riley said.

"Yes," Granger said.

"Has your positioned changed?"

"No."

"Where are you right now?"

"I don't think this is appropriate chatter for such a non-secure venue," Granger said.

"Our communication options are limited, Colonel. Where are you?"

"Qu'Appelle Valley, Canada."

"I'm not familiar with it. What's there?" Riley said.

"Just green grass and us. Not much of anything else," Granger said.

"Do you have shelter?"

"Yes, we're in a secure shelter."

"Have you or any of your men been exposed to the dust clouds?"

He looked puzzled from the strange question as he paused to consider it.

"I'm not sure what you mean," Granger said. "Can you elaborate?"

"You should listen to the radio. Is your shortwave radio capable of picking up standard AM/FM stations?"

He looked at Farrell who was already shaking his head.

"No. We're isolated and off the grid," Granger said.

"How long have you been off the grid, Colonel?"

"Three days until now. What's going on, Sergeant?"

"I don't want to be the one to deliver this info," Riley said reluctantly.

I braced myself for more bad news but I had no idea just how bad it would be.

He continued, "There's been another series of incidents. The east coast of Canada, central Mexico, and both coasts of the United States all experienced intense meteorite showers. There was no warning, not enough to do anything anyway. They were devastating."

Farrell sat down against the wall, holding a hollow stare on his face as his mouth unwittingly hung open. Delgado was breathing deep, sighing as he bent over and resting his hands against his knees. I knew what they were experiencing because I had felt the same way for days. I no longer had to hide the emotion at that point, even if I couldn't completely share their reasons for it. This was just another punch in the stomach for me.

"Casualties?" Granger said.

"Impossible to tell," Riley said. "Worldwide, they estimate well into the billions."

"And Curtis Dixon? I assume D.C was hit then?" Granger asked solemnly.

"Washington D.C. was ground zero, one of many. It was destroyed, as were all major cities on both coasts as far in as New York on the east. Dixon just happened to be visiting schools in the Midwest. He was sixteenth in succession, now he's president of what's left," Riley said.

We all sat still for a moment of silence. I wasn't sure if it was more out of reverence or shock. In a moment like that, I suppose they go hand in hand.

"And the dust clouds?" Granger asked.

"On the fringe of every detonation, clouds of dust have traveled as far away as 200 miles in every direction. There's something in the dust causing a sickness of sorts. Symptoms onset a few days after contact. It's airborne, highly contagious and spreading quicker than we can keep track of. Do you have any form of transport?" Riley said.

"Only our boots at the moment. We have a truck but it's currently on detail," Granger said.

"Try to get your men to Grand Forks Air Force Base, North Dakota. We have a secure set up here and we've become the official communication center for every remaining American base, both domestic and abroad. Satellites and tel-com services are down so we're back to the 1920's over here—we sure could use all the extra hands we can get. In the meantime, just stay inside and keep your distance from unknowns. Carriers of the plague can look healthy and unaffected for 48 to 72 hours after exposure," Riley said.

The other men, my fellow soldiers, all looked over toward me. That's what I thought anyway when I raised my head and saw them staring in my direction. Then I realized they were looking at Eva, checking her out as if she was tainted, evaluating her state of being. I was beginning to feel fearful for her, helpless to defend her should the scenario become ugly against her. Then it hit me that I had been closest to her and I would be just as helpless to defend myself.

Granger kept his eye on us as he spoke, "Symptoms of the sickness? What are they, Sergeant?"

"We don't have too much to go on, but from the intel that's trickled in, it attacks the mind first. Delusions, paranoia, hallucinations, that kind of thing," Riley said. "As it progresses, there's bleeding from the nose and mouth as people become increasingly hostile and in the later stages, it breaks down tissue from the inside out, ending in death."

It was almost too much for my mind to handle. Breathing became difficult and my heart pounded in my chest. Looking back, I think I was beginning to have a panic attack. As we sat there and listened, I was dreading the end of the conversation for I feared it may begin a horrible ordeal for Eva. I needed a drink and I wanted everyone to join me. Just have a drink and relax before doing anything rash.

He continued, "You don't have to worry about that if you can get here though. We've secured the perimeter and locked ourselves in a clean environment—filtered air, water, the whole works. When will your truck return, Colonel?"

"Should be within a few hours, after they re-establish a connection with our contact at Moose Jaw," he said.

"CFB Moose Jaw?" Riley said. "Have you heard from your men, Colonel?"

"Not yet. Why?" Granger said. "Have you communicated with anyone from Moose Jaw?"

"We did, scheduled a check-in every 4 hours," Riley said, "but they went quiet 36 hours ago, nothing but dead air since. You should put your men on alert."

"Copy that," Granger said, quickly turning to Farrell. "Get our boys on the horn, now!"

16
Tainted

"Simmons, come in, damn it," Farrell said. There was still no answer. He'd been at it for fifteen minutes and there was still no answer. Not a peep.

I would say I was beginning to think the worst, but I've come to realize that phrase is a misnomer and, to be blunt, pretty egotistical for anyone to say. Good and bad are relative terms and whatever a person might consider the *worst* will most likely change once something even more horrible comes along. Being an absolute expression, an extreme end to a spectrum, there will only be one *worst* by the time life draws to a close. But, unless they're a god that has already experienced and weighed every possible negative outcome, they won't know which terrible thing that is until they're gone and there's no more opportunities for misfortune. People use that expression to infer death without having to say that ugly word but there are many experiences that make death a merciful escape by comparison. I came to all these conclusions down in that concrete box. It became evident as bad news compiled on bad situations when in reality things were already so much worse than I could have ever imagined. As I watched him make calls through that radio, calls that sounded as authentically concerned as possible to a man whom he acted so angry toward just hours before, I definitely did not foresee my fate.

"Farrell to Simmons. Come in," he said again. Granger sighed deeply, impatiently pacing back and forth behind him. Delgado sat on the side, staring at an empty spot the wall. He hadn't moved or said a word since Riley had brought us up to speed.

Eva didn't leave my side. She held tightly onto my arm sitting close enough that I could feel her breath on my skin. It was very calming. Maybe I should have been afraid that she was infected but I had already been so close to her, it was too late for me, probably for all of us. I figured I may as well enjoy any moments I could before something else happened to take them away.

It made me wonder if she had understood the conversation in the radio transmissions or even the awkward glances my fellow soldiers had given her. I wondered if she realized that danger may not be limited to outside the bunker. At any rate, the brotherhood of military made the potential threat for one of our own seem like a more urgent matter and superseded whatever worries came with her presence. To be honest, while I was not apathetic for the safety of the men that had left us, I was thankful for the diversion.

"Farrell to Simmons, come in," he said for the last time.

A brief hiss of static initiated a response.

"What the fuck you want?" Simmons said.

"Damn it, Simmons. Where the hell have you been?" Farrell said.

"I was taking a shit," Simmons said.

"You left the truck?"

"Well, I'm not gonna shit in the damn truck. I just left the radio here."

"Where are you now?"

"Now, I'm back in the truck!"

"Damn it, give me that thing," Granger said as he snatched the handset radio from Farrell's hand. "This is your commander, Simmons, what happened?"

"Sir, this place was hard as hell to find. GPS can't connect to satellite signals, half the back roads aren't marked and the closest things to landmarks out here are mooses and caribou and shit," Simmons said.

"Are Hanna and Ekwall with you?" Granger said.

"No, sir. I'm waiting in the truck. They went inside to find someone," Simmons said.

"The guard at the front gate didn't direct you?"

"There was no front gate guard. We drove right in and parked out front of the main building. They went inside to find somebody. I stepped outside to relieve myself on a nearby bush and now I'm waiting. I ain't seen no one around nowhere, sir."

"Is it windy there, Simmons? Do you see any dust clouds?" Granger said.

"Dust clouds?" Simmons said. "No. But there *is* a bunch of shit on the ground."

"What do you mean?"

"It looks almost like... like pollen. You know how that shit builds up on your car, like a layer of yellow powdered sugar almost? It's like that everywhere here, except thick enough that it leaves foot prints when you walk in it," Simmons said.

"Stay in the truck, Simmons, and don't touch that shit with your hands. Did you touch it with your bare skin?" Granger said.

A few seconds passed before Simmons spoke, "No, I almost did, but decided not to so I did not touch it."

"Bullshit!" Farrell said. "He's lying. You heard that, right? That was such a lie!"

"Shut up!" Granger said to Farrell as he pressed the button and spoke into the radio. "Simmons, keep the truck running and get your rifle ready."

"Is there something I should know, sir?" Simmons said.

"Just stay alert," Granger said.

"Why do I need my... hold up, hold up. They're coming out now, at least that freak-show Hanna is. I guess they didn't find nobody. Hanna's walking towards the truck," Simmons said.

"Does anything seem odd about him?" Granger said.

"Everything about that cat seem odd, but no more than usual," Simmons said. "OK, OK. Now Ekwall's exiting the building... and he's got his gun drawn. Now there's some other dude, coming out a door to his right... he's uniformed and carrying something."

"What's he carrying?" Granger asked.

"Actually there's a bunch of guys coming out that door and... oh, shit," Simmons said.

Then his radio went quiet.

"Simmons, what's happening?" Granger said. A few more long seconds passed.

Simmons started transmitting again and we could hear the monstrous truck engine growling like thunder through the speaker, almost overpowering his voice, "They're attacking him, beating him!"

"Who?!" Granger said.

"Get in! Get in!" Simmons said before the radio went momentarily quiet again.

"Granger?!" Hanna said through the radio. "They're attacking Agent Ekwall! They're killing him!" Behind his voice, the truck roared and rattled along and we could distinctly hear loud gun shots. They weren't deep enough to be rifle shots, and I could only hope they were coming from Simmons' pistol.

"Hanna? Simmons?! Report back!" Granger said. "What's going on?!"

Nobody moved or spoke. I didn't know what we just heard, and knew even less about how to respond. It seemed nobody did. So we just listened in silence, waiting for them to signal back. Granger acted genuinely concerned, his eyes quickly darting around the front panel as if he knew enough to check it for functionality. Minutes slipped away in a mentally draining anticipation.

"Colonel?" Simmons said. "You still with me, sir?"

"Affirmative. Are you hurt?" Granger said.

"No, sir. I'm alright and Hanna's in the truck with me," Simmons said, "but Ekwall, he didn't make it."

"What happened?" Granger said.

"Hanna said they went in and couldn't find no one. The place looked trashed inside and they found rooms lined with dead bodies and a bunch of crazy shit written on the walls with blood. On their way out, a Canadian officer came out holding a fire ax, and he had six more uniforms behind him. Ekwall tried to talk him down but the dude went nuts, took a swing at him so Ekwall blasted him. The others were too quick though. They beat him down, lifted his pistol," Simmons said.

"What did you do?" Granger said.

"I picked up Hanna and pulled my M9. I fired but they kept on chopping him, yelling crazy shit about 'dark spores' and accusing Ekwall of trying to steal their sunlight. I hit one in the shoulder and even after he fell on Ekwall, he kept attacking, started biting him. I mean really biting chunks of flesh out of him, growling like a mad dog while he did it. They just wouldn't stop. I had to kill 'em, sir," Simmons said. "I killed them all, but it was too late."

"Are you sure Ekwall was dead?" Granger said.

"By the time they got done with the ax, his body was almost in three pieces," Simmons said. "There ain't no way he's not dead."

He wasn't one of our own, not part of the military brotherhood. From what I could tell, nobody down there even liked him. Even still, news of his death hit hard. Maybe it was because he was American and that bond meant something or perhaps just being human was enough; a large part may have been that it was such a violent death at the hands of America's northern allies. I think though the biggest jarring factor was that he was safe and alive down there only a few hours before, just like us. And it wasn't a stretch in reason that, like him, any one of us could be dead in a few hours. Our own mortality was dangling in front of our eyes, harshly reminding us exactly how fragile we are.

Simmons continued, "I went over to look at him and somebody started firing at us out one of the windows. Then more guys started coming out of the building, everyone of 'em running toward us."

"Where are you now?" Granger said.

"I jumped in the truck and we hauled ass. We're on the road, heading back now if we can even find the damn place. This is some fucked-up shit, sir."

"Seems so," Granger said.

"There's one more thing," Simmons said. "That powder, the shit you said not to touch, it was hard to walk on, almost like sand but slicker. Well, when Hanna was running, he tripped and fell face first, and now he's covered in it."

Granger closed his eyes in discouragement and sighed, looking to the ground as he thought. "It will be OK. Just get back here," he said. "Over."

Nobody spoke at first but the silence couldn't last long. While no one wanted to be the first to open their mouth, we sat and looked around at each other knowing the inevitable words someone would have to own.

"We can't let them back in here," Farrell said. "You heard what he just said, right?"

Granger looked at him solemnly.

"We can't do that to one of our own. Hanna, that bastard can walk back to America but Simmons didn't touch it," Delgado said.

"That's bullshit. He was lying when he said that and you know it. But let's pretend for a minute that *was* true at the time—he's spending two hours locked in a truck cab with some guy who, no doubt, is dusting himself off right now," Farrell said. "You think Simmons is going to hold his breath the whole time?"

"What about that bitch?!" Delgado said pointing to Eva. "We should throw her ass to the wolves too. She was on a plane with people that were infected and she could just as easily be a time bomb set to go off and kill us all."

I have to admit, I once had that thought as well but, it felt so good to have her beside me, I pushed it out of my head. I naively hoped no one else would bring it up. Really, I should have known it was only a matter of time though. As Delgado spoke, Eva squeezed my arm tightly and pushed her face into my shoulder. Her English may not have been perfect but she understood what he said and she was going to look to me for protection. My allegiance was being intentionally stretched and I was beginning to fear I'd soon have to tear it apart myself.

"You're some piece of work," Farrell said. "What about all that pious confession bullshit you were spouting? Now you want to throw some young girl out in the middle of nowhere to fend for herself? Hanna is covered in the shit that's making people go nuts. This girl's been away from the crazies for at least a day or two and she seems fine to me."

"First off, you don't know that whatever Hanna fell in was the same dust making everyone sick. As for her, down here eating our food, not contributing shit, I guess we'll find out in another day or so just how healthy she is. Damn, at least Simmons would be functional when shit goes down. What if it was you out there, brother?" Delgado said.

"If it was me, I wouldn't risk infecting my whole troop just to avoid camping outside for a few days," Farrell said turning to Granger. "How do you call it, sir?"

Granger quietly listened to Farrell and Delgado, looking at them like they were a cartoon angel and demon pair sitting on his opposing shoulders. I wondered if he and I would agree on who was which.

"We need them to return," Granger said. "The trip will take them a couple of hours at least and by then, I'll decide whether or not they come back in."

"If you haven't decided yet, why do we need them back?" Farrell said.

"Whether they survive or not," Granger said, "we need that truck."

It was a cold sentiment, as true as it was. We couldn't live down there forever and that truck would greatly help our chances for survival. It still made me feel a little depressed to hear him sound so callous.

"So they come back and what? We thank Simmons and Hanna for dropping off the truck and desert them? Wish them best of luck as the world's creepiest odd couple while we scramble back to whatever states are still united? They're both reasonable people. I'm sure they'll understand," Farrell said.

"That's bullshit. What happened to 'never leave a buddy behind' commander? I'm not leaving Simmons," Delgado said.

"And if they come back in, I won't stay down here just to wait for Dr. Rainbow to finally hop over the edge and start gnawing on somebody's face," Farrell said. "Shit, and the truck? Forget it, that thing's tainted now. I'm not planting my freckled ass behind the wheel of a three-ton Petri dish."

"Shut your mouths!" Granger yelled. "Shut your damn mouths! Out of respect, I cast lots with you all and I help with responsibilities that I could just as easily assign away but don't mistake yourselves as my peers. This is not a vote. You will abide with whatever I decide. I am still the high ranking officer here and you still serve in the Army of the United States."

"There's not much of a United States left," Farrell said defiantly.

Granger quickly stepped up to Farrell, putting his face close enough that their noses nearly touched, but Farrell didn't back away. He had to feel some saliva spray as Granger continued to yell. "Well until every feather's been plucked from that bird, you will obey my orders because you have an obligation to serve your country. After that, you'll do it out of respect to me. And after that, you'll do it because if you don't, I'll kill you where you stand."

His words made me shutter. Granger always seemed level-headed, stern and serious, but unfluctuating in control even when challenged. To see him lose his composure, to threaten one of his own men was unsettling. The feeling was amplified into distress, however, once he turned his attention toward Eva.

"Sorry to break up date night, Princess, but you and I need to talk... somewhere more private."

17
Breaking Boundaries

G ranger looked around the room briefly before locking eyes with Delgado. "Go in the cell and slide him out, chair and all," he said.

"The prisoner?" Delgado said. "Sir, are you sure?"

"I'm not going to repeat myself. Do it," Granger said.

I didn't think any of us knew what he was contemplating, but he was breaching protocols and leading us to join him. The mission parameters seemed to have changed towards a new end, one more focused on survival. In reality, the goal was information extraction as it always was but, with the prisoner and Eva having switched places, I thought the mark had changed. I was as wrong about that as thinking that the bound man wasn't key to the whole mess.

"What are we doing with him?" Farrell said.

"You'll do nothing. Just let him sit," Granger said.

"Then why are you bringing him out here?" Farrell said.

"Damn it! Don't question my orders, Sergeant," Granger said, his bark sounding more aggressive with every word.

The sound of wood sliding against concrete reverberated throughout the bunker as Delgado drove the chair from the cell into the assembly room, facing the prisoner towards a corner. Still bound by his extremities, the man sat calmly as he was pushed even though he looked like he'd been dragged through the deepest puddle in hell. While he had no exposed wounds to speak of, blood covered his shirt and was spattered all over the surface of his thighs. Entry wounds abound on his pants, encompassed in red circular blobs as if he'd been stabbed multiple times and his exposed feet were coated in dirt and soot. I still couldn't see his face, only black hair that peeked out from underneath the cloth sack that covered his head once again. He was a horrible sight to see, no more for anyone than Eva.

She whimpered as he was brought out. I thought maybe it was for example at first. Perhaps Granger thought she had something to hide and wanted to scare her. Had that been the case, I'm sure it would have worked—it scared me on her behalf. He walked over to us and held out his hand to her as she still gripped tightly onto my arm.

"Come with me," he said.

She didn't move. I couldn't blame her. I wanted to draw my pistol and demand he not lay a hand on her. I pictured myself standing up and grabbing her by the hand, holding the others at gunpoint while we both left that place and ran away to an unknown future in what was becoming a foreign and very dangerous world. Instead, I froze. I didn't fight back or even say a word. It was Lin and Uncle Lee all over again.

He pulled Eva's arm, forcing her to stand up. She resisted but Granger dragged her into the cell, gripping her arm above the elbow. Farrell hopped up and moved toward the cell door, but Delgado stood in his way, his brawny chest as much a wall as the concrete that surrounded us.

"Oh, what the fuck is this? Is this what we've become?" Farrell yelled.

"Just take it easy. This has to be done," Delgado said. "We have to make sure she's told us everything she knows and that she's telling us the truth."

"You knew he was going to do this?" Farrell said.

"He mentioned questioning her again, yes," Delgado said. "I didn't know it would be in there but so be it."

"You're OK with it though? She's a young girl, man. She's innocent!" Farrell said, his voice exuding a frustration I shared.

I couldn't sit there. Without her holding my arm, anchoring me still against the cold floor, I had become antsy and on edge. I walked into the mess room and stood there for a moment, letting the rage eat at me for as long as I could. Then I kicked the refrigerator with everything I had, the steel toe of my boot carving a pointed dent in the door. They must have heard it. Farrell came in shortly after and found me leaning on the table, anxiously rocking back and forth.

"You OK, Amish?" he said. "Don't worry, I don't think he'll hurt her. I know he won't. We won't let him."

Amish, he said. That was a name I hated at first, but it had grown on me to the point that I almost found it soothing to hear. On the surface it was just a silly nickname, but I began to recognize it as a familiarity that comes with the bonds of friendship. I felt drawn into the relationship and I really started to trust Farrell. I'm sure that was his intention. I wanted to tell him why I felt compassion for Eva, compelled to protect her. I wanted to tell him about Lin.

"I lost somebody once, that's all," I said.

"Yeah, I know the feeling," he said. "Who did you lose?"

"I don't want to talk about it right now," I said.

At first, Farrell seemed reluctant to speak candidly, at least not with anything emotionally deeper than a penis joke. But right then, to my surprise, he widely opened up.

"Remember I was telling you about my sister? Jamie was always a little weird but let's face it, who doesn't think their kid sister is weird, right?" he said.

"I guess," I said.

He continued, "I thought we had a great family. My parents were still together, married my whole life. My dad was an elementary school teacher, mom was a grocery store cashier. One day I got home from school, fifteen years old, and saw my dad in handcuffs being marched right out the front door. Turns out, my sister was actually a cousin, adopted as a baby when my mom's sister died of cancer. And my dad had been molesting her for eight years, started when she was six. Jamie hid his secret all that time."

I didn't know what to say. Those wonderful childhood memories he'd shared with me suddenly became sad reflections.

"What happened to her?" I said.

He was slow to speak, but persisted, "She became wildly promiscuous. Started drinking and screwing anyone that would give her the time. Guys, girls, it didn't matter. She left home when she turned seventeen and started stripping. Eventually, she ended up with some yo-boy, gangster-wannabe—a black dude named *Zeus* if you can believe that shit."

"Did she stay with him?" I said.

"For as long as she could. The tool-bag turned Jamie onto crack and started pimping her out," he said. "You know, I tracked her down one time, determined to bring her back home, but once I caught up to her, she was so burnt out, she didn't even know who I was. Her mind was gone. A month later, she was found in an alley, dead. Jamie had gotten so high, she suffocated on her own vomit."

I was speechless but I empathized. It made me feel connected to him, made me realize why he acted the way he did. Where Eva made me see my dear Lin, he saw his baby sister, Jamie. The story made me believe he and I felt equally burdened to protect that girl, maybe a small step toward redemption for letting someone we love slip away from us.

"You want to hear something else?" he said.

I locked eyes with him, giving my full attention as approval without saying a word.

"When I found out a what a piece of shit my ole man was, I stole a gun from his safe. I was going to kill him," Farrell said, grinning sadly. "Fifteen years old and I'm sleeping with a loaded gun under my bed so I can kill my father the next time I see him."

"Did you try it?" I said.

"I never had a chance. He was only in prison for a few days before he used a broken piece of his bunk bed to slice up his wrists. He'd bled out by morning."

I almost told him about my childhood. I thought it may have helped him to compare emotional scars—maybe even make me feel better in the process. But I didn't tell him anything. I was so used to being a closed book, to keeping my secrets buried deep inside me, it felt more natural to remain silent. I wasn't ready to share. "I'm sorry," I said simply.

"I'm only sorry I didn't get pull the trigger," he said.

"You can't really mean that," I said, but I knew he could. I would have felt the same way.

"I do. And I had made up my mind that when I got back from this mission, I was going to find that piece of shit Zeus and I was going to put him under, make him pay for his part in killing my sister. He lived on the West Coast though. He's probably dead now too," Farrell said. "Maybe God *is* looking out for me, taking vengeance out on people so I don't have to face the consequences of doing it myself."

He sat down for a minute, looking at my face, reading my reaction. Maybe he expected me to talk, to say something insightful, but I'm much better at writing than speaking. I had little to offer in the way of comfort. He added, "I never told that stuff to anyone before. It feels good. Keep it between us though. I don't want Delgado to start going off on his 'bearing of souls' rant again."

"I won't say a word," I said. "But, I have to admit. I'm still worried about the girl."

"I'm more worried about what I may have to do," Farrell said. "He's asking her questions, fine. I understand that. We need all the information we can get, especially if she could be infected. But If I hear her scream or I find out he's hurt her, I'm busting in, weapons drawn. I'm hoping if the time comes to take a stand, you have my back."

I nodded my head and I *was* with him, in principle at least. I wondered even then how much backbone I could grow should the time come. We walked back out to the assembly room together, watching as Delgado continued to stand guard. The cell was quiet. I had hoped that was a good sign.

"Excuse me," the prisoner said. We looked around at each other, initially not realizing which of us was speaking. It was the first time we'd heard his voice not screaming through a wall.

"Excuse me, sirs, but I really must use the restroom."

I didn't want to make the call, so I waited for someone else to respond.

"No," Delgado said. "Sit there and shut up."

"Sirs, I don't want to seem insistent, but my body is going to expel solids, regardless of where I am," the prisoner said.

"Damn it, you shit your pants and I will shoot you," Delgado said. Then he thought it over for a moment and looked at me. "Amish, take him."

"What? Why me?" I said.

"Granger put me on duty and Farrell needs to stay by the radio. Last thing we need is someone to drop ass in this room. That's not helping anybody," Delgado said. I really couldn't argue with his logic.

I untied the rope that bound him to the chair and told him to stand as I poked my rifle at his back. Then I slipped the hood off his head and barked at him, guiding him where to go. He stumbled a bit as if his legs were asleep. As long as he'd supposedly been sitting in that chair, they probably would have been.

It was awkward watching him use the latrine; I can only imagine how much worse it was for the prisoner, actually trying to relax sphincter muscles while his captor pointed an assault weapon at his heart. Duty demanded I keep my eyes fully on him no matter how much I didn't want to stare. It was hard to not be a little understanding that he had stage fright even if I couldn't act tolerable.

"Speed it up!" I demanded like my former drill instructor. "No need to celebrate it." He closed his eyes to focus his mind, occasionally opening them again on me, his obligated watchman. I'd never guarded a prisoner before. I hoped my nervousness wasn't apparent.

It was the first time I'd seen his face and to my surprise, there wasn't a scratch on it. I figured with all of the fallout from other detention centers, faces were left unscathed so they couldn't be used to garner sympathy in photographs. His cheeks were unshaven as could be expected for as long as we'd been stuck down there, but his scruffy beard looked to only be a few weeks old.

He was a terrorist, or so I was told, as dangerous as they come. When I looked into his eyes, though, I didn't see evil or malice. He was just a man, a rather polite and respectful one at that, humbly completing the exhibition of a ritual most of us like to keep as private as possible.

"May I please use the faucet?" he said.

I nodded, never taking the aim of my rifle from his chest.

He hobbled to the sink and cleaned himself off, washing his face and sneaking sips of water as it pooled up in his hands. Maybe he was testing my ethical code or the boundaries I'd impose. No matter, I didn't stop him. After what he'd gone through, it felt good to allow him the pleasure of cool water on his lips.

"Amish!" Delgado yelled from the other room. "What the hell's he doing in there? Getting ready for prom?"

"That's enough," I said calmly.

He didn't resist as he slowly walked back into the other room and sat down, taking in what little sights he could along the way. I leaned against the wall and watched the prisoner put his hands together, making it easier for Farrell to tie him up once again. Delgado replaced his hood and there he quietly remained.

I tried to put myself in his mental state, to understand his thought process. He shouldn't have had any idea that the world around us was in turmoil, that it was safer down there than just about anywhere else, but still he was oddly submissive. I assumed he really had no choice but to comply, his conformity merely a result of good reasoning. He was out-manned, outgunned and weakened from days upon days of torture. Resistance would only bring him more pain and I reckoned he already had a lifetime worth of agony squeezed in his short stay with us. Even still, something didn't sit right.

Any suspicions I had floating around in my mind though, were quickly suppressed by the preoccupation I had with Eva. We'd heard nothing. A dark part of my imagination kept trying to render scenarios centered around horrible things that could have been happening to her, but I didn't want to succumb to paranoia. All I had to go on was pessimistic speculation and I tried to force that out of my thoughts. I sat down and took several deep breaths, wanting her to come out of the cell and safely back on my arm. I was hoping it would happen quickly but all I could do was wait.

So I waited.

18
Betrayed by Fate

"Simmons to Granger, come in," he said.

The distinct radio static echoed against the concrete walls. Farrell sighed disparagingly as he picked up the handset, sat back in the chair and put his feet up on the desk.

"Granger's not here," Farrell said. "What's your E.T.A.?"

"What do you mean he's not there? Where the fuck he go?" Simmons said.

"Up his own ass, head first," Farrell said. "How far away are you?"

"I don't know, man. We lost as hell. I'm at a gas station now looking at a map but the damn thing's in French," Simmons said.

Farrell smiled slightly, appearing at least a little pleased with what he'd heard. "A gas station?" he said.

"Get this, we had to refuel so we drove through a town about an hour ago. The whole place was off the meds. People fighting in the streets, running around like they possessed and cutting themselves. I saw one dude sitting naked on top a traffic light, eating actual shit from his own ass. We got the hell out of there and found a little station all by itself in middle of dick-tits nowhere," Simmons said.

"By itself? You mean away from town?" Farrell said.

"I mean there's no one here. No workers, no customers. I had to climb behind the register to turn the pumps on my damn self. Place looks jacked up too, almost like it's looted, but shit's not gone, just kicked over," Simmons said. "Whatever happened at Moose Jaw didn't just happen there, man. It's everywhere."

"I think you may be right," Farrell said.

I wondered how he'd handle that call. It was clear he didn't want Simmons to return but I didn't know what the alternative would be. It seemed we'd be endangered if we left, especially in a truck that been exposed to the madness overtaking the world. But, we could only stay buried in that hole for so long before time would pronounce us dead anyway.

"It's that yellow powder, ain't it? Be straight, man... is Hanna going to lose his shit with me? I gotta know before he comes back inside," Simmons said.

"If I had to guess, I'd say it seems pretty likely," Farrell said.

There was a silent pause that I could only assume was a natural chain of reasoning starting to link together in Simmons' mind, forcing him to face a terrifying possibility.

"Can I catch it from him?" Simmons asked.

Despite their differences, Farrell appeared reluctant to steal hope away from a fellow soldier. I couldn't imagine he'd want to tell Simmons his demise was inevitable no matter how much he tried to argue the case to us. It's not information anyone would want to deliver.

"Well, if I were you, I wouldn't kiss him during coitus, that's for damn sure," Farrell said. "In fact, I'd ditch his ass first chance I got, infected or not."

"Is it too late for me?" Simmons said. I could picture his facial twitch contorting into a full-blown seizure from anxiety.

Farrell open his mouth to speak but stopped short. With difficulty formulating a suitable response, he remained silent in thought.

"Just tell me. Am I a dead man walking?" Simmons said sounding more desperate with every question. "You ain't letting us back in, are you?"

Farrell slowly raised the handset to his mouth, looking at us with a seriousness he rarely displayed on his face. His harsh stance was much tougher to vocalize to the man he argued was probably doomed.

"I don't know," he said. "It's not my call to make."

At the time, I imagined Simmons had to be feeling betrayal, if not by us than at least by fate. An unlucky draw of the numbers had forced him to take a trip that would end in his demise, one way or another. In reality though, we're all captive to that eventual end no matter how much we try to manipulate the odds and postpone that last breath. There's never certainty that our choices actually accomplish this but still we try. Listening to Simmons accept the hastening of his inevitable death bluntly presented a significant probability to me. Down there, our chance for survival seemed greater because of a thin layer of protection against the sickness. It helped keep me voluntarily contained. Clearly, I didn't know this barrier from infection was just an illusion.

"Simmons," Farrell said. "Simmons?"

He didn't respond. Repeated attempts yielded no better results. It didn't take long before Farrell gave up and we all sat there, staring at each other in an uncomfortable waiting game.

I listened carefully, almost hoping for some small sign of trouble from the cell and growing evermore impatient with the duration of Granger's questioning. I wanted the charge to begin, to break Eva away from her predicament. Of course, I was looking for Farrell to lead. The spine I wished to grow was unfortunately still a seedling. It didn't help my confidence to size up Delgado, standing there looking much bigger as obstacle than he did as a friend.

Then I began to feel guilt. I realized the more I thought about Eva, that beautiful French girl who attached herself to me, the less I was thinking about my true love. I had promised Lin to never let memories of her fade but, for a spell, I had temporarily pushed her to the back of my mind. She had run away from my bastard guardian while he cursed her, walked away from me as I shunned her and yet, in my hardest times since, she'd been there. It was Lin's sentiments that had carried me through every tribulation and whether or not I ever saw her again, I wanted to do right by her.

I remember a couple of months after I'd driven her away, I ran to a small section of woods encompassed in a park two blocks away from our buildings. It was the spot we had designated as our meeting place. Being shortsighted kids, we never had a time or even a real plan of course, so it's no great surprise she wasn't there.

But Lin and I had shared stories about our homes and our guardians, and her day to day life was almost as miserable as mine. Together, we fantasized, we would run away from that place and never look back, abandoning everything we'd been force to endure and starting again in a different state. We'd steal just enough money to board a bus or train and find a way to make it on our own. While the plan was never fleshed out, having constantly changing destinations and time frames, it always started the same way. We would meet at a certain tree that stood just inside those woods, the top of which made a perfect crow's nest for the first one there to watch for the arrival of the other.

When I'd get angry or frustrated or sad enough, I'd run to that tree, hoping she'd be there waiting for me. I wasn't prepared to leave the moment we'd reconnect however. Without the surety of leaving right after, I never stole the money for fear of it being noticed by my Uncle Lee before I'd be able to return it. In my mind, though, seeing her there even one time by chance was the first step to turning our childish fantasy into reality. Then we could plan our escape and truly become the masters of our destinies.

The dilemma I found was that she had no way to know I had ever been there waiting for her and I reasoned the same held true for her, when and if she even made a visit. So the next day, before I went out for my chores, I stuck a flat-head screwdriver in the side of my shoe and hid the handle with the leg of my pants just to get it out of the apartment. Then I ran as fast I could to that tree, screwdriver in hand, ready to create a beacon to get her attention. Using a rock to hammer the metal tip through the tough bark, I carved a heart in the tree and in the center, the single letter *L*.

I'd go back to visit it every so often, some weeks more than others. I don't know exactly what I expected to find but I'd run to it looking for her or at least, some sign that she'd been there. When she wasn't, I'd climb the tree, pretending that at any moment, I'd see her running down the street toward me. While I was never discouraged completely, it was hard to not feel disappointment as I looked around and saw nothing time after time.

One day in particular, I approached the tree, running as I always did to make myself as difficult as possible for my Uncle Lee to spot me from our window. She wasn't there. But as I started to climb the branches, I looked down at the heart I'd carved and saw fresh markings. They were lighter and thinner than what I'd done but they were distinct and intentional and wonderful. Inside the heart, beside the initial I had carved, beside Lin's initial, I found she had carved +*K*. She had joined us together, creating a monument that she forgave me for pushing her away and that she still wanted to be with me. That's all it took to make me feel like I'd been saved. That's what she did for me. That's always how she made me feel.

But then there I was, sitting on the cold floor of that bunker, feeling compelled to risk my safety for a woman I hardly knew, a woman that could end up being the death of me in more ways than one. And standing in my way was a man shorter than I by a couple inches but probably twice my weight in Mexican muscle.

"You know," Delgado said, "Simmons and I talked. He wasn't the asshole you think he was."

"That right?" Farrell said. "What kind of asshole was he?"

"Seriously, I'm telling you. He's got a good heart and a clear conscience. Even if he doesn't survive this life, he'll be OK. He gave me a confession before he left," Delgado said.

"A confession? For what?" Farrell said.

"Shit he felt bad about," Delgado said. "He wanted forgiveness... just in case he didn't make it back."

"Oh, fuck you," Farrell said. "Who the hell are you to forgive anybody, you piece of shit? You're standing there making sure neither one of us interrupts that asshole in there doing God knows what to an innocent girl and you want to play Pope?"

"Watch your mouth!" Delgado said. "Regardless what you think, he's our commander, Sergeant, and he's just doing his duty."

Farrell started laughing in sarcastic disbelief.

"Is your memory really that short?" he said, directing his attention to the prisoner. "Let's ask this guy about how far up the ass our 'commander' fulfilled his duty."

Emotions were beginning to intensify quickly. My rifle was just a few inches to my right but it seemed so far away. I wished I had put in on my lap earlier, pretending to clean it or something, anything to already have it my hand the way that Delgado had his. I couldn't pick it up then, though, not without my intentions being blatantly suspicious.

"He's not trying to hurt her," Delgado said.

"You sure about that? What about you and that chip you've carried on your shoulder since we found her?" Farrell said.

And just like that, she screamed.

Farrell quickly drew his sidearm, pointing it at Delgado's chest. Delgado reciprocated with his assault rifle. I stood quickly, reaching to grab my rifle, but stopped when commanded.

"Don't do it Amish!" Delgado yelled, never taking his eyes off Farrell. "Lower your weapon, man. You don't want this to happen!"

"I'm not going to be a part of this! That's what you want, you'll have to do it after you drag my corpse up those tiny-ass stairs," Farrell said. "Amish, you with me or what?"

The stand-off lasted only seconds before the door to the cell creaked open. Eva came out, shaken and crying softly but visibly unharmed. She continued past us and into one of the bedrooms. Farrell and Delgado lowered their weapons as Granger exited carrying a dead mouse by the tail. He looked around at the three of us, all sweating and obviously anxious.

"I heard yelling. What's going on?" he said.

Delgado leaned his rifle over his shoulder and wiped his forehead. "Just a heated debate, sir. Find out anything?"

"Well, before the rodent came in and scared the piss out of her, she told me quite a bit. They could see ground fires from the window of the plane and people on board started to panic. Shortly after, the pilot announced they were going in for an emergency landing but he wouldn't say why," Granger said. "Then, a few people in the back of the plane became violent and attacked a flight attendant before turning on other passengers. During descent, apparently close to the ground, they crashed and she ran out of the door."

"Seems like a lot of time to get a story we already knew," Farrell said, "sir."

The insolence in his voice was as apparent as Granger's responsive anger. He again put his face in Farrell's, almost begging him to initiate a physical confrontation. Possibly more out of a reactive rage than a conscious decision, Granger balled up the rodent in his hand and squeezed it like a stress ball, crunching the bones and releasing some red ooze from between his fingers. It appeared it took all of his effort to hold back his anger instead of unleashing wrath on one of his own.

"You have a problem with me being thorough, Sergeant?" he said.

"Being thorough? No," Farrell said. "But the freedoms we fight for—"

"Freedom is the least of my concern right now. I'm just trying to keep us all alive," Granger said.

"How was being in there with the hostage keeping us alive?" Farrell said.

Granger dropped the bloody rodent and grabbed Farrell by the collar, pushing him against the wall.

"How do you have the fucking grapes to question my authority *or* my methods? Are you so sure of yourself that you presume to know what I was ever even doing in there?" Granger said.

"No, I'm not," Farrell said, "but we could ask him."

Granger released his collar and looked around at all of us. Nobody wanted to bring it up but we all wanted to know. That's how it seemed anyway. And at that moment, he was pushed into the spotlight, forced to make a quick decision.

"Fine. Let's ask him," Granger said. He reached down and drew his sidearm as he walked toward the prisoner. Then he whipped the hood off the man's head and pressed the barrel of the pistol to his temple. "Well, what say you, Murat? Got anything you want to share, you pile of shit? Speak now or forever hold your peace."

The prisoner closed his eyes and sniveled as he shook in fear. He didn't say a word. I can't imagine many men in the same circumstance who would. I felt so uncomfortable and intimidated and powerless. I assumed we all felt that way as everyone reacted by doing the same thing. Nothing.

"Well, now," Granger said. "It seems he's shy in a group setting."

Granger replaced his gun to his holster as he turned back toward Farrell.

"This is the last time we'll have this same conversation in such a pleasant way before things get too ugly to turn back. You hear me?"

"I hear you," Farrell said.

"Excuse me, Sergeant?!" Granger said.

"I hear you, *sir*," Farrell said.

"Put his damn rag back on," Granger said lowly as he snatched the dead mouse carcass from the small blood stain on the floor and headed toward the latrine.

Delgado picked up the hood and placed it back on the prisoner's head. His name was Murat and, as Granger walked away, I could see relief on his face as it was being covered. He was no longer hidden behind a wall; he now sat right there in front of our eyes. It was hard to not feel sympathy for him.

Farrell remained still, watching as Delgado approached slowly, stood closely and talked in his ear. "You almost shot me over a bitch and a mouse? That's going to be hard to forgive." he said. "Even harder to forget."

Farrell didn't ask for forgiveness though. In his mind, the dispute was about principle, about protecting what was morally right even when no repercussions are present for doing otherwise. There's no reason to apologize for that, but Farrell didn't stress *that* point either. It seemed he had provoked enough animosity for the time being.

He did give me a foul look, however. I hadn't backed him up the way he asked for, the way I agreed to, and I suppose a glare saturated with some type of ill will was justified. But his gaze wasn't one that held anger or even irritation as much as disappointment. He was let down by my lack of response and it was a genuine feeling, even if not for the reasons I presumed. He thought our bond was stronger than what I had shown it to be. Farrell thought he'd gotten close to me.

I didn't know what to say to him, so I shrugged my shoulders and shook my head slightly. It was a horrible response, I know, but it was the best I had to offer. Farrell solemnly walked away, turning his back on me as he made way into the mess hall. I hoped I hadn't also created tension, especially with someone who seemed to have trusted me and taken to me as a friend. I had none of those to spare.

19
The Little Things

"R.O. for actual, come in."

It was Sergeant Riley again, the voice traveling through radio waves estimated to be a few hundred miles away from Grand Forks AFB, North Dakota. I began to feel dread whenever information would start coming in as the world around us seemed to fall apart a bit more with each update. My mind was becoming stressed and discouraged, almost to the point of being numb. I began to sneak sips of vodka when nobody was looking just to maintain enough buzz that I didn't panic but my trips to the freezer increased in frequency. If it were up to me, I'm not sure I could have answered the call at all.

Farrell reached for the microphone as Granger swooped in and picked it up before him. They hadn't spoken to each other since their altercation and every physical interaction was layered in friction.

"This is Lieutenant Colonel Granger," he said. "What do you need, Sergeant?"

"Just a status update, sir. Maintaining contacts has become a constant process," Riley said.

"Still waiting the arrival of our truck," Granger said.

"And the health of your men?" Riley said.

"Three went out with the vehicle. Of those, at least one is down and the other two are suspect. None of them have returned as of yet," Granger said, "and Moose Jaw has fallen."

"We deduced as much. That's how we marked them," Riley said.

"Marked them for what?" Granger said.

"We're trying to keep track of the sickness by radio silence," Riley said. "Once someone is infected, it spreads quicker than it can be contained and it's only a matter of time before everyone around them catches it until there's no one left to contact."

"And you've tracked it?"

"The spread of it, yes, but it's become tricky," Riley said. "Communication is broken all over and even towns that aren't infected yet have been overtaken by local militias or gangs, and many of them refuse to cooperate. So we've grown to rely on remaining military personnel to estimate the extent of damage," Riley said.

"How far has it spread?" Granger said.

"It's bad, sir. Do you have any other way to get down here?" Riley said.

"Sergeant, that's no answer. How bad is it?" Granger said.

"I given you all I can—the rest is classified," Riley said.

"Dammit, Riley! Talk to me or put your commanding officer on," Granger said.

"I'm highest ranking officer here right now, Colonel. Most of the others are either working radios or outside, protecting our border," Riley said.

"What do you mean?" Granger said.

"I mean we've started shooting anyone heading toward the perimeter of the base in any manner deemed erratic or aggressive," Riley said. "So if you're heading down here, I need to know when to look for you so we can let you in."

Granger sat down in the chair, his face looking grim as he leaned against the desk.

"You're shooting Americans?" he said.

"We've had no choice," Riley said. "Believe me, President Dixon has been sick about this. We all have."

Granger seemed to be at a loss for words. Sadly, I could only think of one: Hoo-ahh.

Still blinded by his cloth hood, Murat made a sound that could have been either a snicker or a sniffle. I don't pretend to know which one it really was and I don't think any of us knew for sure, but Delgado threatened him for silence nonetheless.

"Look, I'll tell you what I know but I don't want my balls on a chopping block, so this is off the books," Riley said.

"Go on," Granger said.

"The meteorites weren't just rock. They were loaded," Riley said.

"How so?" Granger said.

"A team in Mississippi found a piece a shrapnel from one of the blasts," Riley continued. "It had pieces of metal, refined iron and lead and steel, along with a biological agent and some chemical residue typically used in combustibles."

"They were bombs?" Granger said.

"The outer layer was rock that apparently protected them as they entered our atmosphere. But inside, they were packed with explosives that seemed purposed to disperse the unknown parasite. They may have even have a mechanism that helped cloak them."

"Is it possible they were sent out and programmed to return? Who would have the capability to make something like that?" Granger said.

"They originated from outside our planet, sir," Riley said. "This is an alien threat."

"Are you trying to tell me we're being invaded?" Granger said.

"I'm telling you we're being exterminated," Riley said. "The guys upstairs are convinced invasion will come later... after we're all gone."

I saw Eva poke her head out from the bedroom, summoning me with her eyes. She looked beautiful, almost too hard to resist. Even still, I put my finger up, signaling that I'd join her momentarily. I felt physical discomfort hearing Riley's words, but once they started, I couldn't stop listening. It's a morbid curiosity I suppose, like watching a plane crash, only we were all on board helplessly looking out through a small window.

"And the parasites?" Granger said.

"They've been dubbed *zombie mites*," Riley said.

"Because of the affect on humans?" Granger said.

"Because after they've entered an orifice and traveled through the blood stream, they eventually eat holes in live brain tissue," Riley continued. "The first part they attack makes it difficult for humans to distinguish fantasy from reality—those infected are basically running around in waking nightmares."

"For how long?" Granger said.

"Until the bugs devour enough brain matter that it affects basic motor function," Riley said, "But it depends on the person and how much exposure they've had. Last time they altered their estimate, I was told some people can go from massive exposure to death within a few hours, others may take a week or more."

I saw Granger look at Eva again. I could almost hear the gears twirling in his mind. It worried me.

"Have you found a way to kill them?" Granger said.

"Lab techs are having difficulty studying them without getting infected themselves, but they're working on it. So far, the only effective defense is to burn them. Trouble is, removing them from the host first seems unlikely," Riley said.

The room was solemn. I expected no suggestions or pep talks. We listened, coming to the realization that this was bigger than all of us and we were about to get crushed, ironically, by bugs too small to see with the naked eye. As humans, we learn sooner or later that death is coming for all of us, and instincts push us to fight for survival. The life that *we* were clinging to, however, was one of self-imprisonment just to delay the inevitable, not for decades or even years, but days at best.

"And this is worldwide?" Granger said.

"Not one continent has been spared. Australia and Antarctica were the last," Riley said. "As for us, I have a big map of the United States in all its former glory hanging right in front of me with a red pin marking every town, base or individual I can keep in communication with. The pins have formed a giant circle and I'm about as close to the center of that circle as possible but the circumference is getting smaller and smaller all the time. If I were you, I'd try to head this way as quickly as possible."

Granger said, "How long, Sergeant? How long do we have to get there... before the circle closes up completely?"

"Two days," Riley replied. "We expect full saturation in two days. Everyone here will remain inside and try to wait it out for a few weeks after that until the zombie mites run out of food and eventually die off."

"You know that for sure?" Granger said.

"We know nothing for sure but that's our assumption for what it's worth," Riley said. "We still hold hope that there are other bases like us, maybe more groups of survivors than what it seems like right now."

I could picture it in my mind. We'd all seen the most powerful country on Earth in its prime and nobody wanted to believe it could collapse into such a deteriorated state. But there it was, dying.

"You were right, Sergeant," Granger said as he slumped forward. "It is bad."

It was difficult to forge a thought that had any substance. I was genuinely terrified.

"You know, when we first got hit, there were countries stealing weapons, threatening to send nukes our way and destroy America for good," Riley said.

"I wish I was surprised," Granger said.

"They eventually all got hit themselves. But can you believe that? Humanity as a whole is on the verge of extinction and some people are so damn shortsighted they keep infighting, helping whatever enemy we have out there achieve their goal," Riley said. I began to sense that although he was in a secure base with other people, he felt as hopeless as we did.

Eva was becoming impatient. She kept coming to the door and looking at me, beckoning me to join her. Having her attention was among the best feelings in the world and I couldn't enjoy it for the nauseating pangs in my stomach. I was unsure if she'd understood their conversation or had even heard them talking. I didn't want to explain it to her. I just wanted to feel her next to me. My gravitation toward Eva and the corresponding guilt for that attraction increased in equal measure, as if I was somehow being unfaithful to Lin, a girl whose voice I hadn't heard in years. She will always be so special to me; however, I had accepted that my true love had likely been killed. I reasoned within myself that I would literally never have the opportunity to be with a woman again, especially one as lovely as Eva. So I went to her.

When I walked in the bedroom, she was already in the bottom bunk under the covers, patting the flimsy mattress for me to lie next to her.

"I can't sleep without you beside me," she said.

I sat down and removed my boots, hoping she wouldn't notice the smell of my sweaty feet as I quickly put them under the covers beside her. She pulled our bodies close together and put one of her legs on top of mine. Her arm was across my chest as she rested her head on my shoulders and asked me to talk to her. I didn't know what to say.

"What are you thinking about?" she said.

At that moment, I was thinking how wonderful it felt to have that human contact. Fear had assaulted me in constant doses down there, gripping me into near submission after Riley's last transmission. Even still, it didn't stop the blood from rushing to my penis, feeling as though it would swell enough to rip my fatigues every time she'd graze it with her thigh.

"You just remind me of someone," I said.

That was the truth. It was difficult to be around her without thinking of Lin, wondering where she was or what she was doing when she died. I wouldn't let myself dwell on the slim possibility that she could have survived. To imagine her alive but infected or suffering felt much more dreadful.

"Tell me about her," she said.

So I did. I curtailed certain details, but for the first time in my life, I told someone about my lost love. I told Eva bits about my childhood and the other boys I lived with, referring to them as brothers even though we were only related by circumstance. I told her vaguely about that bastard Uncle Lee, how sternly he disciplined us and the amount that we were forced to work. She said it was abuse. I can't help but agree.

I talked and she listened, patiently interjecting sympathy or silence or a soft laugh when appropriate. She genuinely seemed interested in me and, after having it, I realized how deprived I'd been of that kind of attention, how much I longed for it. The more we talked, the more she reminded me of my dear Lin, both so sweet and gentle and wonderfully feminine. I began to feel comfortable around her and I opened up further than I ever thought I would.

I didn't want the moment to end, but our talk didn't last long. Between sleep deprivation and a bloodstream heavily laden in alcohol, my eyelids were getting heavy. Having her beside me, somewhat on top of me even, I laid still for fear any movement may be mistaken as a desire for personal space. My mind started drifting away until I was powerless from nodding off into a deep slumber.

20
Love the One You're With

When I awoke, I was lying in the same position, as was she. Two hours or twenty, the length of our rest was a mystery to me but, by then, the passage of time was an insignificant detail. I looked over at Eva's face as she slept beside me, and momentarily enjoyed the sensation of her breath on my neck. It was warm and moist and I willingly inhaled it, feeling more intimate with her for it.

I could feel our perspiration combine from the body heat we had generated, having been so close for so long. Parts of us felt adhered together where skin touched skin and I didn't want to separate one bit. Her leg still wrapped around one of mine, her arm still extended across my chest.

She had no deodorant to use after she'd showered and I could detect a slight scent of her sweat coming from under her shoulder. I can't say it was a pleasant smell in and of itself; in fact, had such a musk originated from my own body I'd be embarrassed or from another man I'd be disgusted. But emanating from this perfect woman, there was something very raw and candid and exciting about being exposed to this unfiltered function of human physiology. I inched my nose a little closer to her underarm and deeply inhaled the tangy aroma. I found it quite erotic.

I gently turned my head toward the door. All seemed quiet. There was no discussion, no argument, no stirring at all. I guessed the others asleep, but I was too leery to move about and check for fear of waking beautiful Eva. I turned to face her once again, feeling physically connected as I breathed in the air laced with her presence. Then desire got the best of me.

Nervously, I unzipped my fatigues and seized the opportunity to extract some small amount of pleasure in what would surely be the end of days as I'd known them. I moved my hand swiftly and quietly, working hard to not shake the bed but still achieving enough motion to perform the exercise. I clenched my fist tighter to compensate for the lack of freedom but keeping stealth a priority ensured it was no quick task. Then I closed my eyes and pictured Lin beside me.

My lips nearly touched Eva's armpit as I deeply inhaled her smell one last time and released an ocean of seed onto my belly, basking for a moment in the euphoric state I had achieved. I paused to catch my breath and check to see if Eva had woken up during my carnal fulfillment. Luckily, she hadn't.

Then I turned toward the door to find Colonel Granger leaning against the threshold, watching me intently. He took a swig from the bottle of vodka in his hand, staring at me as I promptly refastened my pants.

"If you're done mishandling your vigor, meet us out here," he said. Then he turned and walked away.

All the good feelings instantly subsided for dread of punishment. I quickly wiped my hand on the sheet, smearing my fluid into a thin layer at the foot of the bed, hoping it would dry before Eva could ponder its origin. Then I peaked my head in the hallway and joined the others.

"Listen up," Granger said. "It appears that our transportation may not be returning so one of us will need to grunt through on foot and find an alternative before the clock's hands turn into middle fingers. Time is not on our side."

"Why don't we all go?" Delgado said.

"One man can make it quicker without the excess baggage," Granger said.

I assumed he meant all of our food and supplies, but I suppose he could have been referring to the gimped hostage and possibly Eva.

"Besides," he continued, "we need to maintain radio contact with Grand Forks for as long we can. The nearest town is the village of Qu'Appelle, forty klicks straight south of us. Any volunteers?"

There was an awkward silent pause as we looked at each other, then focused again on him.

"This seems to be one of the unpleasant tasks you described when you proposed the brilliant number system, *sir*," Farrell said.

His was the only response to Granger's question. Farrell's tone was calm but the comment was passively spiteful as it placed the burden directly on our commander. I expected Granger to retract what he'd said earlier and throw out his unorthodox arrangement. I figured he would take control like a dictator and order one of us to head out, using threats if necessary. That was not only his right but more consistent with his duty as the ranking authority.

Like an angry bull, Granger exhaled a forceful sigh through his nostrils as he glared back.

"I figured as much," he said as if to shame us. "No one steps foot in or out of this place until I say otherwise." He then picked up some gear that he'd already bundled for departure, and walked down the hallway, grabbing a handset as he passed.

To my shock, he kept his word. I found it puzzling why he would voluntary accept such a burden but he did so without debate. Perhaps Granger didn't trust any one of us to return or make critical field decisions in such a dire crisis. That was my guess, the only thing that made sense at the time. As strange as it was, I obeyed my command and didn't question his intentions.

Instead, I clung to the semblance of safety I was given and allowed myself to rest easier in ignorance. I still don't understand the true reasons the drawing existed since we were prepared to follow his edicts. All I know is right then, I silently rejoiced again at my luck of drawing the 5. Having that numbered scrap of paper gave me a sense of security and watching Granger leave made me feel more at ease. Maybe that was reason enough.

We sat quietly for a moment, appreciating our station while he ventured out into a corrupt world. The silence couldn't last long.

"Really? No hug?" Farrell said. "Bastard."

"Shut your mouth, man. I'm tired of hearing your shit," Delgado said. "He's out there risking his ass for all of us, including you. That's more than you ever did, ginger."

"Is that right? You didn't seem so quick to pack up your burro either, amigo. Don't kid yourself. He's saving himself and we *might* get to hitch a ride as a foot-note," Farrell said as he stood to leave. "Maybe he'll steal a pick-up truck so we can ride in the back. It'll feel like just another day of work for you then."

He continued mumbling under his breath as he headed toward the mess hall, for food or vodka I couldn't say. My stomach was grumbling audibly though; I had no idea how long it had been since I'd last eaten. Even still, the vodka sounded more appealing.

Delgado sat against the wall staring at his boots. It was the first time the two of us had been alone.

"I think maybe it's fate," he said.

"Which part?" I said.

"With something out there trying to kill us off, maybe there's a reason we're together. We're all different races and religious beliefs, you know? Maybe God wants to preserve that—maybe He chose us to survive," he said.

"Hm," I said.

"There could be other groups like us and maybe we'll be responsible to replenish the Earth. Like after the flood," he said.

I'd never read the Bible and knew only bits and pieces that had been quoted from others. He didn't seem too knowledgeable about it either but the few chunks he knew seemed to have stuck with him and kept floating around in his thoughts. Like religion in general, I disregarded it as a crutch, a defense mechanism to keep his mind from falling apart in disaster. I couldn't buy into it, but I didn't feel I had the right to take it away or even diminish its capacity to provide comfort to him. I almost wish I had faith. I could have used some comfort.

"You really believe that's why we're here?" I said.

"I don't know. It might be the way it is. Or, we could die any day now. Either way, I need to make peace with God, brother," he said.

I didn't know what to say. It was definitely a conversation I was not equipped to engage in.

"When I was kid and I first discovered my pecker," he said. "I had a thing for one of my sister's friends. She was perfect, bro, smooth legs and nice big titties."

I smiled awkwardly. I had no idea what he was doing.

"Two years older than me but I didn't care," he continued. "She spent the weekend with us a few times and I looked for every chance to get with her... or at least see her naked."

I recognized the look on his face as he stared at the wall and smiled, visualizing the girl from memory. I could relate in my own way.

"Did you get to be with her?" I said.

"Nah, man. I was a fat kid—didn't really stand a chance," he said. "I never found a way to see her naked either but when they were busy out in the neighborhood, I used to sneak into her stuff and smell her panties. I was such a little freak, but damn, dude, it smelled like heaven."

He laughed a little but there was as much shame in his voice as joviality. My smile became a little more uncomfortable.

"Why are you telling me this?" I said.

"Because I've done a lot of bad shit," he said in a more serious tone. "I need to confess it, man. Somebody's got to hear it."

"I'm no priest," I said.

"I got no one else," he said.

"I don't even believe in God," I said.

"I know, brother," he said. "That's why I'm thinking you might need to hear it more than anybody."

Delgado started to unload his evil deeds, whether I wanted them or not. Most of them were petty wrongs, victimless transgressions of a fallible youth, but they weighed on his conscience enough that he remembered them. That was the implication. I suppose to a troubled mind that made them sufficient to warrant absolution. It seemed he desired to save me in the process, to bring him closer to the God he was so adamant to defend, yet so afraid to meet.

I have to admit, I zoned away for a bit. Listening to him launder his soul made my own guilt weigh heavier as past misgivings came to the forefront of my mind.

Eva was still asleep and out of my sight, completely without knowledge of what I'd done beside her while she slept. I felt I'd betrayed her trust as well as Lin's memory and at that moment, I wanted to distance myself from her for shame. I didn't deserve the good feelings either of them gave me.

"And then there was Rita," he continued. "I started juicing and lifting weights. I looked good, man, and I finally got a hot girlfriend."

"That must have felt good," I said.

"It did," he said, "but I couldn't shake my low self-image. Inside my head, I was still that little fat punk nobody wanted and I was jealous of everyone, thinking every guy that talked to her was going to steal her away from me."

His eyes started to well up as he spoke.

"Rita went out with this friend of hers, some dude she claimed she knew forever but didn't tell me about because of how I always acted. By chance, I saw them eating dinner together and I flipped, man. I pulled her away, just grabbed her arm and dragged her down the street behind me and we started fighting."

"What happened?" I said.

"She tried to calm me down and justify going behind my back, but I wasn't hearing that shit," he said staring at the floor. "It was the juice, man, it's an animal. I was livid and frustrated and I lost control and I... I hit her. Punched her hard as I could, right in the stomach." A tear started to roll down his cheek. He wiped it away quickly before I could see it.

I was going to comment but I didn't know what to say. I couldn't relate to violence like that, especially toward a woman. He reluctantly continued.

"She bent over and couldn't get back up. Then she started bleeding. I swear I didn't know, man, not until later," he said. "We were at the hospital for a while and the whole time I'm sitting in the waiting room, I'm still fuming like an asshole. Then the doctor came out and told me she lost the baby."

He leaned forward, hiding his face between his knees and sniveling. I couldn't console him or absolve his sins. I'm not sure I would have anyway. I was having trouble even sympathizing no matter how much emotional pain had buried him.

"I killed my son, my baby boy," Delgado said. "That's why I enlisted. Rita was too afraid to turn me in but I still ran away first chance I got. I've run as far as I could and the guilt ain't ever left. It's gonna follow me into death. Then I'm gonna have to answer for it."

Nothing seemed appropriate. Nothing seemed adequate. Had I been given time to write it down, I could have concocted something sincere enough to satisfy his yearning for mercy and grace. "But such as I have, I give to thee," I said, being fairly

certain that phrase originated from his book of faith. And that's
pretty much what I gave him. Nothing.

One of the handsets started to buzz, then went silent. I was
grateful for the distraction, no matter how brief.

Farrell walked in from the kitchen holding a fresh, frosty
bottle of alcohol and picked up the radio, waiting for a response
but no words came out. He pressed the call button and held it
up to mouth, "Farrell to Granger, you send?"

"No," Granger said promptly, "but I heard it too."

It happened again a few minutes later and again a few
minutes after that. Finally a voice emerged. It was Simmons,
sounding recognizable but somehow different.

"The light is talking to me. They told us what you was
doing," he said.

"What the hell?" Farrell said as he spoke into the handset.
"Farrell to Simmons, where are you?"

"You'd like that, won't you bitch," Simmons said. "You want
but you can't have it. No, you got nothing. I see the flame, I got
the spark! The trees, the dirt. They all mine."

The bizarre rant continued for several minutes. Farrell tried
to talk to him, but Simmons couldn't express a lucid thought.
The further he proceeded, the harder it was to even decipher
individual words much less try to infer any sort of logical
meaning.

And that was it. Aside from occasional strange noises or
incoherent babble, that was the last radio transmission we ever
received from Simmons. We heard it on our end, Granger heard
it on his. We all knew what it meant even if we didn't talk about
it. We simply said goodbye to him with silence while Delgado
made a sign of the cross on his chest. Then we passed the bottle
of vodka back and forth, sucking down large swigs to help us
cope. It felt good to be numb, even better to be oblivious.

21
Shortages

"Dammit!" Farrell yelled.

He was somewhere down the hall, the latrine being my first assumption. He wasn't in the bedroom with Eva, that I knew for sure. I had positioned myself to keep an eye on where she was sleeping so I'd see when she was awake. To be honest, I was drunk and staring, almost obsessing.

Farrell's yelling must have woken her up. I saw her from my periphery after that, waving slightly to get my attention, but I wouldn't allow myself to look directly at her. I didn't know how to act around her and felt a bit afraid to go back in there so soon. I was embarrassed for myself, nervous she would somehow discover what I'd done and hold nothing but disgust for me.

At the same time, I had become addicted to the high she gave me and all I wanted was to be next to her. The way she demanded my attention had me believing she felt the same way. I finally looked at her, waving at me, beckoning me to join her again. I refused quietly and turned my head. After a few moments of unsuccessful attempts to coax me, she gave up and came out to me, snuggling up the way she always did.

Farrell came storming out of the mess, throwing a handful of empty ration packets on the floor. He fiercely scowled as his eyes scanned the room and focused on Delgado.

"What the hell happened to them?" Farrell said.

Delgado looked at the wrappers as if deciding whether or not to play ignorant before finally opening is mouth to speak.

"What?" he said.

"What do you think?" Farrell said. "Hanna's rations, Ekwall's rations, they're all gone. And Simmons only has two left. The rest are fucking gone!"

"I ate a few extra. Who cares?" Delgado said. "They're not going to need them."

"Yeah, dipshit, but we will. As it stands, there's only ten meals left. That's two for each of us," Farrell said.

Delgado thought for moment, mentally forming a defense.

"Granger packed his own meals when he left. You don't need to count him," Delgado said.

"I wasn't," Farrell said.

Delgado looked at Farrell and me, then Eva while he tallied the count in his head. He then looked over at the prisoner and the math became clear.

"We're not wasting food on him. He's a prisoner of war!" Delgado said.

"Are you serious?! It's done, man! When the countries having a war no longer exist, the war is over. Everyone lost this one," Farrell said.

"Bullshit. We're brothers in duty and we need to look after our own first. If him starving to death means we get to live a little longer, I'm all for it," Delgado said.

"Have you given much thought to how this place would smell with a corpse in it, chief?" Farrell said.

"We'll just toss his body outside," Delgado said. "Shit, we stay here long enough, *he* may become the only food we have."

His words made me cringe. I hoped he was kidding or exaggerating for effect, but he didn't give any indication of this when he spoke. And having already witnessed the expanse of his appetite made his statement seem that much more disturbing. Farrell shook his head and walked over to the prisoner, reaching for his hood as Delgado interrupted.

"Hey! What do you plan on doing, man? Don't forget he's the enemy," Delgado said.

"Our enemies are the ones bombing the Earth to kill off everyone," Farrell said. "That makes this guy seem less of a threat, don't you think?" Then he pulled the hood off the prisoner's head and sat down on the wooden chair in front of him. The man looked around the room, squinting at our faces glowing in the faint lights and, no doubt, pondering his fate.

"I heard say your name is Murat. Is that correct?" Farrell said.

"Yes," he said.

"You been paying attention to all the shit going down around us?" Farrell said.

"I've gathered what I could," Murat said.

"Then you know we're under attack. And by that, I mean the whole human race is facing genocide. You understand that?" Farrell said.

"Everywhere? What about my country?" Murat said.

"The answer is yes and I don't even know what country you hail from. It's irrelevant, they're all being attacked. Most are probably wiped clean of healthy, sane people by now," Farrell said. "We're all being threatened, collectively, as a species."

"If that's true, you have no reason to hold me. You can set me free so I can go defend my country," Murat said.

"The hell we will," Delgado said. "We have orders and your ass ain't going nowhere."

Farrell looked bothered as Delgado spoke, but he didn't interject or deny the sentiment. He turned back to the prisoner, trying to convey the severity of the matter in words.

"No one can leave this place, not yet. Disease is spreading everywhere and it's killing everyone. Right now, there's nowhere to go and there's no defense but staying put," Farrell said. "We can't have you going out there and coming back infected."

"Even if I can't leave, you *can* unbind me, right?" Murat said.

Farrell looked at him for moment. It seemed he felt uneasy agreeing with a logic that could backfire on him. He was careful to choose his words.

"We have nothing against you personally. We don't know who you are or what you've done and it can stay that way because it doesn't matter now," Farrell said. "But there's been tension between the U.S. and Middle East since before I was filling diapers so you have to understand why we'd be a little apprehensive to just let you loose right away."

Murat looked down at the shackles and cords that still bound his hands and feet together with the chair that he'd sat on for nearly two weeks. He reached a hole in his pants leg and gently stuck a finger into one of his stab wounds, holding up the bloody tip of his finger.

"I have nothing against you personally and I don't hold you responsible for anything you did not do directly to me. I understand how wars are fought," he said. "But you say I'm no longer a prisoner that cannot leave and I'm a free man you won't unbind. So, you have to understand why I think you're full of shit."

Murat was calm and sharp when he spoke. Farrell remained patient. His hesitation to release a prisoner in that circumstance was certainly justifiable. We didn't know what he was capable of or what had been done to him. Many men in his position might seek revenge. I would.

"You have to be patient until we can trust each other," Farrell said.

It seemed part of him was still holding onto the duty bound with the flag patches on his sleeves. As flagrantly disrespectful and subordinate as he'd been acting, perhaps he still held fear for what wrath may come with the return of our commander. There was no real reason we couldn't let Murat just walk out the gate, but Farrell and Delgado both vocalized necessity for his continued restraint, albeit for different reasons.

I found it ironic. This prisoner that we'd bound up and detained to keep the world safe was now bound and protected to keep safe from the world. We could have let him freely walk into certain death but nothing is certain and I suppose it wasn't worth the risk of him bringing death back to us.

"Tell me then, what has changed with this conversation?" Murat said.

"Well," Farrell said. "Are you thirsty?"

Shortly thereafter, Farrell and I rummaged through the meager pantry to decide on a small peace offering from our limited supplies. We gave him water and, as a surprise bonus, one can of food. Beets. I hate beets.

Murat was grateful for them though. Not letting his bound hands slow him down, he inhaled them like a man half-starved while we sat and observed. Delgado watched too, looking agitated as Murat finished up and slurped down the red juice from the can.

My own stomach growled audibly enough that Eva flinched beside me. She turned to me and asked for food herself, probably just to bond with me. I was having trouble building a genuine bond with her though. The lack of control I exhibited around her was a trouble I wasn't accustomed to experiencing; it made me feel less honorable.

The eyes around the room stared at us as we left to partake in the diminishing ration supply that had just caused such a commotion. It was awkward to say the least. But, putting that aside, we ate that terrible food together and talked alone in the mess. That is to say, she talked and asked questions but I was feeling too distant and spoke minimally. She asked me to tell her some more about my childhood but I didn't want to talk. So she told me about hers.

I didn't pay much attention though. As she spoke, I still thought about Lin.

I remembered how I ran back to that tree to see the initials she had carved and the joy it gave me. After finding it there waiting for me, I returned more often, hoping to see her face but she was never there. Even still, I'd look at the carving to strengthen myself, to remind myself I did have something to live for. Weeks went by before I finally looked down at the base of the tree and saw a red ribbon partially buried in the soft dirt. It was the one I had once retrieved for Lin.

I still wonder how many times I had walked right over it, never noticing the red fabric poking out, trying to get my attention. Once I saw it though, I quickly tugged it, feeling too much resistance to pull it out completely. I scooped the dirt away and found the other end tied to a small tin box buried just beneath the surface. I excitedly opened it to find a pencil along side a note folded into a small square. My little hands fumbled as they pulled it apart. I got goosebumps on my arms as I looked inside to find the words *I miss you* written in her hand writing. I missed her too. I still do.

I don't know what Eva was saying at the time but I'm sure my abrupt response didn't make any sense to her.

"I miss Lin," I said.

She got a puzzled look on her face as she put her hand on mine. My comment was jarring in the conversation she thought we were having, enough to change it completely. In retrospect, I know it was rude but I don't really feel bad about it. It's what she originally wanted anyway: for me to open up.

"I bet you do," she said. "Why would you not?"

I couldn't explain it to her but Lin and I had bonded more durably than most people ever do. I fell in love with her and our shared circumstance helped us understand each other in a way that would be nearly impossible otherwise. It was the one good thing I took from my childhood. She was still with me in my heart. I couldn't betray that—I couldn't even let myself be tempted anymore. The guilt I felt for getting as close as I already had was overpowering.

I pulled my hand away from Eva. She didn't understand. I could see it on her face, a mixture of befuddlement and sincere disappointment. Even still, she was beautiful and that was hard to dispute. I admired her face for just a moment more. That was as long as I was able to do so before the room went black.

22
In the Dark

I was still conscious but for a second I wasn't sure until I heard a chorus of profane exclamations from the others reassuring me it wasn't just my eyes or my mind that had failed me. The claustrophobic feeling, the panic attack I thought I'd overcome, returned in the pitch blackness. Buried so far below the soil without light made it seem as if the walls immediately and completely closed in on me. I could feel the air get more difficult to breathe. I was trapped.

"Don't move," I said to Eva as I got up and frantically felt my way to the door. I could hear commotion from the assembly room as people shuffled around in the darkness.

It was the first time I'd seen the whole place without power and light. It's not surprising I hadn't noticed that the hallway and assembly room were outlined on the floor with the same faint glow strips that lined the steps. While they helped define the walkway, they gave off no ambient light. I focused on them to orient myself in the open void. It was the darkest black I'd ever seen anywhere.

"Everyone stay still," Delgado said from the assembly room. "I don't want to trip over anybody's shit."

I could hear him move across the room toward me, using the walls as guides and knocking into the desk and chairs like a man freshly blind. Then I felt his hand touch my stomach as he passed me and headed into one of the bedrooms for his survival kit, loudly cursing as he bumped his head on the top bunk.

I squinted as a beam of light headed out of the bedroom and shined onto my face. The little LED flashlight emitted a surprising amount of illumination but compared to the blackness that engulfed us, I suppose any light would look brilliant.

"Hey Amish," Delgado said as he handed me the flashlight from my kit. "You know anything about electricity?"

"Other than how to flip switches, not really," I said. Not at all is what I meant.

Farrell and Delgado looked around for a breaker box or some sort of access panel, stopping shortly after Murat spoke.

"It's in there," he said.

Delgado shined his light in Murat's eyes, forcing him to quickly close them.

"What is?" Delgado said.

"The circuit box you're looking for," Murat said tilting his head toward the cell. "I can take a look at it. I may be able to fix it."

"You're an electrician?" Farrell said, inflecting doubt.

"Electrical engineer, actually. I may be able to fix it," he said, "if I had the tools."

"Oh, I bet you could," Delgado said. "Let me guess what you need. Hammer? Screwdriver? Serrated combat knife and semi-automatic pistol?"

"I was thinking more along the lines of wire cutters and electrical tape, but a screwdriver might be needed as well," Murat said.

"You think we're stupid?" Delgado said. "You'd say anything to get out of that chair."

"You're probably right. Let's just sit in the dark then," Murat said. "Just bear in mind, I'll need light to see what I'm doing and the batteries in your flashlights won't hold power forever."

They stood momentarily, counting our other reasonable options and coming up with zero. After some searching, they found a tool box in the pantry and removed anything that seemed too dangerous to give a suspected terrorist with every reason to hate us. That included most everything. Then they gave Murat the freedom to move, but kept his feet bound together with enough slack that walking was possible but running was not.

Eva made her way into one of the bedrooms and slid in the bed, hiding like a scared child under the blanket. I thought I had hurt her feelings. That was never my intention and I didn't want to do that. Guilt prodded me again.

I moved as I was told behind Murat, shining the light where he needed while Farrell aimed a pistol at his back. The gray metal power box stood just inside the doorway of the cell. It was hard to breath in there with the terrible stench of a floor covered in decaying blood and a bucket Murat was forced to use as a toilet. It still idly sat inside, partially covered and filled with his excrement.

Farrell showed genuine interest in what he was doing, asking him questions for every action Murat performed. Maybe it was just to ensure he was working in our best interest but it seemed like more than that. I thought maybe Farrell just wanted to learn, but he would point things out, almost as if to make sure I thoroughly understood it. To be candid, I had no genuine interest in how he fixed it as long as it worked. And Murat didn't get frustrated or angry at him for acting that way. He patiently gave thorough answers, seeming fine having to justify his movements. Murat was just biding his time, looking for opportunity.

"What's the loose wire?" Farrell asked.

"That's the one your interrogator used to give me shock treatments," Murat said, "on my testicles."

Farrell didn't respond. Neither did I. He just asked another question, quickly changing the subject matter but I think Murat wanted to intentionally remind us what we had become a part of. Guilt was attacking me from all sides.

He unbolted a steel conduit that encased most of the wire, breaking it apart into halves. Immediately, a waft of odor poured out, smelling of burnt flesh and hair. A partially fried rodent carcass dropped onto the floor. It appeared that the mouse had chewed through a cable splattered with Murat's blood. He pointed that out too.

As we watched him work, I grew concerned for Eva. She was alone in the bedroom, lying in darkness, seemingly hurt from my rejection. I was beginning to feel so emotionally torn when I should have been focused on survival. I had developed some sort of feelings for her, but they couldn't have been real, not deep like the love I had for Lin. I'm convinced of it. Emotions can only be as sincere as the relationship; if one is artificial, so must be the other.

Even still, I jumped into motion when I heard her scream while Delgado shouted a mixture of obscenities and indecipherable Spanish. By reaction, I turned and moved quickly toward them, leaving Farrell alone in the dark with Murat. He yelled at me to stay but I didn't even consider it. In all honesty, his order didn't register until moments later as my adrenaline pushed me down the hall to verify her safety. He opted to follow the light I carried; I could hear his boots readily slap the the cement floor behind me.

When we reached the bedroom, I pointed my flashlight at Delgado who aimed both his flashlight and pistol at Eva. He looked shaken, but physically fine.

"I knew it! I told you," he said. "Now we're fucked!"

I then looked at Eva who laid in the bed, the whole thing trembling as she sobbed with her face buried in the blanket.

"What the hell happened?" Farrell said.

Eva uncovered her face and cried, "He tried to rape me!"

"You lying bitch!" Delgado yelled. "Just look at her."

Her nose trickled with blood.

"He did this to me. He hit my face and told me to shut up or he'd kill me," she said. "Then he pushed his gun between my legs." She began to bawl as she curled herself up in the fetal position.

"Bullshit! She's lying because she knows she's infected and she doesn't want us to kick her lying ass out!" he said.

Suddenly, the rooms started to light up going down the hall, one after another. Her nose had stopped bleeding and, now in full light, the red stain on the sheet looked fairly insignificant.

Delgado and Eva paused briefly as power was restored, then continued to bitterly argue, each voice trying to overpower the other as if volume would convince us of their version of truth. Farrell and I listened for a moment, dumbfounded and speechless, before the arguments began to escalate into a repetitive circle.

"Shut up!" Farrell yelled as he turned to Eva. "You stay put, doll. Do not come out of this room."

Then he turned to Delgado. "You, essé," Farrell said. "Let's chat."

Delgado, Farrell and I left the room, never fully taking our eyes off of her. The stress was effecting my ability to think clearly and I wasn't sure how much more my mind could handle. It was overwhelming to hear their horrible accusations against each other but it seemed only one could be true.

I didn't want to judge between the two but I knew once an accuser was found wanting, the situation would require an immediate and probably ugly resolution. I felt jittery from the constant tension that seem to rain down in a steady, consistent flow.

We reached the assembly room, even as I contemplated my breaking point, and entered to find Murat taking cover behind a corner of the cell wall, pointing a rifle directly at my chest.

"Drop your weapons!" he said. "Drop them now!"

We jumped at his voice, then paused for a moment as our brains were forced to abruptly change gears. It was too late to redraw our holstered weapons. Nobody would have been faster than the rapid stream of bullets capable of firing out of the M4 rifle he controlled and we all knew it. Farrell and Delgado slowly removed their pistols with the tips of their fingers and bent down to put them on the floor. I put down the flashlight that I was holding. As I said, I wasn't thinking clearly.

"Blades too," he said.

Delgado, the only one who carried it, unstrapped the military issued knife and placed it by his feet.

"Slide it towards me. All of it," Murat said.

We kicked our gear, listening to the sharp rattle of metal on concrete. He picked up the knife and cut the cords at his ankles. Then he motioned toward the side of the room, signaling the three of us to sit down by the desk, facing the wall.

I could see Murat, just barely making out his movements in my periphery. He walked completely out of the cell and put one leg up on the back of the chair. Then he stretched the other. Then his back. Even several feet away, I could hear the sounds of air pop from his joints.

"Where's the woman?" he said.

I could see the rifle pointed slightly upward as he leaned against the wall. He wasn't on his highest alert. Even then I suspected he wasn't used to keeping hostages or holding firearms. He may not have even known how to shoot it, but it was too risky to try anything right then.

"She's sick," Delgado said.

"We don't know that," Farrell interrupted.

"You believe that bitch?" Delgado said. "Over me?"

Murat got quiet as he listened to their disharmony. I wasn't sure what was going on his head. In his position, I may have caused that friction to spark into greater turmoil between the three of us. Some men more evil than I may have even used the girl to increase discord since her presence was such an easily detectable source of tension. That's the strategy I worried about. The thought of him hurting Eva caused me great distress without a hint that he was even considering that as an option. But I didn't know what he was thinking or just how crafty he could be. I never suspected his true motives. I never even considered he could be the one who created the turmoil of the world outside.

I was getting anxious and I wanted to press him but we were trained to never do that. In a hostage situation, it's always best to wait for opportunity instead of forcing action. He was out-numbered and eventually he would have to piss or eat or sleep. He had to foresee that. In the meantime, we didn't want to unnecessarily escalate his emotions and put our lives in danger. Unless he was going to kill us all, we would get the opportunity to regain control with patience. So we waited.

23
Do Unto Others

I had no way to tell, but it seemed like hours passed as we sat side by side, quietly looking at the wall. Murat paced back and forth behind us, an understandable desire for anyone forced to remain sedentary for as long as we'd been down there. The ache in my back pulsated from sitting upright for even that short amount of time; I can only imagine the pain he would have endured. The longer we remained still and silent, the more my mind would zone out. I jumped when I heard the radio static startle me back to attention.

"Granger to team, come in," he said.

We didn't answer. We barely even moved our heads out of position. A few minutes passed without Granger getting the response he requested.

"Delgado, Farrell, Khu, come in. Pick it up," Granger said again.

Murat approached us from behind and stood over us. I could see his shadow on the wall menacingly hover above our own.

"Which of you is the radio operator?" he said.

"That'd be me, chief," Farrell said, raising his hand slightly.

"Answer to him, but don't mention a word about me. Ask when he'll be back," Murat said. "Understand?"

Farrell moved far enough to sit at the desk, picking up the microphone and looking over at Murat as he spoke. "Farrell to Granger... sir, operator speaking," he said.

I thought that was an odd choice of words. It wasn't protocol for radio techs like Farrell and even though the world was appearing to fall apart, habits are hard to break. It made me pay attention to his phrasing.

"What the hell took you so long to answer?" Granger said.

Farrell kept his eyes locked with our captor as he communicated, trying to make sure he wasn't saying something that might warrant repercussions.

"We were in the latrine. I was, I mean. The others are... sacked out, sleeping," Farrell said.

"Well, I've searched all over this damn place. There's nothing of use here. Completely FUBAR. The streets are lined with dead bodies, some from the sickness, most skinned or torn apart into piles of meat. And the live ones, they're more like rabid dogs," Granger said. "It's a bloodbath over here."

"And the vehicles? Did you secure one, sir?" Farrell said.

Farrell was a decent speaker who usually talked properly to our commander but I noticed a pattern in his words. He was communicating an alert to Colonel Granger that something was amiss by ending every sentence with words that started with S.O.S.—the international call for distress. It was a subtle gesture that took me a few exchanges to detect but, just as it was probably intended, I noticed it. At the time I was impressed with his quick thinking; now I'm astonished by the depth of guile needed to include the code at all. Murat didn't mention it. Neither did Granger. At least, they didn't call attention to it.

"There's no usable vehicles. Everything has that same film of yellow dust on it that Simmons described and I think they're too risky to bring back. I found a map though. It shows a large farm about 10 klicks west of the bunker. One of you should head out there immediately and see if you can find something drivable. The clock is ticking."

"Affirmative," Farrell said. "We'll send out someone."

Murat pushed Farrell's chair with his foot, prodding him to speak.

"Oh shit, yeah," Farrell said. "When will you be shoving off, sir?"

We could hear that Granger had pressed the button but there was a long pause before he started speaking. I had hoped maybe Farrell's secret message had suddenly illuminated in his mind. Then I wondered if maybe he wasn't sending his own distress call and we were too preoccupied to pick up on it. I was starting to feel panic again, even paranoia. Just not about the right things.

"I won't be returning," he said. "I was attacked by someone here who was obviously sick. I killed him, but I'd be surprised if I'm not infected too. I'm not going to risk bringing that back home. Get a vehicle and try to make to Grand Forks. Go without me."

Farrell had previously displayed obvious animosity toward Granger. In fact, none of us had the same respect for his character that we once did. Murat should have hated him more than anyone and for good reason. Even still, there was no rejoicing over his inevitable demise. After all, his fate could soon be one of ours.

"Copy that," Farrell said solemnly. "Good luck. Over."

It was discouraging to say the least. Farrell slid out of the chair and resumed his position on the floor. I didn't know what Murat had planned or what he was after. He never seemed as clever as he actually was. A few scenarios played out in my mind, most of them ranging from bad to horrible but I never predicted what he would do.

"What was that you were saying about trust?" Murat said.

"I don't remember. I say a lot of things," Farrell said.

"I didn't do anything directly to you, right?" Murat said.

"Right."

"And yet you don't trust me."

"We didn't do anything to you either?" Delgado said.

"Is that so? Because I remember the feel of men forcing me on a helicopter, pushing me down some dark stairs and tying me up so I could be tortured and sodomized," Murat said. "Was that not you?"

"We didn't know that would happen," Farrell said.

"Then you're fools!" Murat said.

I was waiting for him to open fire, to start executing us one after the other. He stood behind us, close enough that we could hear him pace but still far enough away that we would not have been able to wrestle the gun away before some, if not all of us would get shot.

"How bad is the damage to the U.S.?" Murat said.

"From what we've heard, it's been devastated," Farrell said.

"And Massachusetts?" Murat said.

"What?" Farrell said.

"Boston, Massachusetts. Have you heard anything?" Murat said.

"Both coasts were wiped out," Farrell said.

His shadow dropped slightly as he lowered his gun and began to pace again. He appeared agitated and distressed and worried. It was an act though. He knew the answers they would give before he ever asked.

He voice sounded weaker as he spoke. "Americans. They always come in peace. Then they steal and leave a trail of blood in their path," he said. "I should shove this rifle up every one of your assholes and make you taste a bullet as it exits your mouth for your part in what happened to me—for what was stolen from me!"

We remained silent. I didn't want to dispute him as his emotions were rising on their own. Deep inside, I knew we had no argument anyway. If someone treated an American the way he had been treated, we'd be outraged. And afterwards, fellow

Americans, comfortable and safe in their own homes, would demand swift justice from those in uniform.

"Do any of you have children?" he said.

Nobody answered.

"Do you have children?!" he said angrily.

We all shook our heads. I thought Delgado might claim the son he'd conceived and ignorantly destroyed but he didn't.

Murat wasn't just exhibiting rage for what had been done to him. He was also showing grief. It felt like he was building up pressure to a violent climax, the way a volcano shakes before it spews out lava and destroys everything around it. There wasn't much around Murat at that point but us and nobody wanted to call attention to themselves as a volunteer to take his wrath.

"Well, I have three. I had three. Rafi was my son, Aamira and Safia my daughters. My brother and I brought our families out of Syria to get away from the savagery and we ended up building a life in Boston. I should have spent the last several weeks going home to my children and kissing them good night. I would have been there, holding them when they were afraid and guiding them to the safest place. I should have died with them in my arms," he said. "You stole that time away from me."

He was criminalizing us and, at the same time, humanizing himself. He didn't want to be just *the prisoner* in his charade. He wanted to clearly express that he was a man with a life and a job and children. Beyond nationalism, on a grander scale, he was one of us, just a fellow man trying to live a happy life. I understood that. At the time, I didn't know if it was devious tactic or sincere philosophy but it worked on me. I felt the same way he did. I felt sorrow for him.

"I have every right to kill you. I even have the means here in my hands. You understand that?" Murat said. "I won't wear anymore rope for you. I'm free now."

I heard the gun click and I fully expected to be killed. I almost wished it. I was weary in just about every way imaginable and just wanted to be released from whatever kind of life this had become. Even in my head, I pictured Lin's face and said goodbye, hoping for the first time there was an afterlife so I could be with her again.

"Do not forget my mercy," he said.

The sound of light metal scratched its way on the floor, heading in our direction. We looked down beside us to find the gun's fully loaded magazine. We turned to watched him lean the empty rifle against the wall and walk down the hallway. Delgado jumped up as if he were going to charge but Farrell stood in his path.

"No! What the hell?!" Farrell said. "It's over."

Murat didn't leave the bunker though. He headed into the bathroom, turned on the water and stood under the shower pipe for an excessive amount of time. He was washing the dirt away, cleaning his physical wounds; that was probably done in a few minutes though. The rest of the time, the majority of the time, I imagined he was letting his mind cope with his mental wounds, probably wishing the water could somehow wash those away too. We all claimed to lose family and friends in the world's crisis. We all understood.

Delgado walked into the mess hall, no doubt to find something resembling comfort food from the little we had remaining. I was surprised when Farrell didn't yell at him for eating again, but he seemed eager to have a moment alone with me. His mind had already moved forward, rather backward, back to Eva.

"What do you think about the girl?" Farrell said.

"I like her. You know that," I said.

"I mean about what happened between her and Pablo Gigante in there?"

"I don't know. Hard to believe she would lie about that," I said.

"So you think Delgado is lying?" Farrell said.

I could have told Farrell what I knew about Delgado's violent past and his blatant anger toward woman. The rage that had once been ignited by a secretive girlfriend and fueled by body enhancing drugs was in my knowledge to expose. But I didn't.

Eva started peaking her head out of the bedroom door. She looked so sad and my instinctual desire was to be with her. I needed comfort too. Then my heart reminded me of my beautiful Lin. She would want me to survive and she'd want me to be fair. To be openly transparent, the guilt, my relentless and mind-gnawing guilt, made it easier to distance myself from Eva and remove any bias charged by pheromones.

"He can be a dick, but I don't think he's a rapist," I said. "If Eva's sick, maybe it's messing with her head. Maybe she really believes that's what happened."

"You think she's sick now too?" he said.

"I don't know what to think," I said.

Farrell sighed. He seemed frustrated that my hope for her was shaken, that I didn't have complete confidence in her state of mind. I could see disappointment in his eyes even if, at the time, I didn't understand why he had it.

"If your girlfriend really *is* sick, she's a ticking time bomb and she can't be around us," Farrell said. "Are you going to stay away from her?"

I didn't want to believe it. Even then, I don't think I entirely did. Eva still looked so healthy, so beautiful. My emotions were completely polarized over her. Ultimately, it was my unwavering love for Lin that pushed me down the path I chose.

"I don't have much choice," I said.

"Fine. We'll leave her isolated for now and keep our eyes peeled for any strange behavior," Farrell said.

"What about the farm?" I said.

Delgado walked out of the mess hall, sucking the flavor of whatever he'd last eaten from his lips. Farrell didn't answer me directly, instead turning attention to his compatriot, speaking with words unfiltered, the way he often did.

"You're 3," Farrell said.

"What?" Delgado said.

"You're up. You need to head to that farm and see if you can find us a way out of here," Farrell said.

"Bullshit. We're redrawing numbers," Delgado said.

"We don't have time to argue about this. Someone has to go, otherwise we all die here. Suck it up, hombre. It's your time at bat," Farrell said.

"Why not you?" Delgado said.

"I'm the only who knows how to use the radio equipment. No one else can fix it if it breaks. Besides, I drew 4. That lottery was Granger's baby, remember? The commander you loved so much?" Farrell said. "I didn't hear you complaining about the system when Simmons had to go. Or when Granger dragged his shit out of here."

"How about two of us go?" Delgado said.

"And leave Amish or me here with a prisoner five minutes into freedom and a girl that could turn psycho-cannibal any second?" Farrell said. "No. You need to go, alone. If we don't hear good news in a few hours, then I'll leave and head south. The odds for survival are better if we spread out."

Delgado looked like he was trying to think of any excuse to stay. I couldn't blame him. The world was falling apart in front of us. There wasn't much incentive to leave the one place we all felt safest and probably even less to come back if something safer was found. But I held hope that Grand Forks would help us weather the storm, if only we could get there.

"If you want, we can vote on it," Farrell said facetiously.

Delgado looked into each of our eyes and then around at

our dwelling. I was sure the confrontations he'd had over Eva didn't escape his memory. Then he growled and kicked the wooden chair, knocking it across the room.

"Fine," he said. "I don't want to catch whatever that sick bitch has anyway."

Those were the last words he said to us and I thought maybe to anybody. He packed his gear and his cut of the remaining food and walked out. He took a radio handset as he left, but that was just a waste. We never heard from him again.

24
No Place Like Home

Washing fatigues in the bunker was a hassle and everyone was responsible for doing their own. We'd only been given one extra set meaning whichever was not on our bodies, needed to be readied for use later. I had only washed mine once since we'd arrived while Farrell was in the latrine quite often scrubbing his combat uniform in the small sink and hanging it to dry. Given his desire for cleanliness, I was quite surprised when he voluntarily took the clean uniform from his gear and placed it out for Murat. It made me wonder if guilt plagued him as much as it did me.

Murat walked out of the latrine, water still dripping from his hair, and sat on the side of the room opposite from us. There was such sadness on his face.

"I brought you out some clean clothes," Farrell said.

Murat scanned them over for a brief moment, stopping when he saw the American flag patch on the shoulder. He left them alone and rested his head on the wall behind him. "Thank you, but what I have on is fine," he said.

"After that shower, you want to keep on dirty rags? They have to smell like bad cheese and monkey ass by now," Farrell said.

"I'd rather go naked than fly that banner," Murat said.

"Well, I'd rather you stink than go naked, so keep sporting what you got if makes you happy, chief," Farrell said. "But, if you change your mind, they're here."

We sat quietly together for a while, just staring at the walls and each other. Farrell tried to start some conversation but I just wasn't having it then. I had become a vault again, locking everything inside and keeping everyone out. In my mind, I was back at the tree, holding Lin's hand, running off with her to some secret location.

Lin and I had continued writing to each other for the longest time. She had left a pencil inside the tin box with her first note indicating she wanted me to respond and, without a second thought, I did. We were young though. So young. My first few responses were terribly short, but that quickly changed. I attribute that to my studies. The English language was one of the most stressed teachings we received.

It's well known that Americans have no respect for Chinese accents—*Engrish* as it's called. So, the boys and I were forced to learn the language better than the average American, including nuances in slang and various popular dialects. It wasn't perfect, of course. Keeping us separate enough to maintain a Chinese philosophy toward religion and politics and ethics while trying to give us some exposure to American culture for language and popular topics meant some things fell through the cracks. For the most part, I found the teachings reasonably comprehensive and particularly invaluable.

I know the purpose of our education was to effortlessly integrate us into American society in order to find us a suitable job, to ultimately achieve our goals. But, I used that training to help me better communicate with Lin and it wasn't long before our letters increased in length and meaning. I'd scramble to the tree and dig up the box to see what she had written. Then I'd add to it and bury it again. We shared our dreams and hopes this way; I actually preferred it over speaking.

Writing made it easier to choose the perfect words to express my feelings. There was a layer of protection too. We could pour out whole thoughts without having to worry about being interrupted mid-sentence and there was never a worry about her laughing at my silly dreams. They were love letters for sure, but they were more than that. Is was our only way of communicating and therefore the only way to devise our escape from that life. It went on for years too.

A few times we almost ran but something always fouled up the arrangements. One time, just hours before our planned departure, my Uncle Lee stepped on my chest in anger and cracked a few ribs. I'm not sure exactly how many because, despite my nausea and vomiting, I never received medical attention for it. He still made me do my chores that afternoon. At any rate, I couldn't go.

Another time, Lin's Mother Tam punished her by locking her in a closet for more than a day. It seems Lin had neglected to fold and sort the laundry the way she had been instructed. Again, we couldn't go. This continued all the way through our teen years, trying but never finding an opportunity to leave.

Then, I joined the Army. I'd go back and check in on my Uncle Lee and with each visit, I'd update the buried box. In my spare time while gone, I'd write dated letters everyday and bury them in tin when I'd return home. She would do the same. I promised her I wouldn't forget about her and that, one day, we would run away side by side. This past mission was to be my last. I told her when I was expected to return and afterwards, our life together would begin. That was the plan before the meteorites rained down devastation on the entire planet. It seemed most likely that Lin was dead and with her, my hopes and dreams. My heart was broken.

Static burst through the radio again. I almost wanted to turn the damn thing off. I had gone beyond dread at this point and found the calls frustrating and more of an annoyance. Our truck was still MIA and there was no way to get to Grand Forks, no matter how much we would have wanted to go. We had nothing to report, but once I heard Riley's update, it seemed that he wasn't looking to be on the receiving end of news anyway.

"Riley to actual, come in," he said.

Farrell looked like he felt the same way I did. He slowly got up with a sigh, picked up the microphone and collapsed in the chair.

"This Sergeant Farrell, reporting for duty," he said with sarcastic inflection.

"I need to speak to Colonel Granger," Riley said.

"He's gone. Most of our guys are gone. I'm the ranking commander right now," Farrell said.

Hearing him say that was almost laughable. Besides Farrell, I was the only soldier left and rank had become trivial. What's a commander with no one to command? A costume. That's all the uniforms ever were anyway: costumes. Hoo-ahh.

He proceeded, "We still have no way to get to you but the few of us that remain are working hard on it."

"Well, don't," Riley said. "We now have our own situation here."

"What kind of a situation?" Farrell said.

"There's been a breach. Someone here turned out to be infected and he went on a rampage. The sickness is spreading inside the base now," Riley said.

"Are you evacuating?" Farrell said.

"It's not that simple. More and more infected people started approaching the base and we barricaded most of the doors. We essentially imprisoned ourselves as a group."

"Can't you just kill the infected?" Farrell said.

"We did, the obvious ones anyway. We thought we had it contained but it's impossible to tell who's a carrier," he said. His voice was sounding distraught and disheartened. "People look fine and the next day, they start attacking. I watched my colleagues bite and claw at each other with no remorse or intimidation. You can't threaten someone who isn't afraid of being hurt."

"I would run if I were you," Farrell said.

"And go where? Every town and base we've been able to contact is going through the same thing we are," Riley said. "So, just a few minutes ago, everyone was ordered over the intercom to find an empty room, lock the doors and stay put. We are all individually self-quarantined."

"For how long?" Farrell said.

"They told us to remain in isolation for three weeks. Anyone survivors not showing symptoms by then *should* be healthy," Riley said. "Trouble is, we had to do this very quickly with no time to distribute supplies. Where I am, I found a box of cupcakes and two bottles of water. I was fortunate. Some people here ran to rooms that have nothing."

"What are you telling me then? What should we do?" Farrell said.

"Same thing we are," Riley said. "Stay put and survive. Then, cross your fingers the disease dies with the host. If it hibernates inside carcasses or spreads to animals, well, I just don't know."

Farrell rubbed his face as he blankly stared at the wall. That was it. There was no safer haven to strive for anymore. The race was over before it really started and we were already at the finish line. Somehow, being sheltered down there, trapped, it still felt like we lost. Buried under tons of dirt and layered with thick cement, that hole was the safest place for us, the best chance we had for survival. Still, I hated it. The last place on Earth I wanted to be was turning out to be the last place on Earth.

"What's President Dixon saying about all this?" Farrell said.

"President Dixon," Riley said, "he *was* the breach. We don't know how he got infected but he was the first confirmed case here. They had to put him down."

They killed him. They phrased it kindly, the way they do with sick animals as if they ethically euthanized him, ending his misery as favor to him. Maybe they did. Nonetheless, he's dead and they took his life. That was my view. Hearing the horror stories being told about the victims losing their minds, the violence they conduct and the speed at which they do it, I seriously doubted his death was a soft and painless one.

It made me think about Eva. I was beginning to get worried that if she were sick, one of us may have to put *her* down. I wouldn't be able to do it, not even out of mercy. I wasn't confident Farrell could either and all I knew of Murat is that he had a chance to take vengeance out on his captors but he didn't. The thought of it almost made me wish Delgado had stayed just a while longer. Almost.

Farrell and Riley signed off, wishing each other luck as if it had any meaning. Wishes and luck and prayer and God. It all seemed like pointless nonsense to me, especially then after all we'd heard. Life on Earth was dying and if theories were to be believed—which I did wholeheartedly—any people who remained could expect something far worse in their future.

I considered all that humanity had created could be destroyed. The great works and thoughts and innovations of our race—things that we collectively felt proud to admire regardless of petty differences—were being reduced to piles of ash and dying memories. It made me wonder if a species that could kill us off in that fashion would have superior innovations and works that made our own look primitive in comparison. I'd have to assume so. Maybe we didn't deserve to survive if we weren't the fittest.

"That son of a bitch," Farrell said as he walked out of the mess room with a frosty bottle in hand.

Murat and I looked at him inquisitively as he poured drinks for us all, grinning with his mouth but showing anger and disbelief in his eyes.

"Delgado took most of the rations with him," he said.

We knew we'd have to find food in time, though nobody talked about it right then. Of course it was a concern, but the mental drain of the whole situation made worries about starvation seem less pressing. We each cursed Delgado with our preferred word of choice and said no more about plans to rectify the issue.

Instead, the three of us sat together, discussing the plague that was sweeping the world clean of life as we shared the vodka that Farrell retrieved from the freezer. We had only two bottles left and I could foresee it was going to be deflating to see that last drop being swallowed. It was our comfort during trouble, emotional lubricant that took the edge off pain and helped us slide into acceptance. I drank it quickly.

"Dammit, you know what this needs?" Farrell said. He walked away and re-emerged from the storage closet with a box of cigarettes from the mid-1980s. He shredded the plastic, removed a cigarette and put it to his lips. "I found a shit-ton of these by the books."

"You're going to smoke down here?" Murat said.

"Why not? There's an air pump if we need fresh air," Farrell said. "I just need a drag. It's been too long."

Farrell lit it up and blew it into the air, watching it float up and evenly distribute by the cement ceiling. I didn't particularly want to smell the stench of smoke. I hated it actually. But with our numbers dwindling, I felt obligated to avoid as much tension as possible between us. I didn't want to fight. I just wanted the whole mess to be over. If it meant I had to die to do it, I was becoming OK with that.

"How are they? I could use one myself," Murat said.

"It's a thirty year old cigarette. It tastes like shit," Farrell said, "but I want it so bad. In a way, it's the best damn cigarette I ever had."

Farrell passed it to him and laughed as Murat gagged and coughed the smoke out of his lungs.

"That's awful," Murat said. "It doesn't even taste like a cigarette anymore."

"I know. I'm pretty sure all the tobacco has decayed into something far more toxic," Farrell said. Then he puffed on it again making a sour face as he inhaled the smoke. I watched him, contemplating how often people avoid life's enjoyable vices for a chance to live a longer, less gratifying life. If there is a God, this is His great irony. But, with long life seeming improbable for us then, the leverage against dangerous pleasures was gone.

"Be careful," I said dryly. "That shit will kill you."

It was my attempt to be humorous and I'm certain Farrell noticed just how rare those moments could be with me. I'm not completely sure why I even said it but I suppose I was just getting comfortable with them. Maybe I was losing my mind too. I thought maybe we all were.

They both looked at me straight-faced before they started to chuckle, then they laughed harder and I laughed with them. The alcohol undoubtedly played a large part in our sudden burst of high spirits, but it seemed to me that maybe we'd moved on and accepted our impending fates. For me at least, having time to conquer the fear of my imminent death made all worries begin to dissipate. Apathy had set in. One way or another, the pain would soon be over. Even so, I passed on the cigarettes.

25
Talking Shop

The last time I was home was the very last visit I'll ever have with my Uncle Lee. As bad luck would have it, Lin's Mother Tam had caught her sneaking out to the tree and watched as she dug up the letters. She snatched them out of Lin's hand and read the promises of my affection, references to our longtime love affair and worst of all, the schemes we were devising for our departure. They were my letters to Lin and she had no right to read them but she did. And her Mother Tam was livid.

In Lin's defense, after years of sneaking about and not getting caught, it's easy for anyone to get too comfortable, even sloppy. Since our community was close knit, Mother Tam knew who I was and she marched directly over to my Uncle Lee, dragging Lin along with her.

My heart raced when I saw Lin's beautiful face come through my door. Then it dropped when I realized why they had come to our apartment. It was clear when I saw Lin's Mother Tam enter, her lanky fingers wrapped around the tin box. I was horrified.

At the time, only the four of us were there as the younger boys were doing their chores outside. Lin and I watched our guardians in silence as they discussed our fate with heavy handed discipline in mind. They stood there before us and were unified in their anger.

Then the miraculous happened. There was an attraction between them and the more they talked together, the more they began to calm down. Eventually, the things they were saying had less and less to do with us or the other children they supervised than it did with themselves. They had known of each other for years of course, but I suppose that was the first occasion they had to speak intimately.

Lin and her guardian left after an hour of conversation but her Mother Tam came back later that night. She and my Uncle Lee quickly fell in love and decided that they wanted to change their lives too. So they ran off, together, leaving us and the other children behind forever. Lin and I were still separate, but we were finally free of them.

People are much like chemicals in that it's sometimes difficult to predict how they'll react until they're mixed together. I never would have suspected that those two people, each capable of such sadistic cruelty apart, could also be capable of life-altering love when united.

I felt the same way as I watched Farrell and Murat begin to talk. Farrell was outgoing and his personality had an inviting, lively social factor. It was contagious. His way with words encouraged people to interact with him and each other. While not everyone became or stayed his friend, he opened people up to reveal the traits they concealed. I never saw the detriment of having him around. It seemed helpful, even if I couldn't relate to him on every level. Without Farrell, I'm sure I wouldn't have given Murat a chance.

Murat seemed so reserved at first, understandably very different than Farrell. After all I'd seen go on down there, I never figured he would become friendly with any of us, much less me. I didn't think I could relate to him.

Once he began to share though, Murat told a tragic but compelling life story. He and his family lived in Iraq during *the war on terror* as it was called in America. Luckily for him, he was able to get educated as an electrical engineer, financed by his brother.

During that time, U.S. propaganda was pushing a facade that terrorist activity had been quelled in the region. Murat said he was hired to help rebuild the damaged electrical systems.

However, violence continued to escalate between policing officials and savage rebels. "Bastard dogs" he kept calling them. They would open fire with American soldiers in crowded streets using civilians as cover, cowardly hiding behind them for safety. They put their own people in harm's way to turn Iraqi citizens against the occupation and blame the U.S. for inciting the violence. Percentage wise, these bastard dogs were just a small segment of the Iraqi population. Most people over there were the same as most people everywhere. They were just trying to earn a wage and provide food for their families.

During one particularly nasty series of suicide bombings, Murat ditched the reconstruction effort and fled to Syria. There's no way he could have predicted that a few months later, Syria would experience civil war; he once again saw violence that made him fear for the lives of every member of his family.

It culminated to a breaking point when a local boy, only eleven years old, was kidnapped and gang raped by a group of sadistic soldiers. Murat and his family fled again. Most people headed toward Jordan or Turkey or Lebanon, but Murat's brother used the remainder of his saved money to have their families smuggled into the United States. Once inside the border, they resided in Boston.

He talked fondly of his children but often stopped abruptly as if he caught himself showing more emotion than he intended. I thought maybe the vulnerability made him uncomfortable. Maybe he was just reading my reactions and adjusting his speech for my comfort. He seemed like a caring father and after hearing him talk, it made me miss ever having that kind of nurturing paternal figure in my life.

Murat was very candid about mistakes he had made, things he'd done that riddled him with guilt because of the affect they had on his kids. He had a brief sexual affair that ended his marriage after his wife discovered it. "I was weak and foolish," he said, "and she deserved better than that." Although they were surrounded by the American culture, she didn't leave him out of honor. But, the trust was broken and they never truly recovered. He carried a heavy emotional burden as a result.

His stories were not what I would have expected from someone originating from Iraq where woman are typically treated as less than human. He seemed surprisingly humble and honest and reasonable. There was something very endearing about him and the way he candidly described his past as if without bias. I can't quite describe it other than to say that it drew me in and made me trust him. Stupidly, I trusted him.

I should have put my gun up to his head when I had the chance, pulling the trigger and letting pieces of *his* flesh decorate the walls. I could have easily buried a blade in his neck before anyone could have stopped me. But I didn't see through his act and I had no way of knowing that he was setting me up to fuck me over. I genuinely liked him.

Murat seemed impressed with me too and, at first, I couldn't understand why. He was a very educated man and, intellectually my superior even on the surface. Still, I began to notice his tendency to generously give me compliments, admire me even. It was all part his plan.

It started with a conversation about hobbies. I had none. Truth is, I had many interests but no one had ever been interested in me so, more accurately, I had no hobbies I thought anyone would find interesting. He *was* though. After Murat and Farrell chatted through many frivolous topics, most of which I couldn't relate to, they began to talk about the fourth of July.

We were three men with three different perspectives. Farrell of course, felt patriotic about its meaning but nostalgia took precedence once he again started sharing memories about his dead sister.

Murat said he was envious that his home country could not have been so lucky to claim such a grand unifying holiday. "For all its faults, the path your country took to freedom appears as though paved by the Almighty, if such exists. I'd rather live among my own people, but I cannot deny life in America is more abundant. Well, it *was* more abundant," he said.

I didn't really care about the meaning of the holiday at all and I had no positive family memories to relate, but I was always excited by the fireworks. I don't like to admit it seeing as how it tends to feed into an Asian stereotype, but I can't help who I am and I love fireworks. The ability to control such a violent spectacle, to engineer its chaos, inspired my fascination for the science behind it all. The English language was always stressed in my teaching but I felt inherently drawn to work in chemistry. In another life, under different circumstances, that is the study I would have pursued; as it were, I was allowed no such option. Once we started talking about the explosions and colors and sounds though, I recalled that passion and began to spout out various tidbits. All the while, they seemed amazed with the knowledge I had.

"Add strontium to make it red, copper to make it blue. Mix them and they burn purple," I said.

"Damn, Amish. You seem a lot more Asian to me now," Farrell said. I know it sounds derogatory, but I didn't take it that way. That was his version of a compliment. I accepted it as such.

Murat continued to prod me and I continued to spill information. It's easy to persuade someone to talk about something they love and once they found my button, I let down my guard and began to open up. They patiently listened and it felt good to be heard.

I rambled off recipes for making homemade sparklers and smoke bombs and black ash snakes. I talked about making soda bottle bombs with chemical pipe cleaner and aluminum foil. I told them it was something I loved to do as a kid. Truthfully though, having no opportunity, I never tried making anything like that until I was a young adult in transit to the military and away from my Uncle Lee.

"Aluminum powder and rust is another favorite, just because it's so easy to make," I said.

"Thermite, you mean. You're a brave man. That's dangerous stuff," Murat said.

"What is it?" Farrell said.

"Just two metal particles mixed in a 8:3 ratio and once ignited, boom," I said.

"So an explosive?" Farrell said.

"No, not an explosive. It just burns but the reaction is brighter than I've ever seen elsewhere. It's amazing. It melts through almost anything," I said.

"Well, anything with a melting point below about 5,000 degrees Celsius," Murat said.

Farrell seemed lost in the conversation as it progressed, being able to give very little meaningful input. He appeared to be more surprised by Murat's knowledge of the topic than mine, giving him strange looks every time he would talk.

"How the hell do you people know about this stuff? What class did I miss?" Farrell said. Murat and I smiled lightly, bonding over the knowledge he and I shared as if it somehow made us special. Then Farrell looked to Murat and blatantly spoke with a somber voice, "Why were you brought here?"

Murat took another drink from his cup. Any casual expression of social enjoyment subsided from his face as he reluctantly spoke. "I thought it didn't matter," Murat said. "That's what you told me."

The radio static burst through the speakers one last time. Riley's cracking voice began to slowly dictate strange passages regarding "morning ejaculation" and "moldy castle walls." His voice was strained as if he were trying to speak in as low a register as possible, then he mumbled baby gibberish. We listened for a full minute before Farrell reached up from the floor and gently pushed the power button, shutting down the whole system. It seemed to serve no more purpose.

"It doesn't matter," Farrell said to Murat. "The world has changed. Our countries are dead and so are any loyalties. The flag on my sleeve is just a memorial now. That's the way I feel anyway. What do you say, Amish?"

I nodded. I didn't just agree so Murat would talk either. At that point, after everything we'd been through, that's honestly how I felt and I couldn't have phrased it any better than he did. Country be damned.

"Then there's no reason to talk about it," Murat said.

"There's no reason to be shy about it, either," Farrell said. "You seem like a decent guy. I just want to know for my own curiosity. No judgment."

Murat knocked back his liquor and held out his cup again. Farrell gladly refilled it.

"They took my brother," Murat said.

"Who did?" Farrell said.

"Whoever your government uses to take people," Murat said. "They said he was a terrorist. They were wrong. I tried to have him freed and they took me too."

"And that's it?" Farrell said.

"That's it," Murat said.

"Wow," Farrell said, "that is some pile of bullshit."

"Are you calling me a liar?" Murat said.

"I'm saying that is way too short of a story to end up with you being tortured out in the middle of maple country," Farrell said. "Fuck semantics. Call him a terrorist or freedom fighter but if you got dragged out here, your boy got caught doing something and so did you. Whatever, man. Take it to the grave if you want but saying nothing makes me think your brother was Bin Laden himself."

Farrell's suspicious thoughts provoked a spark of tension once they transformed into words exiting through his unfiltered mouth. His blatancy was prone to bring out the best and worst in people and, of course, every coin has those two sides. I didn't want anymore tension though, and I watched for Murat's reaction, hoping his mindset was like mine.

"He had a sordid past, I admit," Murat said. "It had become hard to make a living in our war torn country so he freelanced his help to certain groups, many labeled as enemies of the States over time. He was just a hired gun though. He didn't believe in their causes."

"He was a mercenary," Farrell said.

"He was a father and a husband," Murat said. "He did what he thought was best for his family. Mine too. He risked his life for the people he loved. Don't minimize him as a barbarian."

"I meant no disrespect. He needed money and he helped you. I get it," Farrell said.

"No, you don't. Being poor in America means you ask for government assistance or charity. There, in the middle of a war zone, being poor meant you watch your children slowly starve. Instead of playing, they would pick through garbage for anything valuable enough to trade for food to help our family. And there was never a day I didn't worry one of them could be killed in a bomb blast or shot by soldiers fighting for one side or the other," Murat said. "Unless you've been there, you don't get it."

Farrell didn't reply but I could see the contemplation on his face. Desperation can be a difficult feeling to imagine, but easier than a trying to artificially muster the emotions that comes with fatherhood. I couldn't fully understand that either, but my respect increased greatly the more I listened to Murat speak and heard the pain in his voice.

"The pay was decent but he had an opportunity and he took it without hesitation. He was asked to assist a trade between al Qaeda and a Russian arms dealer. He took the money and got away with it," Murat said. "We fled on stolen blood money."

I was eager to hear the rest and watched as Murat opened his mouth to continue, but said nothing. Instead, a frightened expression overtook his face as he looked up behind us. Farrell and I turned to find Eva, standing in the threshold of the hallway, blood pouring down her chin and onto her shirt.

I wanted to say something to her, anything to get her to speak normally back to us, but I froze. For a split second, I imagined a possibility that maybe she just fell and hurt herself and she would tell us that. She would ask someone—me, her favorite—to come to her aid and help mend her wound and then everything would be alright. But she didn't. My comprehension of the situation before me quickly set in and logic devoured hope.

"Compos mentis," she said. The rest of her words were indiscernible French as she violently lunged toward Farrell. He quickly stood and grabbed Eva, wrapping his arms around hers and picking her off the floor. She wiggled and kicked and screamed as if he was killing her. It seemed clear though, he was just trying to control her wild movements as he carried her down the hallway toward the exit. It couldn't be real but I saw it with my own eyes.

"Don't get too close!" he said. "Stay ten steps behind me!"

I jumped up and rushed toward them. I didn't know why or what I thought I might do. My head was all over the place;

my mind and spirit felt broken. I didn't care if I died, I just didn't want to see any more suffering. Murat saw me make a move toward them and held me in place.

"Stay back! She will only get you sick too," he said. "Her body is here, but she is gone now."

His words reinforced what I had already suspected when I saw her standing there, void of expression. Deep down, I believed it. She made it obvious. I still wanted to follow them though, and we did, together. Murat stood in front and held out his arm, not allowing me to move in too closely. He couldn't permit that. It was apparent that I'd become emotionally involved; when that happens, logical choices can seem unthinkable. Like anyone would be in that scenario, I was unpredictable. It was a critical moment with no room for mistakes from anybody.

"Ow! Dammit!" Farrell yelled. "Stop biting me!" He pleaded with her to calm down as they ascended toward the surface of the Earth out of our view. I was glad I couldn't witness her actually commit that violence. I didn't want that nightmare to supplant my positive memories of Eva. Hearing her growl like an animal was harsh enough.

We followed them up the spiral steps, listening to her guttural screams of agony and anger continue. It was impossible to see them for the curve of the staircase; the darkness that enveloped it only added to that certainty. Murat stopped me at one point as we saw light briefly gradate down the walls. The hatch was open and for a moment, that sweet, far-too-absent sunlight was shining in. It quickly vanished with a heavy thud as the door slammed shut behind them. Murat ran ahead in the blackness and felt for a lever that he wasted no time rotating down, locking them both out.

I had resisted getting close to Eva because of my devotion to Lin. I purposefully distanced myself from the tender human contact I craved out of excessive loyalty. Now she was gone. So was Lin. So was Farrell. There were no more chances to bond with any of them and regrets already started hanging over my head. Seeing that beautiful girl, so young and full of life, being dragged away in that condition by someone who had become a friend, it shattered whatever pieces of my heart still remained in tact.

I had been broken.

26
Unloading Burdens

"Can you hear me?" Murat said, yelling through the steel door.

There was no answer. In fact, there was nothing—no view to the outside world, no method to update ourselves on the status of the planet or anyone who still might be living on it. Communication through radio seemed pointless as there appeared nobody left to communicate with. And Farrell, the man I had related to most was stranded on the other side of a thick steel door and he wasn't responding. I had no hope.

"I'm here," he finally said in a whimpering voice.

"What happened with the girl?" Murat said. "What did you do?"

"Uh," Farrell said before letting out a sorrowful yell. His voice wasn't extremely clear as painful emotion distorted his words. "I did it. I didn't want to, but I did it."

"Did what? Are you alright?" Murat said.

"No. I'm not alright," Farrell said. "I did what I had to do. She's gone now." We could hear the sobbing peaks of lamenting wails as he sat just on the other side of the cold metal gate.

"Do you want to come back inside?" Murat said.

His sobs increased. He was not a man to blubber about like that, but there was no one to impress anymore. No judges or commanders or pressuring peers. Pure emotion was all that remained and I figured that would only last as long as his mind stayed valid. That was what I had gotten used to seeing. He sounded as though he'd broken down in tears. His clear communication wouldn't remain for much longer.

"I can't come back in. The ground is covered with that yellow shit," he said. "I had to wrestle her to the ground and I'm covered in it. It's over for me. It's over."

I sat at the top of the steps with my flashlight for a while, mourning the loss of everybody I loved, everybody I liked, even people I had never met. The world appeared to be breathing its last breath. I began to ponder that mine may eventually be the only set of lungs left to keep that respiration flowing. That thought scared me to no end.

Murat sat there with me, leaning against the door. Had he not been there, I may have just run out into the open air and taken it all in. The sunshine, the wind, the disease. I didn't care. Potentially being the last man alive has a certain set of pressures to it that I didn't ask for and I absolutely didn't want. At that moment, it sounded more appealing to enjoy my final few days on Earth before fading into a painless insanity. With consciousness gone, so are fears and worries and cares. It sounded like a trade worth making.

But there he remained, protecting me from the outside world, playing the role of survival enforcer. I thought he was just trying to keep me alive, keep me from irrationally ending my life earlier than necessary. Part of me figured he just didn't want to be alone. I couldn't blame him. Neither did I.

Farrell eventually went silent. We called to him but he didn't respond and we never heard from him again. I assumed he just started walking because that's what I would have done. Had I been on the other side of that door, I would have headed toward the nearest town to eat and drink anything I wanted, live life to the fullest for however long cognition remained lucid. After that, I would just hope that the mental incapacitation would at least be painless. He didn't say that's what he was doing though, not even a word of farewell. There was nothing substantial left to say anyway. We could deduce his fate and he knew it. I believed it would soon be ours too.

"We're going to die, aren't we?" I said.

"Eventually, sure. Everyone dies," Murat said, "but we can't give up. Not yet."

Murat put his hand on my shoulder, deceptively comforting me like a friend. The flashlight I gripped in my fingers lit up the stairwell enough that I could see the somber expression on his face as he tried to come up with something to say that would give me some small shred of peace.

"I believe I saw one full bottle of vodka remaining in the freezer," he said. "There's no reason to let that go to waste." As superficial as it portrays me to admit, that did make me feel a little better.

We headed down the hallway and I glanced through each room, serene and void of life. He retrieved the last icy bottle of liquor and cracked it open, handing me a cup filled as if it were water. I drank a few large swigs, tolerating the burn down my throat so I could enjoy the warm comfort flowing through my veins. I stared at the ceiling, looking at the ropes that controlled the air pump. It occurred to me for the first time then.

"I guess we can't pump in anymore fresh air," I said.

He appeared genuinely surprised. I'm not sure if it was because he overlooked that detail or because I did not.

"Damn. I didn't even think of that," he said, "but I suppose that *would* bring in polluted air. We shouldn't risk it."

It's a peculiar constant of human nature that when something is out of reach, any desire for the forbidden fruit painfully grows. It was beginning to feel so hot and stuffy down

there—a sensation surely magnified by the alcohol consumption—I just wanted to breath some fresh air. I put the cup filled
with ice cold liquor to my forehead allowing the cool codensa-
tion to run down my face. It was a simple pleasure, the only kind
I had left.

"Does it hurt still?" I asked.

"Which part?" he said.

"Your fingers. That was the worst injury, right?" I said.

He put his palm up in front of his face, looking at the gauze
wrapped so thick there was no longer the shape of a hand but a
blob of dirty white bandages. It seemed like he had nearly
forgotten about it. Maybe he had.

"It hurt like hell when he cut them off, but they don't feel gone
now. It throbs, but it hurts most on the tips of my fingers and
they're no longer there. It's like a phantom limb I guess," he said.

We talked while we drank and the more we drank, the more
open we became. We talked about past relationships and jobs and
life experiences. I remained vague but not once did I ever lie to
him. There was no point anymore. There's nothing to hide when
all the people who'd care to look are dead or insane. And he shared
freely with me too, or at least that's what I thought.

"How'd did you get caught?" I asked.

"What do you mean?" he said.

"You used blood money to come to the States. How did they
catch you?" I said.

He sipped his cup and put the half empty bottle on the desk.

"Well, we got to the States and things seemed good. I got a
legitimate job to support the whole family and we were finan-
cially stable. My brother even found work that didn't make a
paper trail but it didn't matter. Someone in the government had
a connection with one of the groups my brother stole from and
they paid the American contact to find me. In finding me, they
found my brother," he said.

"And they jailed your brother?" I said.

"Not legally. Amir was taken away, brutally dragged out of the house in front of his kids and that was the last time we saw him," he said. "Damn American government. Full of corrupt hypocrites."

But I didn't care about his politics.

"And then they took you too?" I said.

"No, not until I investigated the American contact. I did the only thing I knew how to do. I went back to a different sect from my brother's connections, an enemy of the group he stole from. I convinced them he was on *their* side the whole time and stole the money from their enemy to help *them*," he said.

"Smart," I said.

"They had their own American contact who gave me the information I wanted. After that, I knew who fed my brother to the wolves. I found the man who ruined our peaceful life," he said. "So, I acquired some explosives and threatened to desolate his place of occupation if Amir wasn't released."

"Where did he work?" I said.

"Langley, Virginia," he said. "In the CIA building."

I looked at him for a moment, imagining an Iraqi man placing a threat to blow up the CIA building. It struck me as funny. A lone man, innocent though having family ties to extremist organizations, trying to intimidate the entire department known to take down terrorist threats. It reminded me of one of the biblical tales Delgado once reiterated except this David and Goliath story had a much more likely ending: the giant crushed the annoying farm boy like a roach until nothing remained but a slimy smear in the dirt. It was so absurd, I can't imagine how anyone could expect it would have had any positive outcome. So I snickered. Then I laughed out loud, softly at first then deep from within my belly. I was losing my mind.

"You son of a bitch," he said, laughing nearly as much as I was. "You try taking on the American government. See how far you get."

"Oh, you don't know that half of it," I said. "Damn, the shit I could tell you."

As my drunkenness increased, so did my casual use of profanity. The fit of hysterics subsided and I stared at the bottom of my cup, still holding my tongue with an ever loosening grip.

"Well, don't just leave me feeling like an ass," Murat said.

I took another sip. I could feel it going to my head but I was still alert. I looked at him for a moment, looked in his eyes and I couldn't see a monster. There was no reason that he should have been bound and tortured. He was a decent man. I really trusted him.

"I work, *worked*, for the Chinese government," I said.

"What do you mean?" he said.

"They made me do shit for them, some secret anti-American government stuff," I said.

"You're a spy?" he said.

"Not a spy," I said. "I was a damn slave."

"You got no compensation?" he said.

"Well, I got paid for it, but it was never about the money. I didn't really have a choice," I said.

"But you were sanctioned, financed even, to hurt the American government?" he said.

I nodded.

"You're bullshitting me. You're just saying that to make me happy," he said.

"I swear to you. I've never told anyone that before," I said.

He started laughing. I started laughing. It is funny I suppose, ironic even, to be held captive and later find out at least one of those captors worked for a foreign agency. He got such enjoyment out of it, I kept talking. In fact, I held back nothing.

There was no point to do so anymore. It felt good to make someone else laugh and smile, especially when all hope was lost.

"You're a great man. I would have burned the White House to the ground if I could," he said. "Not for violence against an individual, but because the whole system was so corrupt, nothing could ever change without tearing it to pieces first. I'm glad it's gone. What was your purpose?"

"I helped secure the Dygere servers, the ones that do all the monitoring and calculations for the stock market. I don't know exactly how they work but they're all over, hidden in mountains and bases and shit. I only knew the location for the one I guarded, but I was told there were at least five more spread throughout the country," I said. I could feel my speech breaking apart. The vodka was hitting me heavily and effecting my ability to form words. I assumed it was the alcohol anyway. I can't be sure now.

"What did you do exactly?" he said.

"Me? Not much. They would pay me to get access to a main server and shove a small memory drive into a port. I'd leave it overnight, then remove it the next day and send it back. That's it. I did it a half dozen times or so," I said.

"That's all? What was it for?" he said.

"I don't know, man. I'm just a damn pawn," I said.

"But you had to have some idea," he said.

"I had guesses. The stock market is completely managed by computers now. I don't know if they were trying to influence it to boost investments or control it outright. They may have even been just trying to delay it to get an upper hand on trades. Who knows?" I said.

"That doesn't sound possible from one computer," he said.

"It wasn't. Like I told you, there were at least five other computers all constantly cross-referencing each other and at least five other guards just like me pulling the same shit wherever they were," I said. "I met one of them once. *He* suspected they just wanted enough influence so when they exposed the system's vulnerability, faith in America's superficial economy would collapse and the United States would no longer be the big superpower."

"Using America's own lifeblood against itself. It makes sense," he said. "It's actually quite brilliant."

"Maybe," I said, "but I never knew for sure. It wasn't my job. Honestly, I didn't care."

He started laughing again. Murat seemed as enthralled by my story as I was by his. Somehow, it made our bond feel even stronger.

"It sounds like a risky task," he said. "You know, when I made the threat to blow up the CIA building, it wasn't just verbal. I had already gotten in and planted the bombs. It was easier than you might think."

"How did you get in?" I said.

He snickered as he said, "I dressed as a copier repairman. I bought fake background checks and everything. You believe that? And it worked."

"I released a bird in my facility," I said.

"A bird?"

"Yeah. I didn't have access to the servers, so I released a bird. I had gotten to know everybody who worked there and nobody else wanted to break a sweat to chase it. So I'd catch it and release it into the next part I needed access to until I was in the main server room," I said. "It had gotten to be a running joke since it happened so often and everyone wondered how those damn things kept getting in. They never suspected me though."

"I'm impressed," he said. "If you don't mind me asking, did it pay well?"

My laughter died down quickly and my expression turned somewhat sour.

"It's OK. You don't have to tell me," he said.

"I already told you, I wasn't doing it for the pay," I said.

"Then for your country's cause?" he said.

"Definitely not for the cause. Your brother and I have that in common," I said, trying to give him a reference he'd find relatable.

"Why then?" he said.

I suppose it was obvious that painful memories were rising to the surface. I couldn't even feign a smile as I stared at the wall, refusing to lock eyes with another human for fear that emotion may overcome me. And then I told him, admitted out loud for the first time ever, "I did it to save my siblings."

"I don't understand," he said.

"Forced abortions. They only allowed one child per family in China—any additional children were forcibly destroyed. Wealthy families could pay to have more kids but we were far from wealthy," I said. "I was the second born and I was almost aborted. But, my parents were offered a deal."

"By the Chinese government?" he said.

I nodded.

"I would be allowed to live and my parents could even have more children if they agreed to sneak into America and birth me on U.S. soil so I could work for them from the inside," I said. "Otherwise, I would have been killed by government enforced abortions along with any future siblings. My parents traded my life so they could have more children."

"Damn," he said. "They speak of middle child syndrome but yours must be like no other."

He was trying to make a small joke I think, but I couldn't even grin as a courtesy. It was too painful.

"Did one of them stay to raise you? Your parents, I mean?" he said.

I released a light, sorrowful sigh as I relived my past, looking away in an effort to hide my watery eyes.

"No, I was raised by a horrible man, a genuine asshole. An Uncle Lee," I said.

"Who is Uncle Lee?" he said.

"Not just a who, but a what," I said. "An Uncle Lee is a parental guardian. It's the moniker given by the infiltration program to the men who trained the boys that they forced into servitude."

"Trained to do what?" Murat asked.

"Fit in. Then do whatever they needed. The ones that grew up and got into positions of power or access to classified information were rewarded. I suppose the others were dismissed. Their siblings may have even been killed for failure. I don't really know," I said. "They had a lot of us though, whole groups of us living together in different cities in the U.S."

"All raised by an Uncle Lee?" he said.

"Well, girls had a female version: Mother Tams. These people, evil people, provided only the most basic care and sustenance. There was no love or parental affection with them, just strict training and discipline," I said. "My Uncle Lee was a sadistic son of a bitch and I'm glad he's dead."

"You didn't call him by his real name?" he said.

"I never knew it," I said. "Hell, I didn't even know my own real name if I ever had one. My Uncle Lee called me Kenneth, so that's what I was. My only Chinese identification was a serial number."

I could hold back no more and I began to tear as I unleashed everything. I told him of the abuses endured by the other boys and me. I told him about Lin, my love, and how I wished I could just see her one more time. I told him how I was supposed to run away with her after I got back from this last mission but my hope for any kind of pleasant future was completely gone.

He changed the subject for a few minutes and began to tell me about his kids again. I had a hard time listening though.

After I shed my skin, for the first time revealing the snake underneath, I felt liberated. I could feel tears roll down my cheeks though I couldn't really explain them. I was sad, absolutely, but it was more than that. I was showing myself, opening up everything to someone and letting them see who I was, completely unedited. No more facades or lies. There was a deep down sensation of freedom from somewhere that had previously seemed buried. I felt the soul I'd always been told about and never believed in, but it was there. And it was naked. If that was real, perhaps God could be as well.

Maybe it was just the alcohol. We almost finished off the entire bottle but I think I drank most of it myself. The numbness was overtaking me and I could feel my eyes get weak as we continued talking. I don't even remember everything I said verbatim, but I didn't hold back and neither did he. Whatever I asked, he gave up answers freely and I did the same in return. Every feeling, every secret, every desire.

At one point, my eyelids became too heavy to lift and I talked and listened with them shut. Once my consciousness slipped into blackness though, it was all over. My sins had been confessed and I was baptized in Russian liquor. I slept like a newborn.

27
Coming to Light

I hadn't remembered the moment I fell asleep but I suppose that's not a memory even possible to make. When I awoke, I still wasn't completely sober but the hangover had already begun. My head was pounding and I felt too lethargic to move. I laid there on the ground for several minutes, staring at the cement ceiling, waiting for my sluggish mind to recuperate, at least partially.

The cold floor had chilled my achy back and I had made a decision to go and lay down in the bedroom that Eva hadn't contaminated. I can't say that I really cared about dying at that point, but purposefully putting my own life in danger, knowing that the decision is irreversible, is not an easy thing to do. The survival instinct is a powerful one and truly difficult to ignore. Regardless of my decision, I found it easier for my brain to give my body instruction than it was to inspire it into actual motion. The liquor had taken quite a toll on me, more so than it ever had before.

Murat didn't say a word. I thought he was probably sleeping as well, but I didn't want to turn my head to find out. It just seemed like too much effort. I finally forced myself to stand upright and look around the room, vacant except for me. The nearly depleted bottle of vodka sat on the table next to where I last saw Murat but he was nowhere in sight. I figured he had probably claimed the sole uncontaminated bedroom with squatters rights. It annoyed me. I reassured myself that there were two bunk beds per room and I'd soon find my weary body on a mattress, even if it was only slightly softer than the concrete I'd slept on for hours. It really shouldn't have been a problem to share a room full of beds. I just hoped he didn't snore.

The clean bedroom was empty though. It puzzled me that he might take the bedroom where Eva had slept but I peaked inside to verify. Of course, he wasn't there either. I checked the mess and even the latrine. I finally went down to the end of the hallway to the cell, the last room in the whole bunker. Following what I considered a logical chain of reasoning, I slowly slid the door open with my foot, dreading that I may find the deceased body of a man who'd had enough and ended his own life. When I looked inside, blood abounded but it was days old. Murat was absent.

I began to panic. I didn't want to be alone. I ran up the corridor, grabbing my flashlight along the way and shining it up the spiral steps until I reached the steel door. It appeared he had gone and left me behind. I was ready to live the last few days of my life freely roaming the countryside until the disease devoured me like it had done to everyone else. I didn't spend much time thinking it through, however. I didn't even give it a second thought. I just wanted out. So I grabbed the lever and pulled with all my strength. It wouldn't budge. I ran my fingers over the entire length of the handle, feeling for a lock or some obstruction, but I could find no cause for it to defy movement. Somehow, for some reason, my survival enforcer had hypocritically departed and locked me in from the outside.

I tried to think of motives he may have had. Perhaps he was getting more food or looking to find a vehicle that had eluded the others. There's a chance he was feeling ill and left in case he had gotten infected. Or, maybe he was getting some small amount of revenge after all. I contemplated every rationale I could muster but nothing seemed logical and worse, nothing seemed fair. There was no reason to leave me behind. I was no longer his enemy. We had bonded and if one of us were to go, there's no reason we both could not.

Locked down there, running out of food and dwelling all alone, I was doomed. Getting outside seemed impossible and even if I had managed to escape, the future was bleak. There was no more hope. This was my mindset.

Even still, I gave him some time. I sat on the bed and listened for him to come back with some plausible explanation that I hadn't been able to conjure myself. In the quiet stillness, I even began to have audible hallucinations. I would think I'd heard a click and I'd check the steel gate just to see if he was trying to get in. Then I'd recheck the door thinking maybe I had missed some reason for the door to be sealed. But I missed nothing. And he never came back.

I even tried my hand at using the radio. I powered it back on but all I heard was static. I turned knobs and flipped switches and moved sliders but nothing seemed to have any effect. I should have paid attention to Farrell more carefully. I know that now.

Finally, after great deliberation and internal debate, I was ready. I could easily have just killed myself, but I felt my responsibility even then. I found a scrap of paper and a plastic ball point pen in the mess and looked around for a last meal. Nothing looked appealing.

Besides, I figured in the off-chance that someone would find that place in the middle of nowhere and stumble inside with a desire to survive, they deserved the food more than I did. It shouldn't go to someone about to throw in the towel. I couldn't let a stranger's fortune waste away in my belly. It's just more organic matter to rot and decay and stink up the place when they find my body. I've heard that muscles relax and fecal matter tends to slide out during death. Finding a cadaver is an awful thing but made slightly worse if the last thing that cadaver did was shit himself. I could almost hear Farrell telling me to eat everything I could find as one last big practical joke to the unlucky bastard who would happen to stumble on my corpse. I didn't do it, but as twisted as it sounds, it made me smile to imagine him encourage it.

I walked back into the assembly room, grabbed the virtually empty bottle of vodka and planted myself against the wall next to my gun. I looked at the cheap pen for a few minutes, feeling almost as disposable. No remembrance of me would be left behind in this world. No children, no accomplishments, no legacy. This suicide note would be it. And after years of learning the intricacies of the English language, I had trouble producing that first word. I guess my mind realized finishing the letter meant my life would soon thereafter be over. Even still, once I started writing, my thoughts flowed freely.

★ See ASSESSMENT EXCERPT ★

I can honestly say, putting the gun barrel in my mouth was the hardest part. Once it's there, pulling the trigger of the M9 was relatively easy. See, there's such a big movement bringing the gun to your lips and willingly opening your mouth widely to take in the thick steel shaft. It takes a lot of coordination and intent. I tried several times, most of them only pointing the gun straight up in the air before letting it fall back down into my lap.

Once thoughts are cleared and the cold steel rests on your lips, squeezing the trigger seems effortless in comparison, probably because you'd expect nothing after the bullet leaves the chamber. That's what I expected: nothing. I thought perhaps my life would flash before my eyes as the cliché promises. Or maybe I'd be overcome with darkness before I get to see the white light we hear so much about from near death survivors. What I got instead was an incredible amount of pain.

I didn't expect to comprehend the loud bang of the hammer hitting the metal jacket yet I found my ears ringing. I waited for life to leave my body, but it clung to this world. I remember having my eyes shut tightly and feeling my heart race as I dropped the pistol on the floor. The taste of gunpowder burned in my throat and the roof of my mouth. I opened my eyes as I coughed out smoke and put my hands across the lower half of my face once I saw the blood pour out. I couldn't cap my lips tightly enough with my palm to keep the red life fluid from gushing freely. Still, death refused to take me.

Seeing that amount of blood come from my body as I repeatedly spit mouthfuls on the gray floor quickly made me nauseated. I tried to relax my thoughts but panic attacks were beginning to set in again. Breathing deeply, I made every effort to calm down so I could assess the damage and figure out what went wrong. I carefully used my tongue to explore my lips and my cheeks. They were sore and charred and blistered but seemed well within repair. It wasn't until I moved my tongue upwards and discovered the gaping entrance wound in my soft palette that the nausea was out of my control.

I began to vomit profusely from the pain and the sight of blood. That only made matters worse as the stomach acid added a second layer of burns to my throat and mouth. I tried to hold it in, but it spilled from my lips and through my fingers. Some even made it's way through the newly acquired wound and out my nostrils. It was the most horrible pain I've ever experienced.

I ran into the mess room and washed out my mouth as best I could, slurping up water and painfully rinsing the torn flesh. It was difficult to watch the tainted water splatter down the sink leaving unidentifiable black and red chunks scattered about the porcelain. I looked around for something to stop the bleeding but saw nothing that seemed as good a fit as the sock on my foot. I quickly removed my boot, balled up my cotton sock and shoved it between my teeth to gauze the wound. Instantly, I regretted not laundering my clothes more often.

It was all I could do to drag my body to the kitchen table. Colors looked gray to me and I could feel myself slipping away, melting in a sweaty mess. I thought maybe death was gripping me after all. Then I realized it was just the shocking pain making me feel faint. The episode passed and I began to become more alert after resting my head on the table. I had avoided blacking out and possibly choking on my own fluids, at least for a while.

I raised my head slightly, looking at the note Farrell had jotted on the table during his card trick: *you picked the stack of 5.* It almost seemed prophetic. I pulled the crinkled piece of paper from my pocket and read the number 5 on it, remembering how fortunate I felt to remain in the safety of that place, protected from harm, insulated by the other soldiers who would put themselves in danger before me.

It made me feel *so* good, in fact, I had kept it in my pocket all that time. Don't misinterpret my thought process—I don't believe in good luck charms. I find the idea of a rabbit's foot or special penny influencing life events quite ridiculous. But, I thought it might remind me that even I could occasionally get lucky. I guess that too was ridiculous. I crumpled the scrap into a ball and threw it in the sink, the surface now messily covered with my blood and vomit.

It took me a few minutes to build up the courage to check the back of my head. There was nothing abnormal. I felt the top, the sides and the back again, but strangely enough, there was no exit wound. It made me wonder if the bullet was lodged somewhere in my head but it felt like I was thinking clearly. Other than the pain of my mouth being on fire and the headache that pulsated like a war drum, I was unscathed. It seemed impossible and I debated whether I was the most fortunate soul in existence or most unlucky bastard to ever live. At that point, my situation had only gotten worse and the only way I could think to assess my fortune was one of the scariest things I could imagine. I was going to attempt it again.

I tried not to think about it too much as I walked back to my pistol. I stepped over puddles of blood to retrieve my M9 and sat at the opposite wall, next to the computer desk. Threads and lint from the sock stuck to my wound and pulled loose flesh as I removed it. I pointed the nozzle in the air again, but I was weak. I couldn't do it. I didn't have the mental fortitude to put that gun barrel back in my blistered mouth and I hated myself for it.

In my frustration, I stood and began to beat dents into the desk with the hilt of the pistol to release my anger, then I turned and cried out as I fired three times at the wall. The gunfire loudly blasted and my ears were slightly ringing, but I was not mistaken in what I *didn't* detect. There was no ricochet.

I put the gun down to the desk, holding the barrel a few centimeters away from the wood and pulled the trigger again. I watched as the muzzle flash scorched the surface, the compressed gas even taking away a small shard of the aging wood, but no projectile emerged. I quickly removed the clip and pushed out a cartridge. The tips were not rounded or flattened points like bullets but were crimped in slightly toward the center. They weren't live rounds. They were blank cartridges. I dropped both the gun and the clip and ran toward the bedroom to find my rifle where I had left it. It too contained blanks.

I calmly walked back into the assembly room trying to grasp the situation. It made no sense to me. I figured the cartridges must have been switched at some point during our stay. I know I had checked to make sure my firearms were loaded when I received them. That's the way I'd been trained. Then again, it was dark when I was given my gear and we were all being hurried along. Maybe I only looked at the back of the jackets. I couldn't remember. It didn't matter.

All my pent-up anger and stress and frustration took control and I kicked the radio onto the floor. Unleashing my aggression felt good but I wasn't satisfied. I flipped the desk and picked up that damn wooden chair and beat the wall with it until it was in pieces and I was gasping for air. Then I bent over and rested with my hands against my knees.

I looked down and saw another crumpled scrap of paper where the desk once sat. I remembered Simmons had angrily thrown it there when we drew numbers and he was picked to go first. Maybe his draw was the lucky charm after all and I needed some new luck. I almost felt silly for picking it up. Nevertheless, I did.

Having released much of my tension, I had calmed down. My mouth was still bleeding, though not as profusely, and I was overcoming the panic caused by my wound and my solitude. But the serenity didn't last. Chills poured down my body like water as I unraveled the wad of paper and saw a single digit that altered my perspective much more than I ever thought it possibly could. It too had the number 5.

I'd been had.

28
Once was Blind

The real trick, I figured, was making me think I had a choice to begin with. I couldn't find any other wads of paper, but I really didn't need to see them to know what they contained. It wasn't hard to deduce they all concealed a 5 so it didn't matter which I chose. It was never about luck for me. My fate was orchestrated.

I began to look around starting in the mess, then the latrines and bedrooms. I flipped mattresses, scattered boxes and tore the pantry apart, but it all seemed as it should. I found nothing. Then I went to the place I dreaded most, leaving the cell for last. Once again, I slowly opened the thick wooden door with my foot. It smelled like feces and burnt hair even still, days after Murat's interrogation. I looked over the tools of torture and the vast amounts of blood stains that appeared sprayed and spattered around. I looked at the bucket of body waste and found the audio player they used to blare heavy metal in his ears. Nothing looked out of the ordinary, that is for a chamber intended for torture.

Then I got a strange curiosity. I put the large ear phones up beside my cheek and pushed play. The music was a disturbing noise featuring a terrible metal band screaming over the sounds of thrashing guitars and accentuated drum beats. I jumped to track 2 and then 3. They were more of the same—obnoxious noise hiding under the pretense of artistic expression.

Then I skipped to track 4 and heard Hanna's voice. Then Murat's screams. It put chills down my spine to recount the recorded sessions until I realized the little audio player had large speakers but no microphone. Unless Hanna had taken equipment with him—which I didn't see him do—these audio files hadn't been recorded down in that bunker. It made me doubt that what I heard was a live interrogation at all.

I examined the visible floor and the patterns of blood. They looked consistent with what I'd expected. I removed the panel to the electrical circuits and saw nothing strange. Reluctantly, I pulled the bucket of waste away from the corner feeling as though I had to be thorough. I cracked the partially effective lid and was promptly hit in face with the most intense fecal odor imaginable. The disgusting cesspool aroma activated my body's natural reaction to dry heave and I quickly replaced the lid to avoid purging my stomach once again. If something was hidden in that bucket, that secret would evade me forever. I refused to explore it any further.

I almost gave up my search and left it at that until I glanced at the corner where the bucket had sat. Strangely, I noticed a thick smear of blood running directly to the edge of the wall, but not up on it. It appeared to be running underneath, as if pulled across when the obstruction wasn't there. I pushed on the wall and I felt only the slightest give, but it was enough to convince me the wall was not a permanent fixture. It appeared to be a movable panel whose seams were disguised by the large cover on the juncture box, the electrical conduits and the storage cabinets. There was nothing attached to the panel to pull on and the room was too little for the door to open inward. I figured it must open away from the cell but it wouldn't move. I pushed all over it, ramming it bluntly with my shoulder, even checking around the room for some kind of release lever. I found none.

Emotion started taking over. I took the claw hammer that hung on the wall and beat the panel until I broke through. The heavy claw easily tore a sizable hole in what appeared to be two layers of cement board separated by a few inches of space. Beyond that second layer was black, empty openness. Shining the flashlight through, I could see it was an extension of the hallway and on the floor, just on the other side of that panel, blood had been tracked in from the very room in which I stood.

My adrenaline temporarily acted as anesthetic and numbed my bleeding face, simultaneously fueling my muscles with a rage-enhanced strength. The more angry I became, the more aggression was used to tear through the panel. I demolished the door and ripped out a two-by-four that prevented the wall from being a usable passageway to whatever was behind it. Then I awkwardly squeezed my body through the hole feeling like a newborn calf pushing his way out of the womb toward freedom. It was a hurried task and not the cleanest escape as I tripped over pieces of jagged board that I'd missed and fell on the hard concrete, face first.

Once on the other side, I looked back at the hinged panel and slid over two bolted locks that made it easily pull open as a hidden doorway to the cell. I shined the light down on the floor and saw a trail of blood leading down the hallway toward rooms that branched off from it. I thought perhaps it was just an old section, one considered no longer viable for use, then covered and forgotten. Then I saw glowing lights coming from one of the far rooms that contrasted sharply with the dark hall.

Nervously, I began to approach the unknown. If someone were down there, I had no doubt they had heard me make my entrance like an overzealous tomb raider. The commotion would have easily given them enough time to prepare a defense or, as a more frightening but equally plausible scenario, an attack. I could feel my heart race and pulsate in the wound of my mouth. I tried to subdue my heavy breathing but my lungs kept demanding more air.

The first room I peered in was another bedroom, similarly stocked as the others except the mattresses were thicker than the ones we were given. The covers on all the beds were disheveled. They had been used. I only briefly shined my light around the room, just to put my mind at ease that no one was hiding within the dark corners. But, it was unoccupied.

I crept close to the wall until I reached next doorway, opening to a storage room of sorts. In one corner, there was a refrigerator while the rest of the walls were lined with stacked shelves. I felt around the wall for a switch and clicked on the light, illuminating the space more brightly than I'd seen in any other room down in that bunker.

I began to explore the boxes, looking over my shoulder every few seconds to prevent a possible ambush. In one box I found canned goods and cartons of nonperishable treats while in another, wads of what looked human hair. Then I found some medical supplies, among them a bottle labeled *SODIUM THIOPENTAL* that made me wonder if I'd been drugged. I removed wads of gauze pads and saturated them with oral anesthetic, then put them on my tongue and pushed them upward against the hole in the roof of my mouth. It stung terribly as though I'd ripped open a direct shortcut to my sinus cavity.

I definitely wasn't hungry. In fact, I don't think it was even possible to eat with my mouth in that crippled state. Still, curiosity and persistence for thorough exploration caused my attention to turn toward the refrigerator. Judging by the upgrade in bedding, I figured whoever slept on those beds would have been given something much better to feed on. When I opened the door, however, I jumped back, startled at the contents I that resided within.

There were trays with body parts shrink wrapped in plastic. Eyeballs, fingers, toes, ears. They didn't belong to Murat or anyone who'd been down here with us. My logical conclusion was strengthened when I found the jar of red fluid labeled *PORCINE HEMOGLOBIN*. Pig's blood. It began to make sense, even then. These biological remnants were probably taken from unknown, unclaimed corpses in war or from bodies donated to science, intended to help medical students learn physiology and researchers cure disease. Instead, they were being used as props to fake injuries and torture.

I continued on until I neared the glowing room. Slowly, I peaked around the corner, scanning from one side to the other until I confidently determined it too was vacant. There were four blank video monitors attached to a computer terminal and some radio equipment, all of it powered on. I slid the mouse across the desk and the monitors woke up and showed images from four different cameras, all of them hidden around the other half of the bunker.

I pressed a channel switch that rested underneath the stack of screens and different views from different cameras appeared. The bedrooms, the latrine, the mess, the assembly room. There was even one near the entrance of the gate, lit with night vision technology. There was no escaping the all seeing eye. I had been watched the entire time.

I turned my attention toward the radio equipment and found there was nothing radio about it all. It was an audio player with a direct line that ran into the wall and most likely to the other half of the bunker. I looked at it for a moment and pressed the play button. It made no sound. Then I adjusted a few channel settings and heard a repeat of something I'd already listened to days earlier. It contained all the static and the strange vocal recordings we tuned into as a group. People begging for help and declaring the end of the world, news about disease and war and destruction. Looking back, web access limited to certain sites began to make sense too as it was probably only truly connecting to one external server and not the Internet at all. Everything had been staged.

To my surprise, I looked underneath the desk and found what I had been wanting to look through since the day we had arrived: Ekwall's briefcase. I slammed it on the desk and tried a few combinations to open the locked latches. Frustration took control once again and used what had become my skeleton key. I beat the latches with the claw hammer, ripped them off and pried the case open. Inside were some of Ekwall's personal effects along with his files.

On top of a stack of files resided a cover letter written to Agent Ekwall from the Department of Homeland Security. It basically expressed the goals for the Dolus Initiative's first mission, primarily to extract information from the mark and prevent the terrorist attack. This had become of utmost priority. Underneath were strategic briefs and personnel files for each member of the hand selected team.

As I looked through them, I felt naive and betrayed and angry and afraid. They weren't soldiers at all, at least not active military. Corporal Reggie Simmons was actually Agent Reggie Simmons, FBI. Eva was actually Agent Evelyn Roth, CIA. I flipped through the pages and found them all there, compiled for Agent Ekwall, the only one who actually was the person he claimed to be. Agents Ignado Delgado and Karl Hanna were employed by the NSA. Farrell and Granger were actually Dr. Thomas Farrell and Dr. Charles Granger, both doctors of Psychology. And Murat, the tortured hostage, the one I had sympathized with and bonded to and trusted was really Dr. Yusuf Murat, not only a fellow psychologist but head of the entire Dolus Initiative.

Everyone that I had contact with in the last two weeks was part of some government agency, including the doctors who were actively contracted as consultants by the DHS. There was only one face I didn't recognize, that of Agent Raymond Riley, CIA. His part was that of a radio operator from Grand Forks and it appeared he actually communicated with us from fifteen meters away on the opposite side of the underground complex.

I was missing from those personnel files though. That is, until I got to the last folder and read over my information. As I expected, I was listed as *the mark*. They knew who I was and where I'd come from the whole time. They knew about my home country's threat, sabotage sanctioned by a sect of China's government, and they had already decrypted the information that was on the thumb drive I first smuggled into their network. I didn't even know how the software I planted for you worked, but they probably did. The report didn't spell out the mechanism or intention of your program, but it said that the damage prediction was detailed in an attached technical report. Unfortunately, that wasn't in Ekwall's briefcase.

What they didn't know was where we operated, how we were motivated and trained and dispatched. They didn't know that children were strong-armed into service or that dozens of moles existed in probably every conceivable branch of military and government. They hadn't heard of the deals of indentured servitude in exchange for lives of family members or the blindness that your soldiers have toward the mission's endgame. They didn't know any of that. At least, not until I gave that to them.

I looked at the names listed on the files and noticed they were unchanged. They had used their actual names with me, probably to make playing the parts easier and more genuine. It's a dangerous thing to do for people working undercover, stupid even. That is, I thought, unless they had no intention of me ever having contact with the outside world again. I was trapped down there and I wasn't going to last long sitting idly. I know my responsibility and I needed to get you this report. I had to find a way out.

I took my flashlight and quickly moved up to the end of the hallway, passing another small latrine. There were no more rooms after that but there *was* another spiral staircase and at the top, I was betting another hatch. All that time people were mysteriously going in and out of the cell or during those shifts when I guarded the gate in pitch blackness, the others were probably sleeping in comfortable beds, eating until their bellies were full or possibly going outside for walks and enjoying the sunlight. I was their fool.

Sure enough, there was a steel door, a rear exit that was locked just as securely as the one I already knew about. I tried using tools but the door might as well have been a bank vault. I wasn't getting through it.

I ran back down the steps and started to panic again as the walls seemed to close in on me. I was hot and sweaty and nauseated. The pain from my mouth was throbbing and I had to feel some cold air on my face or I was going to pass out. I ran to the refrigerator and opened it, putting my head inside, quickly cooling down after sitting still for a few moments and concentrating on breathing normally. As I squatted there, trying not to stare at the severed appendages wrapped in plastic, the refrigerator's vent blew chilled air against my perspiration-drenched clothes. Suddenly, I had an idea.

I ran to the assembly room and looked at the ceiling. The vent to the air pump was covered in a grate that was bolted directly to the cement. I tried taking it off with pliers and a wrench but the bolts wouldn't turn. I jammed the claw of the hammer between the metal vent and the cement but I just didn't have enough leverage to pry it off. I even used a screwdriver as a chisel and carved away some cement. After all that, I was left with a hole as big as my fist, presumably leading up to the air pump at the surface of the Earth. The duct work appeared big enough for me to climb through if I could just the grate off.

I ran into the kitchen and looked through the pantry until I found a government issued bottle of vinegar made of thick plastic. Quickly, I dumped it and rinsed it out thoroughly, then filled it with aluminum foil, chemical pipe cleaner and added a little water. I shook it for a few seconds and shoved it as far as I could into that fist sized hole until it was tightly wedged. I sat back and watched as it began to expand after a few seconds, pushing the grate slightly further from the concrete. Then I walked into the cell and waited for the reaction to unfold, hopeful it would aid my escape.

I had created that same weak bomb countless times before, but it seemed to take a great deal longer than I remember. Then again, I never had so much riding on its successful impact and I suppose stress warps the sensation of time's passing. The loud bang filled the closed spaced and, even from several feet away, I could see the splatter of boiling water hit the wall outside the doorway.

I turned the corner and looked to see that the grate still remained attached, but with one bolt loosened. It was enough though. I grabbed the hammer and pounded on the steel, even hung on it with all my body weight, until there looked to be enough clearance for me to squeeze through. I slid the table underneath and rested for just minute until I heard clatter echoing from the staircase. Someone dropped something metallic against the concrete. People were coming. I figured the small explosion was loud enough to alert them that I hadn't given up and now, they were coming for me. I wasn't sure if it were to execute or imprison me, but I didn't want to stay to find out.

I climbed up and through the vent, kicking the table over when I had enough grip against the thick, sturdy duct work. The sharp edge of the grate rubbed painfully against my ribs and waist and legs until I had climbed far enough up that my entire body was hidden well inside. I waited patiently as I looked down and saw armed men quietly pass underneath. I didn't make a sound even though the remnants of the super heated water and pipe cleaner splatter were creating chemical burns on my flesh. It started as a slow irritation and increased to a sensation similar to matches being extinguished on my skin.

Using my sweaty, sticky forearms and boot soles for grip, I pressed outward, inching my way to the surface. I'd slowly move my arms up, press against the metal to secure myself so I could bring my feet up. Then I'd press outward with my boots and repeat the process with my arms. It was slow and tedious, but it was progress and that fueled my determination. I had no idea where I'd end up but I took great joy in thinking about the team searching the entire bunker and not finding me. It would seem like I disappeared, one last trick and it was played by me. A regular Harry Houdini, I imagined myself.

The higher I climbed, the sweatier I became. At first the perspiration on my skin made it sticky enough to aid my grip but slowly, my arms were so saturated they seemed slathered in lubricant. The more I would sweat, the harder I would have to press with my arms for adequate pressure. My sore muscles required more oxygen and my heart pumped faster. I could feel each pulsating beat in the mutilated roof of my mouth. I was becoming exhausted and claustrophobic.

I would check periodically to see if my pursuers were onto my escape route but had seen no signs that they were. It was only a matter of time though. Vertigo began to set in as I looked down and saw the concrete floor nearly three stories straight below, so I focused upward at the small beam of light I was nearing. There was a right angle bend near the top and it took everything I had to contort my body to squeeze through. The last thing I saw below was a flashlight shining upward. I didn't know if they had seen me or not, but time was against me regardless. I needed to elude them. Then I'd need to hide.

I remember seeing the sunlight for the first time. It trickled in the duct work through small cracks of a dangling flap and two thick mesh screens. I easily punched through the screens and pushed the flap up. Then I came to the final obstacle: a metal canopy system at the end of the duct. It was securely bolted. I was trapped. I pushed it and pulled it and eventually punched it a few times out of desperate frustration, splitting the skin on my knuckles. I had no more options, no choice but to lie there and wait in that square aluminum tube.

Several minutes later, I heard whispering voices and then the sound of metal on metal. The heat was oppressive and I was without any further energy. Then the bolts started grinding. I could see them turning, being removed from the outside. One by one, they slowly revolved out of sight and before I knew it, sweet, brilliant sunshine poured in on my face. I had trouble trying to retain my vision, squinting hard and peering through my cracked eyelids. I could see nothing outside of bright light and blurry colors.

Then I felt hands reach in and pull me. My body, soaked in my own fluids, easily slid out even though my torso, hips and legs ripped onto sharp screws that had held the screens in place. I thumped face-down on the ground as I was dragged out into the grass and pulled a meter or so away from my impromptu exit. My pupils rapidly and somewhat painfully contracted but my surroundings all came into focus. I hadn't seen birds or trees or sunlight in days. It was all so beautiful.

"Where you going, you piece of shit?" he said.

I turned over and saw Agent Ekwall hovering above me. Two strange men dressed in black body armor stood on either side of me, pointing assault rifles at my chest. I was feeling fairly certain *their* guns weren't loaded with blanks.

"We weren't done with you," he said, "but I guess it's a good start."

As I lay there in the grass, he gave me the strangest expression when I looked up and smiled. He didn't expect that and frankly neither did I. Fear and anxiety and depression had been my home for what I could only assume was weeks. I wasn't looking at Ekwall when I gazed up but through him. Above his head were clouds and blue sky. A pleasant wind blew across my face as I realized the ordeal was over. The world was standing as well as it ever had and my Lin was out there somewhere, alive. Instantly, I had resurrected some shred of hope that someday I could see her again. It was a wonderful feeling.

"Get this asshole out of here," he said.

They covered me with a hood and shipped me to a detention center somewhere in Virginia. The security here is tighter than I've ever seen anywhere and I'm being kept in solitary confinement. If there are any other detainees here, I haven't seen them. I've been treated fairly well since my capture but I haven't told them anything since. They've offered me immunity for cooperation but I have refused. In full disclosure, I deceptively agreed to help them and used the computer they've given me to write you this report. In addition, I've generated a full alternate report for them denying your involvement and taking full responsibility for all actions, claiming earlier admissions to Dr. Murat were merely to garner the admiration of a fellow hostage.

I've befriended one my guards and it turns out he is sympathetic to those that confront the oppressive U.S. government practices. He agreed to smuggle the flash drive containing this authentic report out to you. Hopefully I am right to trust him. I'm short on options.

As per our agreement, I've written a very detailed account including thoughts, feelings, and beliefs as I had them in the various stages of my artificially staged detainment to better serve the continued cause and long term ambition of my home country with whom I devote full loyalty.

My one recommendation is to improve the treatment and care of your workers raised from childbirth on. Without diminishing my full respect and honor for the leadership of the program for which I serve, I have found many of my own faults and weaknesses stem from the abuses I received during my training. I believe better care will only strengthen the fortitude of your minions.

I make only the request that you extend the mercy that was promised to my family for my life of servitude. I know my mission was not completely successful but my intent and willingness to accommodate every order has been unwavering. Please bring no harm to my family, my parents or my siblings. If punishment for failure is demanded, I will take my own life for their safety. Most of my life has been taken from me anyway.

Should I ever find a way out of here, I will return to continue my work for you in any capacity I can. I await further instructions as you are able to send them.

Kenneth Khu, #07-21-09-12-05

Epilogue

"So then, the son of bitch threw some of those damn fingers at me. Two dead-ass fingers. Got pig's blood all over my shit. How the hell could I not be pissed at that?" Ekwall said discretely. "I know, I know. I should've kept my cool but that fucking guy, he pushed one too many buttons. I mean, come on, I'm only human."

Director Foster leaned back against the wall, sitting in a chair right outside of the office of Deputy Secretary Woodward. Ekwall sat beside him, looking through the door, waiting patiently for Woodward's phone call to end. They continued talking softly, coordinating their thoughts before it was time to present them.

"Yeah, well, I recommend rewording that to something like 'purposefully aided in creating tension for maximum effectiveness' when you tell that part of the story in your official statement," Foster said.

As late in the day as it was, most Agents for the Department of Homeland Security had already gone home. Only those with urgent matters continued to press on into the evening to secure the country they served. The elevator bell dinged as the doors slid open at the end of the hallway. Dr. Murat exited and walked toward the pair of agents, his cleanly shaved face smiling as he approached.

"Doctor," Foster greeted him. "Congratulations."

"Thank you, I'm glad it was a success for us all," Murat said. "I only wish I had been able to go back in one last time."

"I just want to reiterate my apologies for being reluctant to give my full cooperation," Ekwall said. "No hard feelings, I hope. I admit, I never thought it would work. Obviously, I was wrong."

Murat extended his hand in peace and gave a receptive nod as they shook in their civil accord.

"It worked out pretty well I suppose. We still have a few wrinkles to iron out before next time," Murat said.

"Next time?" Ekwall joked. "Shit. If I'm going to field one of your programs again, I want to play the interrogator so *I* can eat decent food and sleep in the back."

The two men smiled briefly as they endured an awkward silence, waiting for their meeting with the Deputy Secretary to begin. They all quickly peered in the office behind them when Woodward slammed the phone down on his desk, mumbling profanities under his breath. He didn't sound as pleased as they all hoped and sincerely expected. Foster's expression exposed his concern as he knocked on the door and led the other two men into Woodward's office, the three of them sitting on the opposite side of his large desk.

Dr. Murat and Deputy Secretary Woodward swallowed obvious animosity as they locked eyes. Their sour past was quickly becoming insignificant in the current circumstance in which they had found a more mutually beneficial relationship than expected.

"Talk to me. What happened?" Woodward said.

Foster began, "We attained a full report—"

"Not you," Woodward interrupted, then turning to Ekwall. "You. I want to hear it straight from the horse's ass."

"Sir?" Ekwall said.

"You know what I'm talking about. You were the field Agent chosen to observe and document, not lose your shit and attack his team members. You could have blown the whole damn thing," Woodward said. "What? You didn't think I'd find out about your lapse of composure?"

"Sir, I think my actions were misinterpreted," Ekwall said. "That outburst was part of a purposeful, orchestrated display to increase tension for maximum effectiveness."

"Is that right?" Woodward said as he turned to Murat. "He attacked one of your guys. What do you have to say about it?"

Murat looked over at Ekwall who appeared much less desperate for support than he actually felt. Having just made peace and knowing he too may need support at some point during the meeting, Murat had already planned on granting his advocacy. Even still, he allowed a brief pause to first give Ekwall a moment of worry, just a small dose of personal punishment for his misdeeds. Murat had used his psychological studies to perfect the emotional manipulation of those whose desires conflicted with him attaining his own. In the end, he needed Ekwall on his side.

"My guys aren't professional actors, so at times I make private plans with one player to keep the surprised expressions of the rest of the team looking authentic," Murat said. "We're dealing with a complex psychological web of interactive dynamics. Sometimes, the tactics and devices need to contour and react to the responses we observe in order to fulfill our agenda."

"Pardon me if I translated that bullshit incorrectly, but you're saying you knew about it then, right?" Woodward said.

It only looked better for Murat to deny that any part of his control group lost control. After all, Agent Hanna, the team member hand-chosen to fulfill the part of sadistic interrogator was involved in the conflict as well.

"Of course. Agent Ekwall was acting under my request," Murat said. "Any report you heard otherwise obviously comes from someone who wasn't privy to that aspect of the stratagem."

Woodward stared him down for a moment. He didn't really buy into the lie; however, without more sufficient cause to pursue it, he really had no recourse but to drop his case. While the potential for damage was great, Ekwall's actions had no harmful effect. In fact, his impromptu outburst did unintentionally help increase the tense atmosphere Murat was devising. It was a poor decision with a positive outcome. The good fortune did not escape Ekwall's appreciation. Neither did Murat's allegiance.

"Well, Doctor, in the future, remember my agents are not on your team. They're my eyes and ears, not your hands," Woodward said. "You had great liberty in choosing your own staff. Use them."

Murat nodded, taking the small amount of undeserved rebuke with shrewd humility.

"Moving on," Woodward said, "this Choo-chang asshole or however you pronounce his damn name, is he talking yet?"

"He's not saying anything other than what he chronicled in his reports but we really don't believe he was privy to any more than he's already given us. He didn't even know his parents named him Chaoxiang Wei. He's always gone by Kenneth Khu," Foster said. "He's just a peon and whoever is organizing the scheme is slyly vague. They're staying elusive by only giving their people the least amount of information needed to perform their bit task. Did you read his accounts?"

"I haven't finished the second one yet, but they look identical to me. What's the difference?" Woodward said.

"He wrote one for us and one intended to go back to a fabricated Chinese liaison. We intercepted the authentic one using one of our guards posing as an anti-government sympathizer," Foster said. "The reports are largely the same, the main exclusion being any statements that implicate the Chinese government as the primary conspirator. In ours, he denies their involvement at all."

Woodward skimmed over the stack of pages, glancing over the suicide note written by the targeted suspect.

"From a psychological standpoint, that report is invaluable," Murat interjected. "Khu was good enough to thoroughly give every emotion and thought process he had throughout his ordeal. The Chinese wanted reports like that to better prepare their agents. We can use that to fine tune the program for future use in a way we never could have otherwise."

"It's no secret I had my doubts about your methods," Woodward said. "Let's be honest. I thought they were bullshit."

"Your opinion was communicated quite blatantly, sir, but I think there's enough evidence to remove any remaining doubts," Murat said. "I extracted a small excerpt that I think exemplifies the program's effectiveness and moved it to the beginning of the report for quick reference. If he was desperate enough to write a suicide letter and end his own life, he had fully subscribed to the scenario we presented. If you look–"

Woodward interrupted, "Now hold on. Putting a hard screw to a Chinaman's psyche enough that he's willing to swallow a bullet may be sufficient for you to wet your short pants and drop the confetti but that was never really the point. Is his intel panning out?"

"We found his old community in Philadelphia and the building he grew up in. There were at least three cells of kids being raised and trained by virtual strangers, just in that small neighborhood. We're investigating all those groups now," Ekwall said. "God only knows how many cities have identical setups."

Dr. Murat began to grin and nod his head. As the updates continued to support his worth, his abundant confidence began to inflate into arrogance.

"We even found the tree with the carved initials he described," Ekwall continued, "and when we got there, sitting nearby on a fallen log was a young Chinese woman holding a tin box with dozens of handwritten notes inside. It was Lin. We have her in custody too now."

"The whole story about Lin and his planned escape and the contempt he held for his guardian, those were very personal details that would make him look very bad to his Chinese superiors," Murat said.

"Then why would he put them in a document he intended to send back home?" Woodward said.

Ekwall answered, "From his perspective, sir, he had to figure everything he said out loud to anyone down there could eventually leak out. He couldn't take the chance to lie about it. It could get his family killed and that's the only reason he did any of this: to save his family."

"The point is my technique works," Murat continued. "This process of providing a diverse peer system and creating tension to push them into choosing allegiances is effective. You slowly eliminate the peers that don't bond with the mark and you're left with a formidable comfort zone tailored to their opinions and personalities. You've caught, what, four other Chinese moles?"

"Five," Ekwall said.

"Excuse me, *five* other Chinese moles being subjected to traditional interrogation techniques for two weeks longer than you allowed me and none of them will say a word out of honor," Murat continued. "It's ingrained in their culture. They're dedicated to their families and their country and until they believe those things are completely gone, they'll die before they talk and put them at risk. Without a reason to lie, Khu told us everything to the best of his knowledge. And so far it's panned out to be one hundred percent accurate."

"Well," Foster said, "not *one hundred* percent."

Dr. Murat tried his best to withhold his sudden feeling of confusion. There were no inaccuracies as far as he'd been told. His suspicious mind immediately began unjustly question

Foster's motives for withholding that information until they were sitting in front of the man in charge.

"The day we found Lin, we did a sweep of the area and found the spot they used to bury their tin box. She had it in her hand and the letters dated back for years, so we didn't dig any further," Foster said, "until this morning."

"What?" Woodward said. "What did they find?"

"Two bodies, both older and of Asian descent, one male, one female," Foster said.

"Have they been identified?" Murat said.

"Initially, that was proving to be tricky," Foster said. "Their hands were bound to their heads, postmortem, and completely burned away. There's no facial skin or fingerprints left to look at."

"How do we know this relates to our guy?" Woodward said.

"To burn the skin away, the perpetrator used a thermite composition, the same kind Khu talked about," Foster said. "However, that's not the cause of death. The male was beaten so severely, his facial structure wasn't even recognizable as human. His teeth were in his neck for God's sake."

"A murder that aggressive, it was definitely personal and probably on emotional impulse," Murat said.

"They're labeling it a *crime of passion* to the press—same with the woman. She wasn't beaten to death though. She was strangled with some sort of thick fabric."

"Like a ribbon?" Murat said.

"They did detect traces of red thread under her fingernails," Foster said.

"Hm. I guess old Uncle Lee didn't find true love after all," Murat said. "It makes sense. He couldn't admit to his government that he killed two of their own."

Foster nodded as he turned slightly to Murat, "I wasn't trying to spring this on you. This was confirmed only two minutes before we arrived."

Murat seemed dismissive toward the agent's expression of regret and more concerned with trying to control damage to his programs' reputation during its probation period.

"I would have gotten that confession out of him had I been able to go back in," Murat said to Woodward. "All due respect, sir, I knew you shouldn't have pulled me out that soon."

"I don't think this undermines the validity of the rest of Khu's testimony either, sir," Ekwall said, "We've gotten more verifiable information about their operation from him than anywhere else."

Woodward pressed his lips together, weighing the information and contemplating their next move.

"Can we squeeze his girl?" Woodward said.

"With your permission, we think we can use Lin and Khu as leverage against each other, the murders too. For full cooperation from both, we can offer immunity and even relocate them somewhere they can be together," Foster said. "That is, as long as you can allow those murders to go officially unsolved."

"Oh, I don't imagine it will affect my sleep very much," Woodward said, "but that keg's been tapped. To offer that traitor-shit immunity, what else are we looking to get out of him?"

"We can have him work with us to reach his contacts and see how deep the roots grow in Chinese bureaucracy. Hopefully, they're shallow enough that this won't start a war with the biggest country in the world," Foster said.

The three men sat patiently before Woodward as he paused, deciding how to place his wager as he turned to Murat.

"Doctor, his family is still in danger, correct? Any ideas how all that honor-before-self bullshit will come into play?" Woodward said.

"He has blatant animosity toward his ancestral country. We can exploit that, maybe convince him that he'll be getting vengeance on the country that's controlled his life by holding his family hostage," Murat said. "This is an opportunity for him to get the girl, keep his family safe and live some form of the American dream on taxpayer dollars while you get to keep that dream alive for the rest of America. I think he'll play along."

"We can't let the economy implode, sir. We have to pursue this," Foster added.

"You really think we can trust him?" Woodward said.

"No," Foster said, "but we can keep his leash short."

"I want him choking at the collar," Woodward said. "Get me the paperwork you need and make it happen. Get to it."

The three men began to stand as Woodward knocked on the desk in front of Dr. Murat.

"Hang around for a moment, won't you?" Woodward said, waiting for the others to leave. He then leaned back in his chair and crossed his fingers on his round belly.

"Your concoction seemed ridiculous but hell, I can't dispute the results. It was effective and I'm impressed," he said. "You think your techniques could work on anybody?"

Murat sat back in his chair and looked at him, smirking smugly. "Not this exact experience, no. Culture, personality, family history, and dozens of other factors need to be taken into account when custom tailoring the scenario," he said. "A Muslim zealot, for instance, puts a higher emphasis on religion than a godless culture like Buddhists. In a doomsday scenario, Muslims would cling to their faith more than ever and not say a word."

"So your methods have a limited scope, then?" Woodward said.

"Not at all. Every person on planet Earth is basically an animal. We all have needs and desires, people we love and things we hate. We're all the same. It's just a matter of creating the optimal atmosphere and pushing the right buttons to get people to open up," Murat said. "Everyone has a breaking point."

Woodward squinted his eyes, processing his thoughts.

"Before you walked in, I received a disturbing phone call about a direct threat against some of this country's more prominent leadership. Hypothetically, let's say a terrorist of Irish

Catholic background and a penchant for explosives seems to have found a sudden affinity for a group of Allah's more fanatical followers. Would you have any suggestions?" he said.

Dr. Murat began to gnaw over the possibilities, smiling with his eyes as much as his mouth.

"I have a few ideas I think could work," he said, "but I would need more information."

"Good," Woodward said. "I should have a brief within the hour. I'll send you a copy."

With a nod, Dr. Murat exited down the hallway. He looked at the patriotic iconography hanging on the walls as he passed and felt content. Being part of the great machine established to battle a constant onslaught of threats, he was proud his was a cog that had not failed. But as dangers continually arise, his rest would be short-lived like it is for all those who work in national defense. The endless barrage of hazards meant it was statistically inevitable that something would slip through the cracks of the system. No nation is invulnerable and no empire indestructible. Still, he didn't feel the pressure of the giant resting on his shoulders, only the pride that his life's work had helped the country he loved. The United States would stand, at least for a little while longer.

結束

A Note from the Author

Being a fiction writer, I don't live in reality. The vast majority of the time, my thoughts are somewhere else getting to know people that don't exist. I'll spend days thinking about these characters, then months obsessing over which words best describe them. I sacrifice health, family time, hobbies, and vacations as I bury my nose in a laptop attempting to craft a world that I hope others will visit. It can be a lonely, selfish life and for many authors like me, most of the time, there is little reward for it.

Now, since you've gotten this far, I'm assuming the story interested you enough to finish the book. I'm deeply grateful that you gave it a chance and I truly hope you enjoyed reading it. Please feel free to contact me with comments or criticisms. If you did find it worthwhile, please recommend it to a friend and rate my book online at www.amazon.com or other online retailers. It's the biggest compliment you can give. Thank you for your support.

Oh, and if you found the two hidden codes buried within the text, I'd love to know. There may even be a little something in it for you.

Humbly and Sincerely,
David Lineberry
ashenpawn@gmail.com

Visit Us:
www.ashenpawn.com
ashenpawn.wordpress.com
Ashen Pawn Publishing is also on Facebook.

ASHEN
PAWN
PUBLISHING